Death of the Eleven-Toed Man

ALSO BY GAYNOR TORRANCE

JEMIMA HUXLEY SERIES
Book 1: The Cardiff Killings
Book 2: The Briarmarsh Close Killings
Book 3: The Caerphilly Mountain Killings
Book 4: The Leighton Meadow Killings
Book 5: The Marquess Club Killings
Book 6: The Rhymney Valley Killings
Book 7: The Boy in the Reeds

WYE VALLEY WIDOWS
Book 1: Death of a Ghostwriter
Book 2: Death of the Eleven-Toed Man

DEATH
of the
Eleven-Toed
Man

GAYNOR TORRANCE

JOFFE BOOKS

Joffe Books, London
www.joffebooks.com

First published in Great Britain in 2025

Cover art by Cherie Chapman

ISBN: 978-1-80573-302-7

CHAPTER 1

It was the time of year when the pressure was on. The Wye Valley Village of the Year competition was less than two weeks away and the members of the Monksworthy Action Group had to pull out all the stops. After all, when it came to winning the competition, the devil was in the detail. And it required a great deal of effort to ensure that everything was just so.

The MAG committee kept the village in tip-top condition year-round. Picking up litter. Planting flowers. Cutting the grass on the village green. Ensuring dog walkers cleared up after their pooches. But everything ramped up in June and they were determined to win this year.

Tonight, the MAG was meeting to discuss any final projects that needed to be tackled, to make sure everything would be in place before the big day. There were plenty of items on the agenda. However, a few minutes into the meeting, committee chair the Reverend Tobias Daniels had all but given up on the idea of calling the meeting to order, such was the excitable mood around the table.

'C'mon, Gwen,' urged Anthony. As the owner of the Monksworthy Garden Centre, the annual competition was his chance to shine. It was his carefully chosen blooms that filled the village with colour and heady fragrance. But his updates on the state of the delphiniums and larkspur on the roundabout and the flourishing hanging baskets would have to wait. 'Give us the low-down on Abbotsmead. What the heck happened there?'

The village had been buzzing all day with rumours. He leaned forward so as not to miss a word.

Gwendolen Singh's eyes sparkled with excitement as she glanced at each of her fellow members. She ran the village shop with her husband, Rohan, which meant she was the go-to person for any juicy gossip. And it was apparent to everyone that Gwen was relishing her moment in the spotlight.

'Well, the only way to describe it is a massacre!' She spoke slowly, living up to her position as leading lady in the Wye Valley Players, the local amateur dramatic group. Duncan and Liz gasped in unison, and buoyed by this reaction Gwen continued. 'Believe me, we are lucky it didn't happen here. From what I've heard it was absolute carnage. No word of a lie, it was dev-a-station. Completely ruined their chances at being Village of the Year.' Despite her tone of voice being measured, she struggled to mask her delight, as on a couple of occasions her lips twitched almost gleefully. Though appreciating that some would undoubtedly find it distasteful, she managed to control herself sufficiently so as not to smile.

Elsie, who was the most empathetic of souls, stifled a squeal, and dabbed her eyes with a crumpled tissue.

'There, there, my darling.' Tobias reached out and patted his wife's shoulder. 'Don't go getting upset.'

'So, you've been there? Seen it?' pressed Sir Barnaby. Despite not technically being a villager, the heir of the nearby sprawling Cavendish-Mortimer estate had been a keen member of the committee for years.

'Oh, no. No, no, no, I haven't,' replied Gwen. Sensing heat rise to her cheeks, she lowered her gaze. 'It didn't feel right to intrude. It's only what I've been told.'

The local lord harrumphed loudly. He had no time for idle speculation. Before he had the opportunity to say anything else, Gwen speedily took up her tale once more.

'I don't think—' Sir Barnaby began, but he was stopped short by a sharp kick under the table.

'Let her speak, Barney.' Sylvie glared in his direction, warning him not to interrupt again. There were very few people who could get away with using his nickname, much less kicking him. But Sylvie Franklynn had been close friends with Barney since childhood. Barney opened his mouth to speak again but thought better of it and instead took a bite of cake. As he munched, he rolled his eyes at Liz Morgan. Liz was Barney's other closest friend in the village. She ran the Delicious Desserts Tearoom with Sylvie, and the three of them were thick as thieves.

'Thank you, Sylvie,' said Gwen. She nodded her head appreciatively. 'I've no reason to think that it's anything other than the truth. I can assure you it's come from an impeccable source. Indeed, it was Ezra Tiverton himself who told me all about it.'

'Well, we certainly have a different understanding of the definition of "impeccable source", Gwen,' interjected Brendon Forbes. 'Ezra Tiverton's got the morals of an alley cat. You can't trust a word that comes out of his mouth.'

Ezra Tiverton owned the Spotted Pig pub, known locally as the SP, and the establishment was located in the neighbouring village of Abbotsmead. The rivalry between Ezra and Brendon was well-known, as Brendon ran the Monksworthy Arms with his husband, Duncan. Although the two villages were separated by a few miles, it was inevitable that the two pubs came into direct competition.

'We all know there's no love lost between you,' said Gwen, as she dismissively flicked a hand as though shooing away a pesky fly. 'And I know Ezra's not above playing the odd dirty trick when it comes to attracting punters, but I believe every word he said about this. After all, why would he lie?'

'Go on, Gwen. Don't keep us hanging,' said Sylvie. Usually, Sylvie and Liz would have been updated on any local crimes by Liz's younger brother, Simon, who was a police sergeant. But as luck would have it on this occasion, Sergeant Simon Porter had taken a much-needed holiday and was sunning himself on a beach somewhere along the coast of Menorca.

'As I was about to say, Ezra popped into the post office this morning. He was after a couple of stamps — it's his sister's daughter's baby shower in a couple of weeks, bad timing with the Village of the Year competition — and he was all of a tizz about what had happened on the weekend.' Gwen loved the sound of her own voice and had the propensity to include all sorts of irrelevancies into any narrative whenever she was given free rein to gossip. With everyone's eyes upon her, she knew that she had this audience in the palm of her hand, which was every leading lady's dream. This wasn't by any means comparable with the thrill of being centre stage with the Wye Valley Players, but nevertheless she was still holding court, and it felt good. Taking a deep breath, she continued. 'Apparently, a stag party had spent hours drinking at the SP. He was happy enough at first, as they were spending a lot of money. But then they started playing a drinking game. I think it was Truth or Dare.' Gwen paused for dramatic effect, looking at each of them in turn. 'And that's when they started to become rowdy. It upset some of the regulars, and there was some argy-bargy. It all kicked off when one of the lads kissed old Mrs Prendergast on the lips. Apparently, she went rigid and began to wail like a banshee.'

'I'm not surprised,' said Liz. 'She's only just had new dentures fitted, and she's been having trouble with them. By all accounts they've been hurting like billy-o.'

'Oh, the poor woman. It doesn't bear thinking about,' said Elsie. 'I've got a couple of hours free tomorrow, so I'll make her a jelly and buy a tub of vanilla ice cream. Everyone likes vanilla and it might help soothe her gums.'

'Personally, I prefer peach sorbet,' said Barney.

'Chocolate's my favourite,' added Sylvie.

'Order! Order!' called Reverend Daniels. 'This is not the time to discuss ice cream preferences. We've a lot to get through and we all want to hear what Gwen has to say.'

'Thank you, Reverend.' Gwen nodded appreciatively. 'So, as I was saying, with old Mrs Prendergast upset and clearly in pain, Billy Muldoon took it upon himself to voice his displeasure and demand that the lads leave. Now, Ezra knew that it was in his interests to side with his regulars. He told the party they'd overstepped the mark and ordered them to drink up and go. Let's face it, it's the locals who are the bread and butter of small business owners in these parts. You can't afford to upset them.'

There were nods of agreement from those committee members who owned small businesses in the area. They understood the fine line you had to tread between attracting passing clientele and keeping your regular customer base happy.

'Well, anyone could have told him that,' sniffed Brendon. 'You need your regulars to keep up a steady cash flow, which means making sure they have a good time and good reasons to come back. We didn't start the weekly quiz night to pull in tourists.'

'Precisely! Anyway, about an hour before last orders, Ezra asked them to leave,' said Gwen. 'He thought it best to give them time to leave the village before the locals headed home, to minimise the risk of things escalating out on the street. Well, the lads weren't happy about it, but as a compromise, he sold them a bottle of vodka to take out.'

There was a collective gasp at the stupidity.

'I'm glad they weren't in our pub,' said Brendon. 'People like that might very well put a lot of money through the till, but to be honest, Duncan and I could do without the aggravation.'

'I hope they didn't drive after drinking that much,' said Liz. 'There have been a few nasty smash-ups on local roads.'

'It wasn't a smash-up on the roads they caused, from what I heard,' said Anthony. 'But did they really . . . ?' Anthony could barely bring himself to say it out loud.

'Well, that's what I'm getting to.' Gwen's frustration was evident.

'So how did they establish that it was those lads that did it?' asked Sylvie. It was a reasonable question. There was no obvious reason to link them to the devastation, apart from the fact that they were strangers to the area and had been both obnoxious and drunk.

'I asked Ezra the very same question,' said Gwen. 'And he told me that all the police had to do was follow the trail.'

'What trail?' asked Tobias. He cocked his head, eager to hear what she was about to say. He hadn't heard much about what had happened, and he wasn't one to gossip, but such was the magnitude of what had occurred in Abbotsmead that he surely owed it to his congregation to learn the full story. To counsel them should they seek his help and guidance.

'To where they were staying, of course,' said Gwen impatiently. 'From what I was told, the lads in question were from Hereford. Not that that has any bearing on what they did. I'm sure there are many lovely people living in Hereford. But it seems that they returned to their digs and carried on drinking.'

'Does anyone know where these louts were staying?' asked Barney.

'I heard they'd rented the Joneses' Airbnb for the weekend,' said Liz. There was a ripple of gasps and tuts of disapproval.

No one knew for certain how Rob and Angela Jones, who owned the Airbnb, made their money. The forty-something couple had moved into the village just ten years before. No one could remember seeing either of them ever heading off to a place of employment. But everyone was sure the couple had money behind them. Shortly after moving to Abbotsmead, they'd snapped up another property at the far side of the

6

village that was about to go on the market and turned it into an Airbnb.

The thought of such a venture being foisted upon their beloved village didn't go down well with the locals. Though instead of making their concerns and objections known by speaking directly to the Joneses, the aggrieved villagers did what many people are prone to do when confronted by something they don't like. They sniped about it behind their backs.

'Serves them right,' said Sylvie.

'Oh, don't say that!' Elsie looked distraught at the idea.

'Well, if what I've heard is correct, we know they ruined any chance of Abbotsmead winning this year's competition.' Sylvie folded her arms stubbornly.

'But what's this about a trail?' asked Tobias.

'If you'd all just allow me to tell you what I know.' Gwen gave each of them a hard stare. 'Where was I? Ah, yes. In the middle of the night, they went back out into the village and set about destroying all the floral displays. They stole every hanging basket and tore the heads off flowers in every front garden.'

Anthony looked pained. 'Awful, just awful. Not that their floral displays would have been a patch on ours. I kept my finest stock for our own use.'

'But you still haven't explained about the trail,' interjected Liz, her voice tinged with impatience.

'I'm getting to that!' Gwen snapped. 'They took the hanging baskets back to the property, and they weren't exactly careful about it. There were clumps of soil and leaves and debris that led all the way back to the cottage.'

'Just as well it hadn't rained,' said Elsie breathlessly. 'Or the trail would've washed away.'

'Precisely,' said Gwen. 'Anyway, the police were called in early the next morning when people awoke to discover what had happened. They got in touch with the Joneses, who gave them a key. Apparently, when the officers went in the lads were still fast asleep.'

'Undoubtedly hungover, if they'd drunk to excess,' Tobias interjected.

'The evidence was all there. Hanging baskets strewn across the floor. And each of the lads covered in dirt. Soil-stained hands. Apparently, the prospective groom had even strewn some of the stolen flowerheads across his bed.'

At that, the reverend was finally able to bring the meeting round to its intended purpose. The revelation of recent dastardly events at Abbotsmead was a stark warning that such wanton thuggery could occur anywhere. No doubt, this was a wake-up call. Each person around the table appreciated that the prudent course of action was to improve security throughout the village. A lengthy discussion ensued until they came up with a workable strategy to minimise the risk of such a thing ever happening in Monksworthy.

Eventually, having exhausted this urgent matter, the reverend announced that they needed to move on, as they had only booked the village hall for another forty minutes and they had a lot to get through. The rest of the agenda items were discussed in a record amount of time.

There was an update on numbers signed up for the litter-picking rota. A date set for community painting of the cricket pavilion — weather permitting. Decisions arrived at on the date and location of a car boot sale to raise funds to support their entry into the Village of the Year competition. As for Any Other Business, there was none.

'Well, I guess that's it, until next week's meeting. There's a lot for us to think about and act upon. Thank you, everyone,' said Tobias. He nodded to Elsie, who as committee secretary dutifully set about collecting the paper copies of the printed agenda. In recent years, each of the members, at one time or another, had tried but failed to convince Tobias that there was no need to have copies printed. Almost all of them made sure they had the agenda on a tablet or their phone. But the reverend was set in his ways. He was a traditionalist, and besides, as the chairperson of the MAG, he ultimately called the shots.

'Pub, anyone?' asked Brendon. He was headed there no matter what, as he knew that Duncan would appreciate a hand pulling pints and indulging in small talk with their customers.

'Absolutely,' said Barney. 'Ladies?' He addressed this directly to Liz and Sylvie.

'Well, I've nothing to rush back for,' said Sylvie. She had been widowed less than a year ago, and her husband's untimely death had come as a shock. Though he had spent a significant amount of time away from home for his work — and for other reasons which had come to light more recently — throughout their marriage of almost forty years, she missed him dearly. And their adult daughter Annabel had long since moved out too.

'Count me in. I don't need to be asked twice,' added Liz, as she pulled on her coat. 'I think we could all do with a stiff drink after that.'

'Will Harriet be there?' asked Barney.

Harriet Joyce was a newcomer to the village. She had met Sylvie under the most awful of circumstances the previous year. During that time, Liz had got to know her too. Shortly after becoming acquainted, the three women had gone out on a limb to catch a murderer. Sylvie and Liz had welcomed Harriet into their friendship group, and recently, Harriet had moved into a cottage in the village.

'Unfortunately, no.' Brendon was the first to respond. 'I bumped into her earlier, and she said she was up against it with work commitments. She's always very cagey about what she does. You know me, I can usually get anyone to spill the beans, but no matter how hard I've tried, she always manages to sidestep the issue. Do any of you know what she does?' he asked.

They all shook their heads, but Barney was the only one of the three who answered truthfully. Liz and Sylvie both knew what Harriet did for a living but were sworn to secrecy.

CHAPTER 2

Stepping inside the Monksworthy Arms at this time of the evening was like turning up at the home of a favourite relative, where the welcome was always warm and genuine. No matter how hard a day you'd had, it was guaranteed to lift your mood as you felt the stresses and strains drain away. You would always find someone to chat to and wile away a few hours in pleasant companionship. So it was unsurprising that this was the place where villagers congregated.

Duncan, being more practical than his husband, had worked hard to turn the pub around since he'd taken over the licence fourteen years earlier. He'd been a project manager before packing it in and opting for a different lifestyle. Upgrading fixtures and fittings, introducing craft beers and hiring a chef with a reputation for producing high-quality fare were all his handiwork. He'd also introduced a weekly quiz night and a weekly folk night with live performances. They'd proved to be shrewd business moves as, when word spread, they brought people in from all across the valley. It kept the kitchen busy, the drinks flowing and the till ringing. More importantly, there'd been no complaints from the villagers as it meant that they had something to look forward to every week, right on their doorstep.

Brendon was the first to enter the pub, and within seconds his husband spotted him.

'Great timing, Bren. Get yourself around this side of the bar. There're pints to be pulled,' called Duncan. He waved and shouted a welcome to Barney and the ladies.

'As usual, no rest for the wicked,' said Brendon. He made his way to the bar, stopping at a couple of tables and collecting a few empties along the way.

'You're a love. I don't know what I'd do without you,' said Duncan. 'It's been manic in here tonight. We've a couple of groups come in for food. Haven't seen them in here before. Right, Barney, what can I get you?' he asked, as he handed another customer their change.

Sylvie and Liz found a table towards the inglenook fireplace and were chatting away contentedly when Barney came to join them. 'Bren will bring the drinks over when they're ready. Got you both the usual,' he said, as he handed them each a menu. 'I take it you haven't eaten?'

'Not had time,' said Liz. 'I'm ravenous.'

'Me too,' added Sylvie.

When Brendon brought the drinks over, they placed their food order. In recent months Duncan had launched an app for the pub which gave customers the option of ordering food and drink without leaving their table — 'to keep up with the times'. It was easy enough to do once you had it set up on your phone. But the three friends always enjoyed the opportunity to have a chat and so opted for the more conventional route of simply telling Brendon what they wanted. After all, what was wrong with speaking to people?

Food ordered, Barney picked up his pint and savoured the first sip. He was about to say something about the events in Abbotsmead when their table was approached by Ian Wyde. Ian had lived in the village for more than thirty years, having moved there when he took up a post as a history teacher at a local high school.

Ian's passion for the past was well-known. He had even set up a local history group, as well as a detectorist society. He'd discovered the hobby as a student, fuelled by boyhood dreams of discovering artefacts from civilisations long past. The news was full of reports of amateur historians uncovering hidden hordes, treasure troves that offered incredible insights into how people once lived, and Ian longed to become one of them. Now he led a group of six dedicated enthusiasts who joined him most weekends in a search to hit the jackpot. Rain or shine, they could be spotted somewhere in the valley waving a metal contraption over the earth, systematically scanning an area which they'd divided up into a grid.

Ian held up a hand and smiled uncertainly. He cleared his throat. For a man who spent his working life in a classroom, facing down recalcitrant, disinterested and sometimes hostile teenagers, it seemed ridiculous that he was feeling so on edge. And it suddenly occurred to him that the last time he'd felt this jittery was back in his student days when he first asked a girl if she'd like to go out on a date.

Sensing Ian's awkwardness, Sylvie dived right in to put him at ease. 'Hello, Ian. Haven't seen you for a while. Would you like to join us?'

The unexpected offer immediately relaxed him.

'Hello, Sylvie, Liz, Sir Barnaby.' He found himself unable to prevent himself nodding deferentially at Barney, and as soon as he did it, he silently chastised himself. He had an image of serfs doffing their caps to the landed gentry. 'No, no, I wouldn't want to impose. I'm having a quiet drink with a few friends, but I wanted to ask a favour of Sir Barnaby.'

'Oh? Well, you have my attention.' Barney's tone was friendly, and he raised an eyebrow in a questioning manner.

'In that case, I was wondering if you'd allow the village detectorist group to scan some of your land?'

'Well, I don't see why not, old bean.' Barney smiled affably, playing up to his role as lord of the estate. 'I've often wondered what you chaps discover in these parts. It seems to me that you get plenty of fresh air. Communing with nature, that sort of thing. You never know, perhaps I might join you. I've been looking for a new hobby to take up. After all, there're only so many rounds of golf one can play. And you never know, this detectorising malarky might just do the trick. Nothing ventured, eh?'

It was immediately clear to both Liz and Sylvie that Ian had not expected such an enthusiastic response. It seemed to take him a few seconds to recover. But then he pressed his lips into a smile. Though the result appeared to be more of a grimace than one of genuine happiness.

Barney was still speaking, unaware of any discomfort in his audience. 'You know, I've just recalled something from my school days. I do believe that Squirrel Tuffnell had one of those contraptions.'

'Squirrel Tuffnell?' echoed Liz. She raised an eyebrow questioningly. 'Who's he when he's at home?'

'If you must know, his name was Timothy Tuffnell. The masters used to call him Tufty. Which led us chaps in the inner circle to assign him the moniker Squirrel.'

'You've lost me there,' said Sylvie. Her brow furrowed as she tried to make sense of what Barney was saying.

'Oh, keep up!' said Barney. 'I was never one for popular culture, but even I knew about the Tufty Club.'

'Was that a branch of the Truffle Club?' asked Liz.

The women had only learned of the existence of the Truffle Club a few months earlier. It had been a night they would never forget. Barney, Liz, Sylvie and Harriet had driven for hours to warn someone from Barney's past that his life might be in danger. And if that hadn't been bad enough, they had ended up finding themselves staring down the wrong end of a shotgun barrel. Miraculously, Barney had managed to diffuse a situation which could have rapidly spiralled out of control, by grunting and squealing as he imitated a wild boar and then chanting a bizarre combination of words which had apparently been the mantra of an unofficial organisation called the Truffle Club.

Not for the want of trying, they had never really got to the bottom of what the Truffle Club was. Or learned the reason why Barney had been a member of it. All he would say on the matter was the trite phrase '*What happens in the Truffle Club, stays in the Truffle Club.*' It was so unlike him to be evasive. If anything, he was prone to overshare. In the end, they gave up trying to get an answer out of him. It was most likely some sort of private school thing, they decided, which they were better off not knowing.

'What's the Truffle Club?' asked Ian. He looked from one to the other.

'Best not to ask,' said Sylvie. She shook her head.

Barney ignored the question and sighed. 'Are you seriously telling me that none of you have heard of the Tufty Club? Come on, people, you must have heard of Tufty Fluffytail.'

When both women shook their heads, he continued. 'Tufty was the greatest squirrel in the history of squirrels. He saved children's lives.'

'I believe he was a RoSPA creation,' said Ian. 'A cartoon character.'

'What's RoSPA?' asked Liz.

'The Royal Society for the Prevention of Accidents,' said Barney. 'Didn't you have a Tufty Club in your school, to teach you about road safety?'

'Not that I can remember,' said Liz. She glanced at Sylvie, who shook her head.

'I had the honour of being the first in my year group to get a Tufty Club badge,' said Barney. 'The other boys were so envious. I believe I still have it somewhere.'

'You're still a big kid at heart,' chuckled Sylvie. She playfully punched his shoulder.

'Nothing wrong with that,' said Barney. 'Anyway, I digress. Squirrel Tuffnell had one of those metal contraptions. Used to go around the school grounds with it. Never understood the fascination at the time, but perhaps Ian and his group of enthusiasts will open my eyes. Plus, I own a lot of land, and it would be quite nice to have a bona fide reason to explore some of its more remote areas. In fact, I know the perfect spot to start. So, when were you thinking of venturing up there?'

'Saturday morning, if that's OK with you?'

'Sounds good to me. I'm free all day. Shall we say ten o'clock? Give me a chance to have a hearty breakfast. You can call at the house, and I'll lead the way.'

Ian nodded.

'Do I need to purchase any equipment?' asked Barney.

'No, not immediately. I've a few spare metal detectors. You can borrow one of them. See if you take to it first, before you shell out on one.'

'Good-oh. See you at my place on Saturday morning, old chap! Ten o'clock sharp. Don't be late.'

As Ian headed back to his friends, he wondered what he'd let himself in for.

CHAPTER 3

Saturday in the Wye Valley turned out to be exceptionally clement, bringing plenty of visitors eager to explore and make the most of the good weather.

From the moment Liz and Sylvie opened the doors of the tearoom, there was a constant stream of customers. Fortunately, they had a healthy supply of cakes, scones and biscuits to keep up with demand, but both knew that they would have to put more in the oven as soon as things quietened off.

The lunchtime rush had extended into late afternoon. But now that it was over and done with, and the next batch of baked offerings were in the oven, a mouthwatering aroma filled the tearoom as Liz and Sylvie were taking a much-needed break.

'Never mind the ten thousand steps health officials keep banging on about. We must have done at least double the amount and then some,' said Sylvie.

'You're not wrong,' agreed Liz. 'It's certainly been an endurance test today. Still, it's good for the profits.'

They had just sat down to two steaming cups of tea, along with a selection of scones and all the usual pots of jam and clotted cream, when the door opened.

Liz, whose back was to the entrance, sighed and muttered. 'Oh, here we go again. Look sharp, Sylve.'

Sylvie glanced towards the door and smiled. 'Don't worry, it's not a customer. It's only Barney.'

'How did it go with the detectorists? Did you have a good time?' asked Liz, as she turned round to look at their friend. 'Everything all right?'

'No, everything's far from all right.'

Barney glanced around the tearoom to make sure it was just the three of them present, and sighed, as though he was carrying the weight of the world upon his shoulders.

'I was so looking forward to today,' he said. 'I love trying out new things. It started out well, but I ended up having the worst morning of my life. It's all kicked off up at mine, and I don't know what to do.' His brow was furrowed, his normally ruddy complexion pale.

Sylvie jumped out of her seat and raced to his side. Placing an arm around his shoulder, she guided him to a seat at their table. 'C'mon, Barn. Sit down and tell us what happened. Whatever it is, you're not alone now. We've got your back.'

'I'll get you a cuppa,' Liz said. 'A strong cup of tea and some of our scones will take the edge off things. We'll help you through whatever this is.'

Barney shook his head. 'I don't think anyone can put this right. I think I'll have nightmares about it for a long time. But I need to tell someone, and you're the only people I really trust. That's why I came straight here. I don't suppose you've anything stronger than tea or coffee?'

'Sorry, Barney. We don't have a licence to serve alcohol,' said Sylvie. It was concerning to see their friend so distressed. For as long as they'd known him, Barney had been unflappable. Even as a teenager, his first response in a crisis was to adapt to new circumstances by finding ways around problems, which was the reason he'd grown up to become such a successful businessman.

Barney flopped onto the chair, as though his legs were too weak to support him. He placed his elbows on the table and rested his forehead against the palms of his hand. 'In that case, I guess I'll have a coffee, if it's not too much trouble. The stronger the better. I need something to take the edge off, and I don't think tea is going to cut it.'

'Coming right up. I'll get you a couple of pastries too. You look like you need a quick sugar rush,' said Liz. She and Sylvie shared a worried glance. Neither had ever heard Barney admit to being so troubled.

'I just don't know how this could have happened,' he muttered, more to himself than to anyone else. 'You do someone a favour and then . . .' His voice trailed off mid-sentence. He sat back in his seat, shaking his head in disbelief as he tried to make sense of recent events.

In no time at all, Liz had placed a cup of coffee and a selection of pastries in front of Barney. She sat across from him and looked at him expectantly.

'So, c'mon, Barney, are you going to tell us what's happened?' asked Liz.

He sighed, then rubbed his cheeks as he sought to ground himself. His friends sat in silence until he eventually spoke.

'You remember in the pub when Ian Wyde asked if his crowd could have a go at scanning my land with their metal detectors?' Liz and Sylvie nodded. 'I had no hesitation agreeing to it. After all, he's a thoroughly decent chap with a harmless, if somewhat strange, pastime. I even said that I'd join them, as I'd not tried detectorising before, and I thought it might be fun.'

Sylvie nodded. 'You told him to get to yours at ten o'clock.'

'That's right, I did, and he turned up on time along with the rest of his group. Anyway, we headed off to one of the more remote areas of the estate. I'd selected that particular spot as we have a wedding at the manor today, and I didn't think it would be good for business. Nobody wants their wedding pictures or the videos of their happy day full of people tramping about in the background with their metal detectors. Bleepers going off every time they hover over a buried ring pull from a can of lager.'

'That's understandable,' agreed Sylvie. 'Not when you've paid thousands for your wedding. After all, you get your bookings because of the exclusivity you offer, not to mention the gorgeous grounds.'

'Precisely,' said Barney.

'Arg! Stop it, you two!' admonished Liz. 'Just get to the point, will you, Barney? I can't stand all the suspense. My imagination is on overdrive here, and I've no idea what you're about to tell us.'

Barney looked at her in surprise and was about to respond, when the door to the tearoom opened once again and Harriet entered.

'Should I be offended that you're meeting without me? Is something going on that you're trying to keep from me?' They could immediately tell that she was joking.

'Barney's got the weight of the world on his shoulders,' said Sylvie.

'Nothing serious, I hope?' asked Harriet.

'He was just about to tell us why he's so upset,' said Liz. 'Can I get you something to drink?'

Harriet sat down and accepted a cup of tea from Liz.

'As serious as you can get,' said Barney. 'You'll undoubtedly hear about it before the day's out. Simon's up at mine as we speak.'

'My Simon?' asked Liz.

Barney nodded. 'I don't know any other Simon.'

'So it's a police matter?' pressed Liz. 'Must be serious.'

'It is, and I'm not sure where to begin. It's been an extremely traumatic few hours.'

Sylvie remained quiet, but reached out and grabbed his hand, squeezing it tightly.

Appreciating the gesture, Barney attempted a smile. 'As I was saying, Ian loaned me one of his detecting contraptions.

He showed me how to use it, and explained that if it started to bleep, it meant that there was metal beneath the surface. At that point, it's time to stop scanning and start digging.'

Barney cleared his throat and took a sip of coffee.

'Ian divided the area up into a grid and allocated a reasonable-sized plot to each of us and we got started. To be honest, it was quite tedious at first. The most anyone found was ring pulls and a discarded five-pence piece. Hardly elusive treasure.

'Anyway, after about forty minutes or so, my machine sounded an alert. I had a rush of adrenalin, which got the old heart racing. So I placed the machine on the ground and removed a trowel from the rucksack I'd been carrying. As I started digging, my imagination ran wild about what I was about to find. I knew it was unlikely to be treasure but I still couldn't stop myself fantasising about being the one to find something important — the Wye Hoard, I imagined it being called. And I'm afraid I got ahead of myself. In those few minutes, I pictured myself doing the rounds with the media. Being a guest on various talk shows. Putting the place on the map. Then I came crashing back to earth, as after digging a few inches into the soil, I hadn't found a thing.

'So I scanned the area once more and the device bleeped again, and that's when Ian came over to help. He scanned the spot with his machine, and it picked up something too. We knew at that stage that the machines weren't faulty. We realised that whatever was setting the detectors off must be further into the ground.'

'And what was it?' interjected Liz.

Barney's voice trembled as he spoke. 'It was a . . . It was a body.'

20

CHAPTER 4

'What precisely do you mean by that?' Harriet asked.

Harriet was used to being faced with a wide array of bizarre, sometimes convoluted occurrences and conundrums. As a secret agony aunt, she had learned that even the most self-reliant of individuals occasionally felt overwhelmed by perhaps the most basic of problems. And it was her job to provide impartial, common-sense advice. So it was perhaps unsurprising that she was the first of the three women to recover her composure.

The tremor in Barney's voice continued. 'What I just said. I found a body. If I hadn't been the one to dig it up, I would have thought it was some sort of hoax . . .'

'Ooh, I wonder if you've found a body of a Roman centurion or Neanderthal!' enthused Liz. 'They could have been buried with treasure. It could be priceless.'

'I think you've got hold of the wrong end of the stick,' Harriet told Liz. 'Barney didn't say anything about Romans or Neanderthals.'

'I thought the same thing, Liz,' said Barney. 'I admit that for those first few moments I was blinded by the thought of it being an ancient burial ground and how I could monetise the situation. My imagination ran away with itself. I thought it would put us on the map, increase visitor numbers. I'd open a new side to the business, a museum. But the illusion was quickly shattered. Ian called the police — you have to, apparently, if you find a body, even if you think it's a Roman. You must follow procedure, or else you could find yourself in all sorts of trouble. Anyway, Simon turned up with a couple of colleagues, had a look and immediately called some sort of specialist who deals with that sort of thing — and it turns out the body was buried there within the last twenty years. Possibly even more recently than that. Apparently, they could tell by the clothes. Don't ask me how. They looked like rags. So they're treating it as suspicious.'

'You mean that someone might have buried that poor soul on your estate within our lifetime?' Sylvie's eyes widened with alarm.

Barney nodded. 'Now you can understand why I'm concerned. I know for a fact that no one was given permission to bury a body there. My father would never have agreed to such a thing, and I certainly didn't agree to it. Which means that it was buried there without our consent.'

'Whoever did it was trying to hide something by covering up a death,' said Liz.

'Which suggests something terrible happened,' said Barney.

'I hate to say it, but it's likely to be murder,' added Harriet. 'And, if that's the case, I'd guess that the killer was someone familiar with this area.'

'What makes you think that?' asked Sylvie in an unnaturally high-pitched voice. Her heart missed a beat at the mere suggestion that there could be yet another murderer at large. It was only recently that her own life had been threatened by a serial killer.

'Well, if you kill someone, and want to dispose of the body, you're hardly likely to drive around with it, searching for an ideal spot to bury it. Common sense suggests that even if you're a careful driver, the longer you keep a dead body in your vehicle, the greater the chance that you would be stopped for some traffic violation and discovered,' said Harriet.

'Yes, unless you're some sort of professional killer, chances are you'd be so worked up that you wouldn't be able to drive carefully. After all, your mind would be on other things. Such as not getting caught with a body in the boot,' added Liz. 'Though I suppose the person could have been killed on your estate, Barney.'

'I certainly hope not. I wish I knew what the police know, now they have the body,' said Barney. 'Though I don't want to risk coming across as trying to insert myself into their investigation. After all, the body's been found on my land. I guess that must make me suspect numero uno, so to speak.'

'Surely not. There's no denying that you're an astute businessman, some might even say a shark, but you're an old softie at heart, and we love you even more because of it,' said Sylvie.

'I wish I had your confidence. I really do.'

'I think you're right,' said Harriet. She addressed this remark to Barney, choosing to ignore Sylvie's emotional interjection and concentrate instead on practicalities. 'You should stay out of it. Let the police do their job, without any interference.'

'I suppose I'll get a sense of which way the wind's blowing if Andy is still up for our usual round of golf,' said Barney miserably. He and Andrew Young, the chief constable, had played a weekly game together for years. 'If he starts to make excuses, I'll have reason to be concerned. In all the time we've played together, he's hardly ever missed a round.'

'Fingers crossed it stays that way,' said Sylvie.

'How about for everyone's peace of mind I have a quiet word with Si?' asked Liz. 'See if I can get the low-down on what's going on. You know what he's like. He's never been able to keep anything from me.'

'Oh, I'd very much appreciate it if you did,' said Barney. He reached out and squeezed her hand.

'Just you wait and see, Barney. There'll most likely turn out to be a simple explanation as to why a body was buried there,' reassured Liz. 'Are you coming to quiz night this week?'

'Unfortunately, no. I'm afraid the Yabbadabbadoos will have to do without me on this occasion,' said Barney, referring to their quiz team. 'I've a meeting with my accountant. He couldn't fit me in at any other time. But I assure you I'll be there next week.'

The weekly pub quiz had become a popular and hotly contested event ever since Duncan had got it up and running ten years ago. The four of them, along with Simon, had been battling for top spot against the Doom Raiders since Christmas.

'Well, I'll let you know if I find anything out before then,' said Liz. 'Because of his shift patterns I'm not due to see Si for a few days anyway.'

'You never know, we might get lucky tomorrow evening,' said Sylvie. 'It's book club night, and you know what that's like.'

'Certainly do,' said Liz. 'Too much gossip and very little discussion about what we're supposed to have read.'

'Anyway, I'd best be off,' said Barney. 'There're a million and one things requiring my attention, and this latest development has been a distraction I could do without. And I'm sure that after all these years, the killer will be long gone. He'll have wanted to put some distance between himself and his victim. So we should all be able to sleep soundly knowing that there's not a murderer on the loose. At least not around these parts.'

CHAPTER 5

The Monksworthy book club was in its sixteenth year and still going strong. Unsurprisingly, membership had changed over time. But for the last three years, it had proceeded with a faithful core. True, there were very few actual bibliophiles among them. And as with all such clubs, it wasn't unusual to discover that at least a couple of people hadn't bothered to read more than the blurb. The genre of choice tended to be raunchy bonkbusters, but in order to be fair to everyone they selected from a wide range of literature.

The book club was Brendon Forbes's baby. He was a committed bibliophile who favoured true crime. Liz was the only other obsessive reader among the group, whereas most of them only read the occasional book from cover to cover if the mood took them.

Hannah Walters had already messaged to say that she was unable to make it. Being in her late thirties, she was the youngest member of the group by far. Since her early teens she'd had an entrepreneurial streak. Despite being academically gifted, she had decided not to go to university and instead set up a dog-walking business, which proved to be extremely popular among pet owners from across the Wye Valley, not to mention quite lucrative. Tonight, she had booked to meet a new potential client and their pooch, which clashed with the book club. But business came first.

The book club met at the village hall. Sylvie walked in to find that Harriet and Brendon were already there and were discussing an upcoming shopping trip to a new outlet which had recently opened near Oxford. Although they had only known each other for barely a year, the pair had become fast friends and often ventured into Bristol or Cheltenham to browse high-end boutiques and occasionally returned home with a purchase or two. Brendon glanced up and smiled as she approached. 'Hello, Sylve. How're you doing?'

'Hi, Bren. I'm good. And you?'

'Just planning the next outing with my favourite shopping pal,' he replied.

Before Harriet could add anything, the door opened once more and Liz, Elsie and Gwen arrived together. They were talking nineteen to the dozen about the latest episode of *Coronation Street*.

'No Ian tonight?' asked Brendon. It was immediately apparent from his tone that he was unaware of what had happened on the Cavendish-Mortimer estate.

'It's not like him to be late,' said Gwen.

'I take it you haven't heard?' said Sylvie. There was a moment as the words left her lips that she regretted being the one to reveal what had occurred. But knowing that the news would inevitably come out sooner rather than later, she thought it might cause some bad feelings if the others were to learn that she, Liz and Harriet had sat on the information.

'Heard what?' asked Gwen. Sensing that she was about to hear some juicy news, she made no attempt to mask her excitement. Dropping her handbag on a nearby table, she plonked herself down on the nearest seat and leaned forward, eager to learn what had happened. 'Come on, Sylve,' she urged. 'Spill the beans. What's happened? You can't keep us in suspense.'

The others were keen to know too. It was not unusual for weeks or even months to pass in the small village without any real excitement or even mildly unusual turn of events to occur. Indeed, such was the routine nature of village life that it was commonplace for speculation to become rife if a villager swapped a regular order of semi-skimmed milk to a plant-based alternative.

Colour rose in Sylvie's cheeks. As soon as the words were out there, she wished she hadn't said anything. But there was no taking it back. It was impossible to backpedal, as off the top of her head she couldn't think of anything else to say which would sound plausible. She surreptitiously glanced at her two closest friends. Harriet gave her a hard stare of disapproval. Liz merely shrugged her shoulders.

'C'mon, Sylve. There're no secrets between friends,' urged Brendon. He leaned forward in anticipation.

Sylvie cleared her throat before she said anything else. 'I don't know much, but what I can tell you is that Barney allowed the detectorists to have access to a section of his land, and—'

'Oh! My! Word!' interrupted Elsie. 'They found some treasure! There's been rumours of some being buried in this valley. Oh, this is so exciting! I can't wait to tell Toby. He'll be over the moon about this.'

'No, no. Stop it, Elsie. That's not what I was about to tell you.' But before Sylvie could say anything else, the door opened once more and in walked Ian, looking remarkably calm.

Everyone turned to look at him.

'I take it you've heard about the body?' he asked in a very matter-of-fact way.

'Body? Did you say body?' Brendon gripped the arms of his chair. 'You all heard him say they found a body, didn't you?' As he uttered those few words, his voice rose by at least an octave.

'Calm down, Bren,' said Harriet. She reached out a hand and he gripped it.

Gwen patted the vacant seat next to her. 'Sit down, Ian my love, and tell us all about it. I'm sure it must've come as an awful shock. Believe me, I know from personal experience that in circumstances like this it's best to share the load and allow your friends to support you.'

Harriet suppressed a smile. She very much doubted that Gwen had ever chanced upon some random dead body, or until now, knew anyone who had. Yet here she was trying to convince Ian that she knew exactly what he was going through.

In the end, however, Gwen carried out what could only be described as an interrogation, though she elicited no more than the three friends had learned from their conversation with Barney. They still only knew that a body had been found, and the police were treating the death as suspicious, unless their enquires proved otherwise.

Once everyone finished speculating about what might have happened to the poor unfortunate soul, their attention returned to the book they were supposed to have read. And as things drew to a close, they chose their next book.

'Do you both want to come back to mine?' asked Harriet, as she, Liz and Sylvie headed out of the village hall. 'I've finally finished decorating the lounge and thought you might like to take a look at it.'

'I'd love to, but I can't,' said Liz. 'Simon's calling around. He should be at mine in the next—' She glanced at her watch. 'Oh dear, it's later than I thought. I'd better run, or else he'll be waiting for me. I promised to make him supper and I'm going to try to find out what's happening with that investigation.'

'You go. Don't worry, and good luck,' called Harriet. 'Do you fancy a cuppa, or perhaps something stronger at mine, Sylve?'

'I don't need asking twice. I've nothing else planned,' Sylvie said, and she reached out to link arms with her friend. As they strolled along in companionable silence, her thoughts turned to the two recent unsettling events: the trashing of Abbotsmead and the discovery of a body. And when it occurred to her that it was often said that bad things happen in threes, she shivered despite the warmth of the evening.

CHAPTER 6

Early the next morning, Sylvie ambled along the pavement as she headed towards the tearoom. As they lived on different sides of the village, she and Liz rarely bumped into each other on their way to work.

She was mostly unaware of her immediate surroundings as she was concentrating on texting her daughter. Annabel was a wedding planner, and a substantial number of the events she organised were held at Barney's purpose-built venue. The Cavendish-Mortimer estate offered a prestigious and beautiful backdrop to any special occasion, and no matter the time of year or the weather, there was always some optimal location for the coveted photographs to be shot.

Given how closely Annabel worked with Barney's team, Sylvie figured that it was possible that her daughter would have some intel on the latest developments regarding the uni-dentified body. After all, it was not unreasonable to expect a wedding planner to have their finger on the pulse of local news, as it was crucial to the success of their business. With such high expectations for the big day itself, no bride, or groom for that matter, would want their wedding to be held anywhere near a location where there had been grisly goings on. And if it turned out that dastardly deeds really had been committed on the Cavendish-Mortimer estate, then it wasn't only Barney whose business might suffer because of it. Such a thing could quite easily affect Annabel too.

'Cooee!' Liz's voice shattered the relative quiet of that time in the morning.

Sylvie had been so focused on her phone that she hadn't spotted Liz. She raised a hand, waved and smiled. Then she quickly gestured towards the windows on the upper floors of nearby dwellings, as she knew that her friend's enthusiastic greeting risked annoying those neighbours who were still languishing in their beds.

'Oops!' Liz immediately clamped a hand over her mouth and looked at her watch. Her complexion reddened as she realised how early it was.

They usually arrived several hours before opening to make sure everything was ready for the first customers of the day. But with the Village of the Year competition just days away, they needed to make sure the whole shop looked as perfect as their freshly baked scones. Thankfully they no longer had to do all their baking in the little kitchen at the back of the shop. Liz had finally agreed to outsourcing a large proportion of their baked goods to a few small startups located in villages throughout the valley, which had each gained her trust for their ability to bake to her high standards. Although, Liz still refused to let anyone else use the recipe for her renowned brownies and blondies, and a few other baked offerings too. But she and Sylvie were both at an age where they agreed that there was more to life than work.

As Sylvie opened the tearoom door, there was the sound of rapid footsteps coming up behind them. Glancing over her shoulder, she saw Harriet, who was heading home after completing her daily morning run. 'Fancy a cuppa?'

'Give me half an hour,' Harriet replied. 'I need to shower and get changed first. Don't think you'll thank me for sitting inside when I'm this hot and sweaty. Not the sort of aroma you want your customers to face!'

'Fair point,' said Liz. 'We certainly don't want to risk putting customers off. But you'll need to hurry as I guarantee you'll want to hear what Simon said about the investigation at the manor. Of course, they're supposed to be keeping it all hush-hush till they can make an official announcement, but you know what Simon's like. Can't keep anything from me once I set my mind to finding out something.'

'OK, I'll be as quick as I can. Half hour, tops. But promise not to start without me — I don't want to miss anything.' Harriet set off towards her house and the two tearoom owners went inside to start their day.

Twenty-five minutes later, Harriet had returned, freshly showered, and the three friends were sitting around a table at the far end of the tearoom, sharing a breakfast of croissants, pain au chocolat and steaming cups of freshly brewed tea.

'C'mon, Liz, it's time to spill the beans,' prompted Sylvie. 'You've been looking like the cat that's got the cream since the moment we arrived, and you're obviously dying to tell us what you know. It's safe to say you've got our attention. I just hope it's not going to be a let-down.'

'Believe me it's worth the wait.' Carefully replacing her cup on the saucer, Liz leaned forward. The others mirrored her, keen to know what she had found out.

'Simon didn't say as much, but odds on it's murder. The skull was damaged. Which could have happened at any time I suppose, given the amount of time the body's been in the ground. The body is male, and has likely been buried in that section of the grounds for about ten years,' said Liz. Seeing their questioning looks, she explained. 'I asked Simon how they know he was buried there for that amount of time. He said they'd been informed that the scientists examining the remains had reached that conclusion. He had no idea how. Apparently, they bring in specialists for that sort of thing. And those scientists are trying to establish the cause of death.'

31

'So if the damage to the skull was the cause of death, we really might have a killer living in this area.' Sylvie's complexion paled at the thought of it. 'It could be someone we know.'

'Let's not get ahead of ourselves, Sylve. We don't have any facts about what happened. And even if the poor man was murdered, the killer could just as easily be a stranger,' said Harriet. She was the most pragmatic of the three. 'It was ten years ago, after all.'

'But it's just like you suggested, Harriet. Simon said whoever buried the body must have been familiar with the area in the first place,' said Liz.

Sylvie shuddered.

'I don't think there's anything to worry about at the moment,' reassured Harriet. 'Unless . . . They haven't found any other bodies up there, have they?'

'No. Simon told me that they've undertaken a thorough search of the immediate area. They used special GPR equipment. So they're confident there're no more bodies.'

'What on earth is GPR?' asked Sylvie.

'Sorry, I forgot you're not an obsessive like me.' Liz spent her spare time watching TV crime shows and reading copious amounts of crime fiction, which meant that she was familiar with the lingo and acronyms used by the police. 'Ground penetrating radar. It's used to scan beneath the surface to see if there's anything buried there that shouldn't be.'

'Makes sense,' said Harriet. 'From what Barney said, this body was buried quite deep, wasn't it? It took the detectorists a while to dig down far enough to realise it was a body.'

'Should we investigate this?' asked Sylvie. Her colour had returned, though she still looked a bit peaky. 'Perhaps we could try to find out who this poor man was.'

'I don't know,' Liz replied, looking uncertain. 'Simon assured me that the police have everything in hand. They're the professionals. They're not going to want us poking our noses in. And we've got more than enough on our plates what with work, the last-minute preparations for the competition, and making sure that no one sabotages our efforts. We don't want to become another Abbotsmead.'

'I agree,' said Harriet. 'But I also think that Sylvie's suggestion of trying to find out who that poor man was, has some merit. After all, he was someone's son, and I'd hate to think of his poor parents fretting about where he is. I've no doubt they'll be devastated when they learn that he's dead. But still, it'd be torture not knowing. Always waiting for the phone to ring, or the knock on the door. I know that I couldn't bear it if either of my kids were missing.'

'My thought precisely,' said Sylvie. 'No matter how old your kids are, you still want to protect them and be part of their lives. I think we should make some effort to try and find out who he is. I'm not suggesting we drop everything else, but we could do something.'

Harriet nodded. 'I know it was a totally different set of circumstances, but you've only got to think back to what brought us together in the first place. If we hadn't have carried out our own investigation, at least one more person would have died.'

'But those were exceptional circumstances,' protested Liz. 'You'd both had your lives upended. You needed answers. We had to do something.'

'And this poor man's family have had their lives upended too. We've mentioned his parents, but there could have been a wife and children too,' said Harriet. 'That body has lain there undiscovered for ten years or more. Do we really think that the police will pull out all the stops to try to find out who that victim was? I'm sure they'll allocate some resources to it, but let's face it, they're always complaining about being overworked. It's not as if they manage to solve every current crime, so I doubt they'll have enough people to divert onto a cold case like this.'

'Harriet's got a point, Liz,' said Sylvie. 'Simon notwithstanding, the police don't have the resources to investigate burglaries, or other crimes they routinely used to follow up on. These days they just seem to want to have quick wins, so their crime statistics look good. We'll steer clear of anything death-related. Just concentrate our efforts on trying to find out who he was. And if we can establish his identity, it might even help the police.'

'I propose that we investigate,' said Harriet. 'His family deserve to know what happened to him.'

'Seconded,' said Sylvie.

'But we don't know enough to be able to investigate!' said Liz.

'Not yet, we don't,' said Sylvie. 'But that's where your Simon comes in. It's the pub quiz tonight. We'll tackle him then.'

CHAPTER 7

Brendon was a busy bee, focused on ensuring that the Monksworthy Arms's hanging baskets, window boxes and other planters were in tip-top condition. As a man who cared deeply about his appearance, he also took pride in his surroundings. And as his husband was working his way through a list of tasks to ensure the smooth running of the pub, Brendon was determined to get its external aesthetics as perfect as possible.

With secateurs in hand, he pruned some rogue foliage. He'd already deadheaded the pansies and petunias, swept up and binned rogue cigarette butts, and soon would begin the task of watering the floral displays. These last few days before the judges arrived were always hectic and stressful. But community spirit was high, and everyone was determined to play their part and do what needed to be done.

'You're doing a sterling job, Brendon! The displays are magnificent,' called Tobias. He was dressed in a pared-down version of his vocational attire — smart trousers, black shirt and dog collar.

'You caught me by surprise. I didn't realise you were there,' said Brendon as he did his best to stifle a yawn.

'You're looking tired.'

'Not been sleeping too well since we heard about that body being found. To be honest, it gives me the creeps just thinking about it. Duncan's complaining. Says I'm tossing and turning all night. Though it doesn't seem to stop him snoring.'

Tobias nodded his head. 'Elsie's having difficulty sleeping too. She's exceptionally jittery at the moment. I've told her it's best to keep busy. Less time to dwell on things out of her control. Hopefully the police will get to the bottom of things soon. Anyway, must get on. Parishioners to see. Keep up the good work. I've a feeling we'll be in with a good chance of winning it this year.'

With Brendon's help, Duncan had transformed the Monksworthy Arms from a business on its last legs, to one of the few thriving hostelries in the area. It had taken a significant amount of blood, sweat, tears, imagination and money, but they were a formidable couple with no intention of giving up on what had been Duncan's dream. By hiring a talented chef, renting out rooms on a B&B basis, and adopting a variety of themed nights, the business venture went from strength to strength. Their most popular event was the weekly quiz night. Teams came from all over the valley to participate, and the competition could get quite fierce.

As usual, Harriet was the first of the Yabbadabbadoos to arrive for the quiz. Her work as an agony aunt for various publications meant that she had the luxury of setting her own hours, whereas Sylvie and Liz were constrained by their opening hours, and occasionally by their customers, usually tourists, who sat nursing a long-cold beverage or nibbling on crumbs. And when that happened, all they could do was drop a couple of subtle hints to get them moving. After all, a village tearoom relied on word of mouth and having a reputation for a friendly ambience. And no small business wanted to get a bad review on TripAdvisor.

Harriet now watched as Brendon weaved through various groups of customers, with the usual pleasantries and warnings to 'mind your backs' as he carried the tray of drinks to Harriet's table. Unusually for a quiz night there were only four drinks on the tray, which meant that one of the team wasn't planning to attend tonight's event.

'No Sir Barnaby tonight, then?' asked Brendon as he placed the drinks on the table.

'How did you guess?'

'No GBD — gin mixed with dandelion and burdock.' Brendon grinned. The cocktail was a Barney special. Throughout the entire time Brendon and Duncan had run the pub, Barney was the only person who had ever been known to order it. And for some reason, he only ever insisted on having it on a quiz night.

'Work commitments,' said Harriet. 'You still on for next week's shopping trip?'

'Naturally. Wouldn't miss it for the world.'

'I've just learned there'll be a sale at my go-to boutique on the same day — could we add it to the list? I'm hoping to pick up a bargain or two. Remember that handbag and matching shoes?'

'The aquamarine ones, with the killer heels?' Brendon's voice sounded almost dreamy as he evoked the memory. 'Is that where you got them?'

'Those are the ones.' She smiled and nodded. 'Oh look, Sylvie and Liz are here.' Harriet waved and indicated that she had already got the drinks in. 'Just waiting on Simon now.'

'I'd better head back and give Duncan a hand. He's rushed off his feet and even from this distance I can sense his baby blues boring into the back of my head,' said Brendon, grinning. He said a quick hello to the others and headed back to the other side of the bar.

For once, Simon arrived long before the quiz was due to start.

'Got you one in.' Harriet pointed at his ale as he sat down.

'Much appreciated.' He gulped down an inch or two of the amber-coloured liquid, then gave a satisfied sigh. 'Right, let's get it out of the way, because if we're to stand any chance of winning, we need to be focused. I suppose you want an update?'

The three women nodded.

'First off, I know you've got the sleuthing bug after finding Bertie's killer, but believe me, this is different.' Simon looked sternly at them. 'There's nothing linking any of you to this case. If you want my opinion, the safest thing for each of you would be to sit back and allow the police to get on with it. Whoever buried that body went to a great deal of trouble to ensure that it wasn't discovered. Which means that if the killer's someone who lives in this area, they're going to be panicking.'

'You just said killer!' said Liz.

'Shhh, keep your voice down, sis.' Simon glowered at each of them to emphasise that he was serious. 'Yes, word came through this afternoon that it was murder. They'll no doubt release a statement in a day or two. So, until then, keep schtum, because I could get into all sorts of trouble. Do you understand?'

They all nodded agreement.

'So leave the investigation to the professionals,' persisted Simon.

'We weren't thinking of poking our noses into a murder investigation,' said Sylvie. She spoke quietly so as not to be overheard.

'But we were thinking of trying to find out who that poor man was,' said Harriet. 'We're just thinking of his family. They must have been to hell and back over the years, wondering where he was.'

'Sorry, Si. I'm with them on this. It can't do any harm for us to dig around and see what we can find. If we come up with anything, we'll let you know immediately,' said Liz.

'You're all impossible,' sighed Simon.

'But you wouldn't have us any other way,' said Liz, as she placed an arm around her brother's shoulder and pulled

38

him close. 'C'mon, Si. Perhaps we'll be able to help. And we promise that we're only interested in finding out who he was. Finding out who killed him will be down to the police. After all, you're the professionals.'

'And if we find out who he was, we'll tell you straightaway and even let you take the credit for it,' added Sylvie. The other two nodded their agreement. 'See, Si, you've nothing to lose. Now, there's not long until the quiz starts, so has everyone switched their phone off?'

'Fine. I'm sure you can't do any harm trying to identify him. But I'll expect regular updates.' He glanced at his watch. 'We've still got a few minutes before Duncan makes a start, so I'll let you in on some top-secret information which mustn't become public knowledge.'

Simon leaned forward to bridge the gap between them. When he spoke, his voice was barely audible. 'The body was fully clothed when it was buried. Of course, the fabrics have degraded, so they'll need to do formal tests to establish whether they can get anything useful from them. During the post-mortem, they removed the shoes and discovered something which could turn out to be a huge help in establishing the victim's identity.'

'What did they find?' asked Sylvie.

'The left foot had six toes.'

All three women coughed and spluttered as their drinks went down the wrong way.

CHAPTER 8

Having completed her usual five-mile early morning run, before most of the villagers had even left the comfort of their beds, Harriet had set about showering, then put a wash on and had breakfast. Since moving to the village, she frequently joined Liz and Sylvie at the tearoom to enjoy a leisurely breakfast before the establishment opened to the public. However, this morning, Harriet had three reasons for breakfasting alone.

Firstly, she had an exceptionally large amount of correspondence to reply to. For the last few weeks, requests for Aunt Aggie's sage advice had been arriving in her inbox thick and fast. Not only that, but the magazines she worked for regularly forwarded her copious letters sent through the more traditional snail-mail route.

Secondly, the tearoom would be crazily busy that day thanks to an anticipated coachload of tourists. And finally, Harriet had scheduled in time to find out as much as possible about people born with an extra toe.

Harriet was never happier than when she had some meaty problem to get her teeth into.

There were many things she could have chosen to do with her life. Things which could have made her a great deal of money. However, she valued job satisfaction over wealth.

It was this determined streak and good old-fashioned common-sense approach which had aided Harriet in her chosen career of an agony aunt. She genuinely cared about people. Even those she had no personal connection with. And unlike many people, she had honed the ability to cut through emotional noise and offer valuable advice in a dispassionate, yet non-preachy way. Which was the reason that so many readers turned to her.

Having worked her way through twenty-four requests for help, Harriet felt the need to clear her mind before she set about researching the unusual phenomena of people born with more than five digits on any or all limbs. Some fresh air was just what she needed to get into the right headspace, so she decided to mow the front lawn. The back garden needed doing too, but she'd hung freshly laundered clothes to dry on the line, and she thought it best to leave that section of grass until later.

As she pushed the mower back and forth across her front lawn, she breathed deeply. The smell of freshly mown grass was invigorating, and the lines created by the rotary mower provided a sense of satisfaction of a job well done. The warmth of the sun kissed her bare arms. It made a pleasant change from the comparative coolness of indoors.

'Hello, Mrs Joyce, I've got another parcel for you,' called John Morris, the postie.

'Thanks, John.' She wiped her hands on her jeans before reaching out to take the parcel off the younger man. It was her next consignment of letters from readers asking for Aunt Aggie's advice.

'Why do you keep getting so many parcels? They're sent to you so frequently. At least three times a week. You're not some kind of celebrity, are you?' He wrinkled his nose in puzzlement.

'Nope. Just an ordinary run-of-the-mill person, I'm afraid.'

'Somehow I doubt there's anything run-of-the-mill about you Mrs Joyce.' He winked suggestively.

Harriet averted her gaze as she felt her cheeks flush. She knew his flirting was harmless, but it was an ego boost, nevertheless. After a short conversation about the upcoming competition, the postie returned to his van none the wiser about Harriet's chosen career. Life in this village was such a change of pace from the soulless town Harriet had recently left behind. It was strange to think that until little over a year ago she'd never even heard of Monksworthy. Yet villagers had welcomed her with open arms and treated her as one of their own.

After learning about the devastating events at Abbotsmead, Harriet realised just how fortunate she had been. It was obvious from what had been said about the Joneses that not all new arrivals in small communities were made to feel so welcome, whereas Harriet had landed on her feet. Strangers had soon become friends. She was happy with her lot in life, and she believed that it was the best move she had ever made.

As she cleaned the lawn mower and lugged it back to the shed, Harriet thought about everything that had happened in the last year. She was just approaching the back door when she heard her phone ping. Keen to know who had messaged her, she stopped in her tracks and repositioned herself so that the sun wasn't shining directly on the screen.

It was a message to their quiz team WhatsApp group from Barney. *Sorry to have let everyone down with last night's no-show at the quiz. How about a catch-up at the old AP? Tonight. 7:30. Don't be late. RSVP. PS — I've already arranged catering and it's not to be missed.*

Harriet smiled as she read the message. It so was typical of Barney. It was a standing joke that he referred to his home as the old AP — the old ancient pile. And as for him arranging catering . . . Well, that was code for 'posh nosh'. Most likely a dinner party which would be in a completely different league from their usual takeouts. She responded immediately, telling him that she'd be there.

The thought of spending the evening with friends filled Harriet with joy. Her life had improved immensely since she had got to know Sylvie and Liz. Her subsequent relocation to Monksworthy had transformed her life and she was happier now than she had ever been.

Nevertheless, there was still a lot to be done before she headed off to Barney's place. And top of the list of tasks was for her to undertake some research to learn everything she could about people born with an extra digit.

CHAPTER 9

As usual at that time of day, the approach to the Cavendish-Mortimer estate was lit up like an airport runway. It was one of Sir Barnaby's rules. The lights were timed to come on well before sunset. With the various commercial buildings being so far off the beaten track, it was essential to see where you were going. It was fortunate that the size of Barney's ancestral estate allowed him to house many of his commercial ventures. Those which he could see from his residence were in converted barns and a coach house. Others which required more space, such as his newly built conference centre, were far enough away so as not to impinge on the wedding venue, the day spa, or more importantly, Barney's privacy.

The last thing Barney wanted was for some chancer to claim that they'd had an accident caused by his negligence. He'd heard plenty of horror stories of responsible business owners being sued by unscrupulous clients who saw it as an easy way to bleed some money out of a successful entrepreneur.

Following a short confab, the three ladies had decided to share a taxi. None of them drank that heavily, but Barney's dinner parties were known to get quite boozy. Whenever he got caterers in, it was because he was trialling them for the wedding venue, or because they wanted to change their menus. Inevitably, there would be various wines paired with each course. Barney valued his trusted friends and relied on them to be honest about what they were served. The caterers might make a big song and dance about new menus; it was the business they were in. But Barney knew that it only took a few disgruntled guests to post a bad review for his bookings to be seriously affected. He had a vested interest in getting it right, and if it meant sharing a tasting with his friends, all the better.

Barney opened the huge front door and greeted them with a smile. 'Welcome. Welcome. Come in. Don't stand on ceremony.' Usually his housekeeper, Elisa Pendlebury, would be there to greet them, but she clearly was not working that evening. 'Before you ask, there'll be just the four of us. Simon can't make it after all, as he's working. Though perhaps it's best under the circumstances that we maintain a low profile with the police.'

'How're you doing, Barney?' asked Sylvie. 'Got over the initial shock yet?'

'Oh, you know me. I'm quite a resilient sort. I must admit that I was shocked to the core at finding the corpse on my first attempt at detectorising. I don't think I'll join them again. Not really my sort of thing. I soon concluded that the possibility of finding buried treasure is far too remote to be worthwhile.'

'You should refer to them as detectorists, not detectorisers,' said Harriet. 'They get quite sniffy if you don't treat their hobby with respect.'

'I'm sure they won't mind if they don't know,' said Barney, with a dismissive flick of his hand. 'It's not as if I have any intention of joining their group again.'

'What's for dinner?' asked Liz. 'We've been rushed off our feet all day. I haven't eaten for hours.' Her stomach growled at the thought of food.

'It's not my traditional sort of fare,' said Barney. 'We're having a buffet. There'll also be wine, or soft drinks should you prefer.'

'Oh?' muttered Liz.

Spotting the look of ill-disguised disappointment on her face, Barney did his best to suppress a smile. 'Don't worry, old thing. It's not a selection of sandwiches and sausage rolls. Not that there's anything wrong with that per se,' he quickly added. He appreciated that there was a chance he was on course to offend his two oldest friends. He knew they served both at their tearoom alongside their famous baked goods, and there were often leftover cakes, pastries, sandwiches and sausage rolls on offer whenever he visited their homes.

'The wedding world's moving on, and the younger demographic — which we are obviously trying to court, as they make up the majority of our clientele — are open to more informal dining options. The days of stuffy silver service formality appear to be on the decline. I've been advised that street food buffets are the way to go. Plenty of delicious culinary fare, and less traditional English snobbery. I'm sure you'll all become converts as soon as you see what's on offer. It's a mix and match of food from around the world. I promise you, it's an absolute gastronomic delight.'

'Well, I for one can't wait to try it,' said Sylvie, rubbing her hands in anticipation.

Barney led the way to the dining room, where numerous hot plates had been set up to keep the food at optimum temperature until they were ready to be sampled.

'Where are the caterers?' asked Liz, as she looked around expectantly.

'Oh, I sent them home after they set everything up. Told them I was hosting a top-secret meeting. Couldn't risk any state secrets being leaked. And it was in their interests not to remain on site.'

'And they believed you?' asked Harriet.

'I'm very convincing. Couldn't believe how quickly they headed off. Of course, the downside is that I'll have to shoehorn them in first thing tomorrow, to give them feedback. But if this gastronomic offering tickles your tastebuds this evening, then I'll award them a contract.'

For the best part of an hour, everyone wandered around helping themselves to samples from many different parts of the world. Throughout that time, there was little conversation, just the sound of *oohs* and *aahs*. And once everyone had had their fill of the savoury dishes, Barney wheeled in a wide array of desserts.

'Told you you'd love it,' he said. 'Now, I'm afraid I have no intention of entirely discarding tradition this evening. Who'll join me in a glass of the finest port and some rather tasty Stilton?'

Everyone agreed that they would love to indulge. 'In that case, I suggest we head to the drawing room, where we can round off the meal while we sit and chat in comfort.'

'How did your fact-finding mission go, Liz?' asked Harriet. It was something she'd wanted to ask about as they'd shared the taxi ride but thought better of it, as she thought it wasn't wise to discuss such matters in the presence of a stranger.

'Fact-finding?' asked Barney. 'You've piqued my interest.'

'Simon told us that the poor soul you discovered had six toes on one of his feet,' said Sylvie.

'Six toes on one foot, eh? The death of the eleven-toed man . . . It could almost be a title of a Sherlock Holmes mystery,' said Barney. 'Now, he was a fine detective.' He nodded his head approvingly.

'You do realise that Sherlock Holmes was a fictional character?' asked Liz. Which was quite rich coming from her, as over the years she had frequently referred to herself as a modern-day Miss Marple, and bristled whenever anyone had the audacity to point out that Jane Marple wasn't a real person.

'Pot, kettle,' said the others in unison, as they all collapsed with laughter.

'That reminds me. Talk among yourselves for a moment,' said Barney. There was a twinkle in his eye as he stood up and began to walk briskly from the room. 'Help yourselves to more port, or whatever else you might fancy from the drinks cabinet. Won't be long!' he called over his shoulder.

It was almost ten minutes later when he finally reappeared. The ladies were mid-conversation and stopped speaking abruptly as all heads turned in his direction. There was a collective gasp of surprise.

'What do you think?' he asked, as he looked at each of his guests in turn. 'Honest opinion. Do I cut the mustard?'

Barney was wearing a long caped overcoat, which looked like something out of the ark. With a deerstalker hat, his full head of hair was no longer visible. And somehow, he had even acquired a calabash pipe, which he placed in his mouth and now sucked on experimentally — even though it was empty and he had never smoked a pipe in his life.

'Where on earth did you get that and why are you wearing it?' asked Sylvie. She was used to Barney's eccentricities, but still . . .

'Oh, I've had this get-up for quite a while. Beatrice sourced it for me.' As Sir Barnaby's PA of many years, Beatrice Cornish had been asked to complete many unexpected tasks, but this surely topped them all.

'Why?' asked Harriet.

'I wore it to one of the murder mystery events held on the estate. Thought I looked quite the part. I seem to recall that I was quite the talking point.' He smiled at the memory. 'Now, if we're going to solve this mystery of the eleven-toed man, then what more could we want than to be inspired by the great Sherlock Holmes?'

'Well, it's certainly a statement outfit,' laughed Harriet.

'You're not wrong there,' said Sylvie, as she and Liz chuckled at Barney's get-up.

Barney continued, unperturbed by their reaction. 'Ladies, I suggest we formulate a plan. To that end, Harriet — an update, please.'

Harriet cleared her throat before speaking. 'As it's a subject I'm unfamiliar with, I had to start from scratch. Really there's not much information out there on polydactyly, and I can't see how it will help us identify that poor soul.'

'Polydactyly?' Liz looked mystified.

'Having more than the standard ten fingers and ten toes,' explained Harriet. 'It's a relatively rare genetic condition.'

'Define relatively rare,' said Barney. His head was cocked as he listened attentively.

'About one in a thousand babies are born with it, and there are different types.'

'What do you mean by different types?' asked Sylvie.

'Well, it can occur on hands or feet, and basically anywhere along the hand or foot. So there could be an extra thumb or big toe. An additional pinkie or little toe. Or even an extra digit somewhere in the middle.'

'I've never really understood genetics,' said Barney. 'I must admit that I used to zone out in science lessons.'

'Do you have a pen and paper handy?' asked Harriet.

'I'll get one.' Barney headed out of the room and returned a few moments later. He handed them to Harriet.

'I'm no expert, but simply put,' Harriet began, 'any living organism, be it human, animal or plant is made up of a collection of cells. For this purpose, all you need to understand is that when a child is conceived, it is formed by characteristics from both parents. Each characteristic is determined by genes, and those genes can be dominant or recessive.'

'I'm not sure I understand,' said Sylvie. Her brow furrowed as she puzzled over what Harriet was saying. 'I get the bit about kids looking like their parents, but it's the dominant or recessive thing that's confusing me.'

'I'll draw it out for you. It might help,' said Harriet. She proceeded to give the others a crash course in basic genetics.

'Humans have twenty-three pairs of chromosomes.' Sensing that Liz was about to question this, Harriet held up a hand before she was interrupted. 'You don't need to understand the nitty-gritty of this. All you need to know is that each of the twenty-three pairs is made up of one chromosome from the mother and similarly one from the father.'

Everyone nodded.

'Now, chromosomes are made up of numerous genes. So, if two dominant genes for a particular characteristic, such as eye colour, are passed on by the parents, then then the off-spring will have that dominant characteristic. If a dominant and a recessive gene are passed on, the dominant one wins again. It's only when two recessive ones are passed on together that the recessive characteristic becomes an issue.' Seeing their puzzled faces, she decided to put their minds at rest. 'Don't worry, you don't need to understand this. I only went into detail because Barney asked about it.'

'You really are exceptionally intelligent,' said Barney. He nodded approvingly. 'Puts me to shame.'

'We all have strengths and weaknesses,' she replied, blushing under his gaze. She cleared her throat again before she continued. 'But I only have the most basic understanding of genetics. I'm just telling you what I learned in school. And I've no idea how it affects things in this instance. Truthfully, it's way too complicated for me. So don't go thinking that I'm a genius, because I'm not. What I'm trying to say is that this man had six toes on one of his feet, but there's no obvious way we can use it to identify him.'

'I guess it would have been easier if he'd had an extra finger or thumb,' said Liz. 'There's a greater chance that someone would have noticed. But with an extra toe . . . Well, most of the time that would have been covered by his shoes.'

'Precisely. Which is why, unless we get very lucky and just happen to come across someone who knew a missing man with an extra toe, we're not going to make any progress.' As she looked around, Harriet saw everyone's disappointed expression. 'Sorry, guys, I did my best, but on this occasion it didn't help.'

'Don't underestimate yourself. This is fascinating stuff,' said Barney. He reached out to squeeze her hand. 'And now we all have a much better understanding of genetics thanks to your eloquent explanation. Though there doesn't seem to be any easy way of identifying our mystery man. Perhaps it's best left to the police.'

'I'm sure they'll check their missing persons database,' said Liz.

CHAPTER 10

Good food, fine wines and pleasant conversation had ensured a lovely evening with Barney. The man was a force of nature whose infectious love of life usually lifted even the darkest of moods. However, as they said their goodbyes, everyone, including the man himself, felt a little downbeat. They had all had high hopes of being the ones to uncover the identity of the dead man, but it appeared that there was no obvious route for them to follow.

Indeed, after talking things through, they'd agreed that perhaps Simon was correct. This was an impossible puzzle for them to solve, and the matter was best left to the police.

In any case, it was a busy time of year, and they really needed to be focusing on the Village of the Year competition. As it was, they were already run ragged trying to juggle their day jobs and MAG commitments.

The judges for the competition would be arriving in a few days' time, and there was still plenty of last-minute preparations to keep them all busy. And given the Abbotsmead flower massacre, the MAG committee had committed to a nightly schedule patrolling their village to ensure that no undesirables got up to mischief and spoiled their chances of winning that year's award. They all wanted the village to look its best, not least to impress this year's celebrity judge.

The next few days seemed to fly by as speculation about who the celebrity judge would be ran riot. The villagers had arranged a sweepstake to see if anyone could guess who it was. Rumour had it the pool had surpassed £200.

It was customary for the celebrity judge's identity to remain a closely guarded secret until shortly before the competition began. The mounting excitement about who it might be ensured that people flocked to the participating villages, and the small business owners saw an increase in passing trade. It was a win–win situation for everyone concerned.

With the judges due to arrive at the village the following day, the MAG committee members had gathered at the vicarage ready for the email revealing who the celebrity would be, along with the full list of who was on the judging panel.

As the Reverend Tobias Daniels was chair of the group, the email would be sent to him. When the message eventually came through, it was apparent that the usual public and corporate officials were being wheeled out to fulfil the role they had undertaken many times before. Though, disappointingly for many gathered at the pub, this year's celebrity judge was not a well-known actor, singer or even writer. It was someone named DJ Juicer.

'Anyone know who this so-called celebrity is?' asked Barney. Judging by the number of shrugging shoulders and shakes of the head, no one did. 'Well, that's a bit of a letdown. I was hoping they'd have someone interesting this year. Jeremy Clarkson, perhaps. He'd inject some pizzazz to the proceedings. As I understand it, this isn't too far from his neck of the woods. Though I suppose he's got his hands full with that farm of his. Never mind, perhaps next year. I can but hope . . .'

These last few words trailed off as Barney stared wistfully into the distance, as his imagination conjured up a scenario of his meeting one of the few people he admired. He had never been a petrolhead, but *Clarkson's Farm* was his guilty pleasure.

His latest line of thought was broken when Liz spoke. 'Found him!' she shouted as she scrolled through information on her phone. Everyone turned to listen to what she had to say. 'Apparently, he's quite big on the club scene.'

'If they were going for a DJ, they should have got someone like Clancy Petfield,' said Sylvie.

'Oh, that would have been amazing!' squealed Elsie. 'We're such fans of *PopTime*. Aren't we, Toby?'

Her husband nodded his agreement. 'Everything stops for *PopTime*. It's our thing. We make a point of sitting down for a cuppa and plate of chocolate digestives.'

'Still, I suppose that by having this DJ Juicer on the judging panel, it'll ensure that the younger generation take an interest in the event,' said Gwen. 'You never know, we might get some younger blood on the committee.'

'Better get out and spread the word,' said Brendon. 'Do you know what time they're scheduled to arrive?'

'We're second on the list,' said Toby. 'They're calling at Abbotsmead first, and we're pencilled in for eleven o'clockish.'

'Given what's happened there, they're not going to pose a threat,' said Sylvie. 'Eleven is good, it'll allow us time to give everything a last-minute once-over.'

'Absolutely. Positive thoughts, everyone!' said Barney. 'I suggest we keep the surveillance rota up throughout the night and reconvene at seven o'clock tomorrow morning. It's the final push. Tomorrow morning, we need this village to be in tip-top condition. Instagram-ready. Experience shows that if there's even a blade of grass out of place, we could end up losing out. We can't influence the judging panel's decision-making. But if we don't end up winning, we'll have the satisfaction of knowing that we've gone down fighting, and it won't be down to complacency on our part.'

CHAPTER 11

It was the morning of the competition. As seven o'clock approached, many of the villagers were already assembled outside the village hall. The sun had risen a few hours earlier, and the weather forecast was for balmy temperatures and sunshine for the rest of the day.

With everyone assigned tasks, it was time for the final preparations to begin. The overall aim was to achieve aesthetic perfection, or as near as they could get to it. There were tiny pieces of litter to be picked. A last-minute mowing of the grass on the village green. The final hanging baskets and pots to be watered. One or two windows to be cleaned. Paving stones that had been missed the day before to be scrubbed. And any flowers that had wilted overnight to be deadheaded. It was events such as these which united the community with a common sense of purpose.

'Any idea who the celebrity judge is?' asked Harriet. She had been too busy to catch up with the others yesterday.

'Someone called DJ Juicer,' said Brendon. 'Word is he's big on the fancy club scene. Not my cup of tea. But he'll no doubt appeal to some.' He and Harriet were on litter-picking duty. They were both dressed down in their so-called scruffs.

Which meant freshly laundered jeans, T-shirt and trainers. Their only concession to not looking smart was the soiled gardening gloves which protected their hands.

'His name sounds familiar, but for the life of me, I can't remember where I've heard it . . .' Harriet was thoughtful. 'No doubt it'll come to me at some stage. Who knows, when he turns up, I might even recognise him. After all, I doubt it's his real name. It sounds far too contrived.'

'You think?' laughed Brendon. 'My money's on his real name being something like Joe Smith. That wouldn't go down well on the club scene. He'd hardly be thought of as being cool with a name like that.'

'Does anyone apart from our age group say *cool* these days?' asked Harriet.

'No idea.' Brendon shrugged his shoulders. They continued diligently working their way through the village and returned to the village hall shortly before nine o'clock. By that time, it seemed that everyone else had completed their tasks too, which allowed sufficient time to shower, change and grab some much-needed breakfast before the arrival of the judges.

As eleven o'clock approached, the committee members had reconvened outside the village hall to welcome the judges. It was not good form to keep them waiting. Not that the MAG committee had ever been that discourteous. But a few years ago, word had reached villages throughout the valley that St Thomas on Wye had lost out on being awarded third place when their welcoming committee had the misfortune to find themselves locked inside the church vestry, an embarrassing incident resulting from a prank by their choir master's eldest son. The judges had been kept waiting for a full ten minutes and were not best pleased, as it put their schedule out for the remainder of the day.

A small convoy of unfamiliar vehicles approached Monksworthy village hall's small parking area. It could accommodate up to twenty vehicles, which made it ideal for the weekly classes that took place there, as well as special events such as birthday parties, anniversaries — and Village of the Year competitions. This morning, the car park was empty until the judges' cars began to park in their designated spots. The murmur of nervous chatter among the awaiting crowd stopped abruptly.

Following the usual convention, each judge had arrived in a separate chauffeur-driven car — five in total. There was no good reason for this, except for the fact that the chief judge, Christine Holloway, insisted upon it. She believed that it elevated the panel's status in the competition. And what Christine wanted, Christine got.

'Here we go. Best foot forward, everyone,' said Brendon. His lips were so tight they barely moved as he spoke.

He wasn't the only one on edge. Most of the committee's faces seemed frozen in a rictus grin.

'For goodness' sake, everyone, take a deep breath and just act naturally,' whispered Tobias. 'It isn't the first time we've done this. They're just people. Think of them as tourists if you need to. Most of you deal with them day in, day out. The judges are here to see how wonderful our village is. You'll all scare them to death, the way you're acting.' Taking a step forward from the others, he readied himself for greeting the visitors. Though it was clear that he too must be rather nervous, as there was a tremor in his voice.

Barney sighed in frustration. 'I suppose I'll have to endure that dreadful woman simpering over me.' He looked around. 'You're all behaving as though you're about to go on a first date. And I should know. I've had far too many of those. Oh well, once more unto the breach, and all that . . .'

As the chauffeurs opened the car doors, Barney squared his shoulders then strode purposefully forwards to stand next to Tobias. He was determined to treat this just like any other business encounter. His smile was warm, welcoming and genuine. That is, until his gaze fell upon Christine, and he had to force himself to maintain the expression.

Christine's haughty manner was well-known by everyone assembled. She had served as a Village of the Year judge for many years. She was an exceptionally tall, overtly self-entitled woman, who looked down her nose at anyone she believed to be unworthy of her time or consideration. This attitude made it difficult for people to warm to her and did little to make an occasion such as this a pleasant experience. The one person who managed to avoid her withering expression was Barney. She'd had romantic designs on him for many years, no doubt because of his wealth and social status. But Barney had never been able to find her attractive in return.

The other judges also stepped out of their vehicles and approached the awaiting committee, gazing around appreciatively. As usual, three of them worked for the county council as public servants in some capacity or another. This year the panel was rounded out by the celebrity judge, DJ Juicer.

The panel seemed pleasant enough, but Christine made Barney's skin crawl, and he knew that, if past years were anything to go by, she would engineer some pretext to get him on his own. Sure enough, she ignored the reverend and made a beeline for him. The chief judge grasped his outstretched hand with her own, like the tentacles of a monster from the deep, looking him up and down greedily. It was as though she was undressing him with her eyes.

'Sir Barnaby, darling,' she purred, 'how lovely to see you again.' She kissed the air around him.

Knowing that at worst he would only have to spend an hour in her company, Barney dug deep and willed his smile not to falter. However, his cheeks flushed with embarrassment at this dreadful woman's unwanted attention and were becoming redder by the second. For one who was usually in control of any social occasion, he found himself struggling to regulate his breathing. As he felt her breath on his face, he felt like a mouse cornered by a cat. He was prey and she was toying with him. Every fibre of his being wanted to run, but he knew he must stand his ground. If he upset her in any way, it could negatively affect their chances in the competition.

Thankfully, it seemed that DJ Juicer had picked up on Christine's predatory interest in Sir Barnaby, as he deftly stepped in to intervene. The DJ was used to having to deal with unwanted attention, though it was usually from girls young enough to be his daughter, emboldened with alcohol or occasionally other substances. Years of dealing with this sort of situation had taught him that there was no point in being polite. The direct approach was best, as embarrassment had a way of making most people think again.

'Whoa, steady on, love,' he said in a jocular manner. His voice was loud enough for everyone to hear what he was saying. 'Have you superglued yourself to his hand or something? If you don't let go soon, you'll have people talking.'

The spell was immediately broken and Christine let go. She shot DJ Juicer a contemptuous look. 'Be quiet, you silly little man. You don't know what you're talking about.' She was not impressed by this year's so-called celebrity judge. Nevertheless, she moved on to shake the others' hands.

Barney breathed a sigh of relief and then mouthed a silent thank-you to the guest judge.

'You're welcome, mate,' he replied under his breath. 'Seems she's got the hots for you, and no mistake. Think you could do with a stiff drink.'

'You're not wrong there,' said Barney, as he watched Christine sashay past the welcome party.

'Do you want a swig of this?' he asked. He held out a sports bottle. 'I've only had a sip or two.'

'What's in it?' asked Barney.

'Not sure exactly. It's one of me wife's concoctions. I'm running on empty this morning and I'm in need of a bit of a pick-me-up. Last night's gig was a late one. You know what it's like, you reach a certain age, and you hit the proverbial wall. Sometimes you just need to have a decent kip. Sometimes you need something a bit stronger.' He held the bottle up to the light. 'This is all it usually takes to energise me, though it tastes a bit different today. Got a bit of a tang to it. Good stuff though. Her recipes haven't failed me yet. I can recommend it.'

'It's a kind offer, old bean, but I'll pass if you don't mind,' said Barney. 'I'm strictly a coffee man at this time of day. But if, as you claim, that's supposed to energise you, I'd suggest you drink it down. You're looking rather peaky, and I've a feeling you've a long day ahead of you.'

'You're right,' he agreed. 'I'll get this meet-and-greet over, then I'll neck the rest of bottle. It doesn't help that I skipped breakfast.'

'Well, I think we can help you there, just as long as it won't be construed as bribery,' said Barney.

'What do you mean?' asked Juicer.

'You see those lovely ladies?' he gestured at Liz and Sylvie. Juicer nodded. He gave the pair a little wave.

'They run the most amazing tearoom in the village — you'll see it on the tour, wonderful display in the window. They have a spread ready for when you go past, but Liz always has a couple of pastries at the ready, and I believe there are a few going spare at the village hall. After all, we can't have you collapsing on us. Reverend Daniels and Christine will be occupied for a few minutes while they confirm the logistics of the tour. So, I'm sure that leaves enough time for you to sit down in the village hall, finish your energy drink and demolish a few of Liz's creations. I assure you from personal experience, they're not to be missed.'

'I'd appreciate that,' Juicer said, clearly brightening at the thought of some food. 'Truth is, I'm feeling a bit light-headed.'

'In that case, get yourself inside. It's open. I'll ask Liz to sort you out.'

Barney beckoned Liz over. 'This is DJ Juicer, Liz. You don't happen to have any pastries on hand, do you?'

'Of course,' smiled Liz, 'you know me. I have a spare Tupperware container full of them. I took my Girl Guides oath seriously: I'm prepared for most eventualities, especially if they're cake-related. Come with me.'

She led the hungry DJ inside the village hall, found a paper plate and arranged some pastries on it. Then she left him alone to tuck in. He really didn't look very well, she thought as she stepped back into the sunshine. But it was best to leave him to it. Some people were quite funny about eating in front of strangers. She hoped he would be quick, though. The committee would be ready to begin their tour any moment now.

CHAPTER 12

'Come on, people. Chop-chop. We've a schedule to keep to.' Christine had known for weeks which village was going to be awarded this year's coveted prize. Apart from her, there were only two other people who knew how that decision had been reached. And one of those was proving to be expensively problematic. He would have to be dealt with before things got out of hand, as there was far more than the result of this silly competition at stake. But that was for another time, as for now, there was this charade to endure. She clapped her hands again, and everyone fell into line, ready to accompany her on the village tour. Everyone, that is, apart from DJ Juicer, who was nowhere to be seen. 'Where's that dreadful little club man?' She knew his name but chose not to use it. He wouldn't have been her choice, but this year the mayor had decided to stick his oar in and for some unfathomable reason had asked Juicer if he'd like to be the celebrity judge. Which meant that Christine was stuck with the man.

'Do you mean DJ Juicer?' asked Liz.

'Yes. That's what I said.' Christine shot Liz a withering look. 'Where's he gone? We're on a tight schedule and can't afford to waste time.'

'He was in the village hall a few moments ago,' said Liz. 'He was feeling a bit under the weather. So he's eating one of my pastries as a little pick-me-up.' She didn't like this pugnacious woman. Her attitude might very well be acceptable in the day-to-day running of the local authority, Liz thought, but here in Monksworthy, people treated each other with respect.

'He should have taken this role seriously and readied himself by having a proper breakfast to enable him to undertake his duties. It's my understanding that he had very little sleep last night. Out enjoying himself instead of getting to bed at a reasonable hour to ensure that he's on top form today. It's such a disrespectful attitude,' said Christine.

Sylvie harrumphed loudly and there were other audible mutterings of disapproval from those assembled. It was apparent that many of those present did not appreciate Christine's attempt at demeaning a fellow judge.

'Someone go and get him. Now! We've work to do!' Christine was determined not to engage with these lesser mortals.

'I'll go,' said Barney, happy to escape.

'I'll come with you,' said Elsie. It was the excuse she needed to put some distance between herself and that horrible woman. The vicar's wife was the sweetest of souls, but even she had had more than enough of Christine Holloway's rudeness. She worried she might just say something she soon regretted if she remained within ten feet of her.

'That woman makes my blood boil,' she muttered as she trotted along beside Barney. 'She's just awful.'

'Isn't she just?' agreed Barney. 'She's most unpleasant. Still, she'll be on her way soon enough, and we won't have to see her again for another year.'

'I don't know how you tolerate her making a play for you like that,' Elsie said rather bravely. 'She clearly has no shame.'

'It's not easy, believe me, but she'll be gone soon,' said Barney. They had reached the village hall and were about to step inside. 'After you, dear lady.'

Barney stepped aside and held out his hand to allow her to walk ahead of him.

'You always have such impeccable manners,' said Elsie as she entered the building.

Barney smiled appreciatively, then called out, 'Sorry, old chap. The respite is over. It's time to make a move.'

Elsie, who was the first to enter the room, saw DJ Juicer seemingly asleep in the chair.

'Oh, bless him. He's exhausted. It seems cruel to have to wake him.'

'Wakey-wakey, old bean. It's time to go. You've work to do.' Barney touched him lightly on the shoulder but got no response. He suddenly had an awful feeling that the worst might have happened.

'Elsie, my good woman, would you mind stepping outside?' Ever the gentleman, and at pains not to distress Elsie, Barney kept his voice level. He didn't want to unnecessarily cause her alarm. 'I think DJ Juicer needs a minute.'

The vicar's wife looked between him and the sleeping DJ. Sensing something was amiss but not comprehending what had happened, she walked quickly back the way she'd come without a word.

Once she had gone, Barney moved closer and looked into DJ Juicer's face. He knew that no amount of cajoling would get the man to join the rest of the judging panel.

This was the second corpse that Barney had discovered in the space of a week. It was becoming a habit. He felt jinxed.

Over the years, he had learned a thing or two about police procedure through his friendship with Andy, the chief constable. And although he had no idea why DJ Juicer had died so suddenly, he knew that the death would initially be treated as suspicious. He also appreciated that he needed to keep everyone else out of the village hall, as it would inevitably be treated as a crime scene. The poor man had been far younger than Barney. And he may have looked a little under the weather, but he was far from being at death's door.

Barney retreated gingerly towards the door, careful not to touch anything. Then he took out his phone and called Andy.

CHAPTER 13

Barney stood guard at the entrance to the village hall. He cradled the phone as he listened to the ringtone and willed Andy to pick up. As they had cancelled their usual round of golf that day, he had no idea whether or not his friend would be able to take the call. If he didn't, Barney decided, he'd leave a message telling him what had happened and dial 999.

A raised voice intruded upon his chaotic thoughts. He glanced up and saw that it was Christine Holloway, demanding to know where DJ Juicer was. Barney always tried to see the best in people, no matter how badly they behaved, but she had a way of bulldozing her way through life to get what she wanted. He shut his eyes and turned away as he tried to block a tide of rising frustration. The last thing he needed right now was to have a confrontational encounter with that objectionable woman.

'Hello, Barney. I wasn't expecting a call from you this morning.'

Barney was so wrapped up in his thoughts that he hadn't noticed Andy had answered.

'Barney? Is everything all right?'

'Andy, thank goodness. Something awful has happened. I need—' However, Barney's explanation was cut short as someone grabbed hold of his shoulder and attempted to push him aside.

'Stay back! You're not to go in there!' Barney barked, sounding like a sergeant major, and there was no mistaking the fact that this was an order. In one seamless movement, he used his free hand to push away whoever had hold of him. Having momentarily forgotten all about the competition, it was only when she squealed and stumbled backwards that he realised it was Christine Holloway.

A short distance away, the mumbled conversations of the group stopped abruptly. In all the time they'd known Barney, not one of them had ever heard him raise his voice.

Tobias Daniels raced over to defuse the situation. Christine wasn't used to being challenged, let alone confronted in such a forceful manner. She had stormed through life always getting her own way, and suddenly she didn't know what to do. Shocked at Barney's response, her cheeks burned with the understanding that whatever was going on here, she was no longer top dog.

'Get her out of here, and keep everyone back,' Barney told Tobias.

The vicar immediately appreciated that something serious must have happened. He also realised that this was not the time to allow his curiosity to get the better of him. Instead, he did as he was told and led Christine away.

'Barney!' The chief constable was shouting. 'Speak to me!'

'S-sorry, old chap,' said Barney, as his attention switched back to the phone call. 'There's a lot going on over here.'

'Take a deep breath and tell me what's happened.'

Barney experienced a wave of relief wash over him as he succinctly explained the situation to his friend.

'Make sure no one goes in or out of the building. Keep information to a minimum. I'm on my way over, and I'll arrange for the relevant teams to attend. And well done, my friend, for keeping a cool head and doing the right thing. It won't have been an easy situation for you to encounter.'

Sylvie and Liz broke away from the group and made a beeline for Barney. They'd questioned Elsie, but all she had told them was that DJ Juicer was fast asleep. And it seemed that Liz and Sylvie were the only ones to realise that the man must've died.

'What's happened in there?' asked Sylvie. Their friend's dire expression said it all.

'He's dead. The emergency services are on their way.'

'Poor man,' said Liz. 'They'll have to treat it as a crime scene, won't they? He wasn't feeling too clever when I left him. I should have stayed. I might have been able to do something or at least call for an ambulance.'

'You must've been the last person to see him alive,' said Sylvie.

'I know. I feel terrible. He might still be alive if I hadn't left him alone.' Tears welled in Liz's eyes.

'You mustn't blame yourself,' said Barney. 'The truth is that we were all so focused on that stupid competition that none of us thought to check on him. We all neglected him.' They stood in silence; each lost in their own thoughts.

Eventually, at the sound of an approaching vehicle, they turned to see a car pull into the parking area. It was the chief constable. 'You can stand down now, Barney. I'll take it from here.' He nodded a greeting. 'Ladies.'

'Cooee! Chief Constable!' It was immediately apparent that Christine Holloway had regained her composure and was determined to get herself noticed by someone as important as the chief constable. 'Could you tell me what's going on?'

'At this moment in time, no.' The chief constable's words were clipped.

'But we're about to—'

Andy turned to Barney, cutting her short. 'Perhaps you could take all of these people away from here? To somewhere like the local pub.'

'The tearoom is closer,' suggested Sylvie. 'I'm sure we could all do with some refreshments, and we had set it up ready for the judges.'

'That's fine,' said Andy. 'Just make sure that nobody leaves there until we've spoken to them.'

'Absolutely, leave it with me,' said Barney.

Christine Holloway looked aghast. They had a schedule to keep to. As far as she was concerned, the Village of the Year competition was the pinnacle of the calendar. It was the one weekend a year she had to shine. People fawned over her, and she milked it for all it was worth. She still had no idea what had happened, but it obviously had something to do with that dreadful celebrity judge. 'You can't possibly interrupt our schedule. It's far too important an event.' When the senior police officer ignored her, she reached out and grabbed his arm. 'Do you know who I am?' There was no mistaking her annoyance as she demanded the chief constable's attention.

'Take your hand off me and move back, madam! That's an order, not a request.' The chief constable's patience was wearing thin. 'Attention, everyone!' Andy's voice exuded authority. 'I'm afraid that there's been an incident. My officers will need to investigate. We'll need to speak to all of you, and I'd appreciate your full cooperation. If you'd head over to the local tearoom, I've been assured that refreshments will be provided to tide you over while you wait. Until you've heard otherwise from one of my officers, no one is to leave that premises.'

And just like that, the excitement and optimism of the morning evaporated, as all but one of them reflected sombrely on the death of a man they had only met earlier that morning.

CHAPTER 14

Sylvie's hand trembled as she removed the key from her bag and opened the door to the Delicious Desserts Tearoom. Having recently lost her own husband, she couldn't help but wonder about DJ Juicer's family. Someone close to him would have to identify his body, just as she had done for Bertie. As memories flooded back, she fought to banish them. And she appreciated that the best way to do that was to keep herself busy. This should have been a happy day. Not a sad, reflective one, where old wounds were opened.

Putting on a brave face, she did her best to play the genial hostess. 'Come in, everyone. Make yourselves comfortable.'

She stood aside as they filed inside and watched them take seats at various tables. Christine had pushed past to get into the tearoom first, the other judges and MAG members trailing behind. She looked for the best place to sit, but the three remaining judges chose a table located in another part of the room.

'Now, does anyone want anything to eat or drink?' asked Sylvie.

There was a collective shaking of heads, apart from Christine. 'Is it free, or are we expected to pay?'

Sylvie sighed. 'You can have your first cuppa and pastry free. After that, you'll have to pay.

'In that case I'll have a large latte and a Danish pastry,' said Christine. She had a reputation for never turning down a freebie, and true to form, she sat down expectantly.

'Anyone else?' Sylvie turned to the other judges. 'I'm sorry, I don't think we've been introduced.'

'I'm Neil Wetherspoon, and no, thanks,' said a tall wiry man. 'I've lost my appetite.'

'Cyril Bentley,' said a round-faced man. 'Same here. It's a kind offer, but I couldn't face anything at the moment.'

The remaining judge, who introduced herself as Bryony Leverton, declined the offer too.

Across the room, Elsie was in tears and was being comforted by her husband. On reflection, it had seemed odd when Barney had asked her to step out of the village hall, but she had thought that DJ Juicer was fast asleep. She had never seen a dead body before and didn't particularly want to see one again if she could help it. 'There was nothing any of us could have done, Elsie.' Witnessing her obvious distress, Barney was keen to ease her pain. 'The truth is that the poor chap was gone before we entered the building.'

'Most likely a drug overdose,' said Christine. Her tone was dismissive.

'Shame on you! That's a dreadful thing to say.' Tobias's tone was uncharacteristically sharp. He was appalled at her callous accusation. 'You've no proof whatsoever that the poor man took drugs.'

'Oh, wake up and smell the coffee! The man worked in clubs. People like that are all at it,' she countered.

'That's ridiculous!' snapped Barney. 'Using that logic, we might as well say that you're so obviously on the take.'

'How dare you! That's slander.' Christine stood up so abruptly that her chair toppled over and clattered noisily to the floor.

'No more slanderous than what you've just said about that poor man,' said Brendon. 'Sir Barnaby was just making a point, and you . . . Well, you should be ashamed of yourself. You're a public servant and you're behaving despicably. As far as I'm concerned, the sooner you're out of this village, the better.'

'Oh, don't worry. I'm going, and I won't be coming back. Your pathetic village was never going to win this competition.' Christine snatched up her bag from the table.

'How can you possibly say that?' Cyril asked. He looked agog at the idea. 'We haven't looked around yet. Or made any assessment. Let's face it, Monksworthy is the second village on the list. We've hardly started the tour.'

There were murmurs of agreement from all quarters. He had made a valid point.

'It's a figure of speech!' she snapped. Christine's expression darkened. She wasn't used to being questioned and she didn't like the way this conversation was going.

'No . . . No, I don't believe it is,' said Anthony. 'You'd already decided who was going to win the award. Sir Barnaby's right. You're corrupt. You've taken a bung.'

'That's ridiculous,' Christine spluttered. Her face was red and blotchy. She marched towards to door.

Barney stood up to prevent Christine from leaving.

'Out of my way,' she ordered as she tried to sidestep him.

'You're not going anywhere until we've had the all-clear from the police,' he said. 'Now, sit down and be quiet. You're obviously used to getting your own way, but I won't allow you to do that here.'

There were nods of agreement. Elsie and Brendon applauded.

Ignoring everyone, Barney continued: 'The chief constable has ordered that we stay put. We were all present when he said it. If you disregard that order, you're going to find yourself in a whole heap of trouble, and you'll only have yourself to blame.'

72

There was a moment's silence.

'You haven't touched your coffee and Danish, Ms Holloway,' said Liz. She didn't like confrontations and was keen to lower the temperature in the room.

'Fine. I'll have the coffee and pastry. But I don't wish to speak to any of you. I expect you all to leave me alone.'

'I'm sure we'll be happy to,' muttered Bryony. 'We might only have known poor Mr Juicer for a few hours, but I thought he seemed like a good person. And it's awful that he's—' She stopped short as the tinkling bell above the door announced the arrival of the chief constable, with a uniformed officer following a few paces behind.

CHAPTER 15

The chief constable's voice boomed throughout the small space. 'Thank you all for being so patient. I appreciate it's been a difficult few hours, but I've come to update you on the situation. An initial examination of the scene suggests that the victim, known to you all as DJ Juicer, ingested a poisonous substance, which resulted in his death. Until we know otherwise, his death will be treated as murder.'

There was an audible collective gasp, and Elsie began to hyperventilate.

Toby calmly reached into his wife's handbag, extracted a paper bag and held it towards her face. 'You know the drill, darling. Look at me and focus on breathing. Slowly, now. In . . . And out . . . In . . . And out . . . That's it. You've got it. Everything's all right.' The vicar's matter-of-factness and the readily available paper bag suggested that it was not unusual for Elsie to suffer from a panic attack.

For a short while everyone's attention was on the rhythmic rise and fall of the paper bag.

Liz was the first to break the ensuing silence. 'P-poisoned? Oh, the poor man.'

'Have you actually established the source of the poison?' asked Christine. Her tone was devoid of compassion.

'I'm not at liberty to divulge information about an ongoing investigation. That said, further tests will be undertaken on substances found at the scene.'

'If it's any help, I know for a fact that he had a sports bottle containing some concoction of his wife's. He told me it was a sort of energising drink. Even offered me some, but I declined. Under the circumstances, it's probably just as well,' said Barney. 'He told me he wasn't feeling too clever. Apparently, he'd hardly had any sleep, as he'd been working into the early hours.'

'That bottle is part of the evidence collected at the scene, and its contents will be tested at the laboratory,' said the chief constable, apparently deciding he could reveal a bit more. 'There was also a partially consumed pastry, the remains of which were on a plate.'

'I gave him some pastries,' said Liz. 'He was hungry as he'd not had breakfast.'

The chief constable's eyes narrowed as a thought occurred to him. 'Were those pastries baked in this establishment?'

'Yes.' Liz answered the question without hesitation.

'Sshh. Don't say anything else,' whispered Brendon. He had an awful feeling that he knew where this was leading.

'And who was responsible for their creation?' He scanned the room. 'You see, as yet, we haven't established the source of the poison,' pressed the chief constable.

Before Liz had a chance to say anything else, Brendon piped up. 'It was me. I baked the pastries.'

The other villagers caught on quickly.

'No, it was me. I baked them,' said Anthony.

'It was me,' said Elsie, who now looked and sounded more like her old self.

'I did,' said Sylvie.

'They were mine, I baked them,' said the vicar.

'No, I'm Spartacus!' yelled Barney, as he placed a protective arm around Liz. 'I mean I baked the pastries. They were my finest culinary creation.'

'In that case, I'm afraid that you're all going to have to accompany one of my officers to the station, where you'll be questioned under caution.'

'Are you suggesting that that man was poisoned by one of the pastries from this low-rent caff?' shrieked Christine. 'Take me to the hospital now. That woman's just forced me to eat one of them!' She pointed at Liz. 'You won't get away with this. I'll tell anyone who listens that it was your pastries that did it. I'll sue you for every penny you have.'

Pandemonium broke out as Christine Holloway lunged at the chief constable, wrapping her arms around him and refusing to let go. 'Arrest that woman. She's poisoned me, she's poisoned me!'

'Get this woman off me!' the chief constable ordered, as he struggled unsuccessfully to prise her fingers apart. All of a sudden, the thought of picking up a paint brush and getting on with things at home seemed such an appealing prospect.

CHAPTER 16

It was safe to say that the day had not turned out as anyone had expected. Far from being the start of a weekend celebration showcasing the best of village life, the members of the MAG committee found themselves bundled into the back of a police van. It was a first for everyone concerned. Had they thought about it logically, they might have realised that the chief constable's intention was to give them all a short, sharp shock, and make them realise that it was not acceptable to lie to the police. Especially to the chief constable! And he hoped that by them being transported to the station together, it might give them time to reflect on what they had said and realise how reprehensible their behaviour had been.

'Well, I'm all for expanding my horizons and trying new things, but I didn't expect this,' said Barney. 'This vehicle is far from hygienic. I think I'll have to burn my clothes when I get home.' The others nodded their agreement. 'By the way, I'm still not clear on how to make or bake those pastries. And what are they even called?'

'Oh Barney, you do realise that you could be charged with wasting police time?' said Liz. 'That goes for all of you.' She looked around at the fellow MAG members. 'I love you all to bits, it means a lot that you've got my back. I know I had a momentary wobble back there and I really appreciate you stepping up to support me—'

'We absolutely do,' interjected Brendon.

'But the bottom line is I didn't poison that poor man,' Liz said firmly. 'I'd never intentionally harm anyone. And apart from that, they were leftover pastries from the batch that we shared this morning when we were doing the last-minute preparations. If I *had* poisoned them, then how can the rest of us all still be standing?'

'Still, Andy had no right to accuse you of anything,' said Barney. 'It's insulting. You're above reproach.'

'Absolutely,' said Sylvie, to a chorus of agreement.

'Technically he hasn't accused me of anything,' corrected Liz. 'I know from Simon that it's standard procedure to speak to anyone who might have been involved in a crime. If they believe that poor man was poisoned, then it makes sense for them to speak to me. After all, I did make those pastries, and I'm the person who gave them to him. Once they've tested them for poison, they'll realise that the pastries weren't the source of it.'

'But they've shut our business down,' said Sylvie. 'Who knows what damage it will do to our reputation. Once it becomes public knowledge, and it will when people see those forensic officers traipsing in and out of there in their get-ups, customers might be too scared to return.'

'It won't come to that,' reassured Tobias. 'Locals know and trust you. You'll obviously be cleared, and things will go back to normal. As for day trippers, well, they're not going to be any the wiser. This is big news today, but it'll die down soon enough.'

'I'm not so sure that Christine Holloway will allow it to die down,' said Sylvie darkly. 'She's not the sort to let this drop.'

'Well, she's a nasty piece of work,' said Barney. 'You heard what she said. She more or less let slip that it was a done deal that some other village was going to win the award. I think it's corruption, pure and simple. She's made a deal with someone. People like her only ever do things to line their own pockets. They get away with it because no one thinks to look for evidence of corruption. Well, I think it's time to make some noise. Shake a few trees and see what falls out. So don't worry, ladies, she won't be a problem if I have anything to do with it.'

'I've heard a few rumours about her,' said Brendon. 'Customers say all sorts in the pub. They drop their guard once they've had a drink or two. There've been a couple of people who swore that she's slept her way up the ranks in the council.'

There was a collective gasp.

'I know, it doesn't bear thinking about,' added Brendon, as his lip curled in disgust. 'What some people do just to get ahead in life.'

'As my granddad used to say, loose lips sink ships,' said Gwen. 'And I should know, as I can wheedle information out of anyone.'

'Have you heard anything bad about her, Gwen?' Anthony was keen to know more.

'Well, over the years I've heard from three different sources that she's most likely taken backhanders for awarding contracts to certain people. Do you remember that botched job on the roof of the local primary school?'

Everyone nodded.

'Well, she's supposed to have had a hand in that. Apparently, the work went out to tender. They were sealed bids, and Christine was the only one to have had access to them prior to the decision being made, but when the envelopes were opened, some of them looked as though they'd been tampered with.'

'What happened?' asked Barney.

'Nothing much. Apparently, there was an internal investigation, which was over in a flash. They reported back that there was no evidence of wrongdoing.'

'It's always the same in those organisations,' said Liz. 'Everything's hushed up, and if they need to make up for any financial losses they just put up council tax or business rates. It's a disgrace.'

'I'm afraid that there's corruption in so many walks of life,' said Barney. 'Though, at the moment, taking Christine Holloway down isn't top of our agenda. If we're going to keep up this "I'm Spartacus" stance, you, Liz, need to give us all a blow-by-blow account of how to make those delicious pastries of yours.'

'I hope that won't mean that you'll all go off and make your own, and run our business into the ground,' she replied.

'No chance of that,' reassured Elsie. 'We've all got other things to do. Apart from that, even if we practiced making them from now until eternity, I doubt any of us would reach your exacting standards.'

'Well, I'm afraid that I'm still not going to tell you. As I've already said, I didn't poison that poor young man. I haven't poisoned anyone. So there really is no need for any of you to continue with this pretence. Though it is heartwarming to know that you're all prepared to come to my aid. But the last thing we need is for any of you to be charged with wasting the police's time. They've got enough do to as it is. All their efforts need to be focused on finding the murderer.'

In the end, however, it was only Liz and Sylvie who were interviewed by the police. The chief constable was not naive enough to have believed the collective display of blind loyalty to the women. He had seen it for what it was — a close-knit group protecting their friends.

However, he needed to make sure that people knew, no matter who they were, that they could not go about interfering willy-nilly in police investigations.

It was early evening when the MAG members were finally allowed to return home. Through the intervening hours, samples taken from the stock of ingredients, together with samples from their already baked goods, were tested for harmful substances. At the insistence of the chief constable, these tests were rushed through the forensic laboratory, and the results proved unequivocally that whatever had poisoned DJ Juicer, it hadn't come from anything produced at the Delicious Desserts Tearoom. This meant that Liz and Sylvie were in the clear.

The group stepped out of the police station to be met by Harriet and Rohan Singh, who had turned up to whisk them away from their ordeal.

When Barney spotted Harriet, his heart skipped a beat, and he couldn't help but smile. There were times throughout the day when he'd wondered what she was up to, though he was glad that she had not inadvertently found herself caught up in this ordeal.

Harriet waved when she spotted her friends emerge from the police station. 'I've got enough room for four of you. Duncan sends his love, but he's run off his feet back at the pub. I promised to get you back safely,' she said to Brendon.

'I'm ravenous,' said Barney, as they piled inside the car.

'Me too,' agreed Sylvie.

'Didn't they feed you?' asked Harriet.

'Outside of a vending machine that was almost completely out of stock. There was a water cooler and not much else,' said Brendon. 'You should have a word with that chief constable friend of yours, Barney. Damned cheek, keeping us hanging about all day, if you ask me.'

No one responded. They all sat there lost in their own thoughts as Harriet drove them back to the village.

CHAPTER 17

Harriet hadn't been exaggerating when she had said that Duncan was run ragged with the influx of customers. The pub's car park was completely full and there were cars lining both side of the road as far as the eye could see. 'Bye, everyone. Got to get a wiggle on!' Brendon called as he raced across the road towards the pub.

In retrospect it seemed obvious that people would flock to the Monksworthy Arms that night. After the morning's events at the village hall, followed by the entire MAG committee membership being taken in for questioning, villagers would be concerned. Speculation would be rife, and word would have spread. Inevitably, that would have encouraged outsiders to visit the pub too, as they'd be keen to get closer to the action and find out what was going on. It was human nature.

'I've made a pot of chilli, if anyone's up for it?' Harriet announced to the others.

'Yes, please,' said Sylvie. 'I'm starving.'

'I hope you won't mind me heading home after I've eaten, but I've a list of things to do that just won't wait,' said Barney.

'Surely you can put things off until the morning?' pleaded Liz.

'If only I could. But no, I'm afraid I must put the hours in. The inaugural Winning in Wye event is scheduled for a week or so's time. As it's my baby, so to speak, there's a million and one things I need to oversee.'

'What's Winning in Wye?' asked Harriet. This was the first she'd heard of it.

'Putting it simply, it's my chance of giving something back to the community,' said Barney. 'Well, that and an opportunity for me to possibly expand my business portfolio along the way. I've set it up and I'll be hosting it at my conference centre. The delegates will be local business owners, together with a few movers and shakers from larger companies, and people from local government. It's all about networking. Making contacts to help entrepreneurs take businesses to the next level or even diversify.'

'Sounds as though you're up against it,' said Sylvie.

'Believe me, as things stand there are not enough hours in the day. I've research to do and it's time-consuming. I'll be up until all hours as it is. I think the time has come for me to expand the old business empire once more. I've learned over the years that it's beneficial to have a diverse portfolio as it spreads the risk. Plus, I relish the odd new challenge here and there. Flexes the old grey matter. But with a few potential acquisitions on the horizon, I need to familiarise myself with all available information. Do my homework to enable me to make an informed decision should I decide to take things to the next level. Though I can't help thinking it seems rather rude to eat a meal you've graciously prepared and then ship out, so to speak.'

'Don't worry.' Harriet smiled. 'I won't be offended, but it's important you have something to eat, so that you're not distracted by an empty stomach later on.'

Barney's response took Harriet by surprise as he reached for her hand and kissed it. 'You're very kind.'

Harriet blushed. 'It's nothing really. Not after the day you've had.'

Barney was true to his word and headed home as soon as he had finished eating.

At last, with the table cleared and the dishwasher loaded, Liz spoke. 'This has been one of the scariest days of my life. I tried to put on a brave front, but I was so worried for a moment that I was about to be blamed for that poor man's death. I'll never forget the way you all stepped up to protect me. It was wonderful, but reckless.'

'And I don't think I'll ever forget the look on the chief constable's face when we all insisted that we'd baked those pastries,' said Sylvie. 'But we all knew you were innocent. There was never any doubt.'

'I wish I'd been there to see it,' said Harriet. 'Sounds as though it was quite the moment.'

'What did you get up to while we were stuck at the police station?' asked Sylvie.

'Oh, I was busy working when I heard the sirens. It was blindingly obvious something had happened. So, I popped to the shop, and Rohan said that he'd heard the celebrity judge had died. I headed straight back, thought it best to stay out of the way of the police operation. It was chaotic with all the comings and goings,' said Harriet. 'There just seemed to be one siren after another. Which made me think that he couldn't have died of natural causes. So, I used the time to research DJ Juicer. I just couldn't shake the thought that I'd heard of him before. Even in my younger days I avoided the club scene, and he's not someone my kids spoke about when they lived at home. So I wondered if his name had cropped up in one of the magazines I work for.'

Harriet's eyes sparkled.

'You found something, didn't you? Go on, spill the beans,' urged Liz. Having experienced the warm glow of a home-cooked meal and relaxing in the company of her friends, she looked and sounded more like her usual self.

'Possibly. Though as things stand, it's not much yet. I'm still waiting for someone to call me back with some more details.'

'Tell us, then,' insisted Sylvie. She sat forward in the chair, keen to hear what Harriet had to say.

'One of the perks of my job is that I have free access to the online back catalogues of the magazines I work for. I use it quite a bit. It's especially useful for making sure I don't repeat advice too closely,' explained Harriet. 'So, I typed his name into the search bar for each archive. It wasn't quick as I could only search one archive at a time, but my persistence paid off because I eventually found an article about him.'

'Did it mention him having any enemies?' asked Liz.

'Nothing like that.' Harriet shook her head. 'To be honest, it was a typically anodyne interview, if you get my drift. Nothing controversial. More about the club scene and what goes on in the background to enable a DJ to gain popularity.'

'You've lost me,' said Sylvie. 'How is that useful?'

'In itself it's not. But the article was written by someone I know.' Harriet's eyes were sparkling again. 'As soon as I saw her byline, I recalled her telling me about the interview. She'd spoken to him at length but had agreed to omit some of what they'd discussed from the article. I've no idea why that was, but that's what I'm hoping to—' Harriet's phone rang. She glanced at the screen. 'This is what I've been waiting for.'

She stood up and walked out of the room to take the call.

Even though Harriet was in a different part of the cottage, Liz and Sylvie spoke in low voices so as not to distract her. It was almost fifteen minutes later when their friend returned to the room, a shocked expression on her face.

'I think I might know who was buried on Barney's estate,' she said, as she sat down heavily on the nearest chair.

'What—? Did I hear you right?' asked Liz. 'I thought you were speaking to your contact about DJ Juicer.'

'I was,' said Harriet. 'But I don't believe in coincidences. Not when a body that's remained undetected for years is found, and then days later a man is suddenly murdered less than a mile away. If I'm not mistaken, DJ Juicer might very well have known the man with eleven toes.'

CHAPTER 18

The ladies agreed that there was no time to waste. With a killer on the loose, there was no doubt in any of their minds that they needed to update the police immediately. Liz rang her brother and told him that they had some important information. Within the hour there was a knock on the door. It was Simon, and he was still wearing his uniform.

'What's so urgent?' he asked, without saying hello.

'Rude,' said Liz.

'Don't start, sis.' Simon's usual easy-going demeanour had deserted him. 'It's been a full-on day, and we're all working overtime. If whatever you're about to tell me isn't pertinent to the case, I want to know immediately so that I can get back out there and do my job. I haven't got the time for idle chit-chat.'

'We believe there's a connection between the eleven-toed man buried on Barney's estate and DJ Juicer,' said Harriet.

Simon sighed. 'How could you possibly know that? Do you have any proof?'

'Not definitive proof. But hear me out, please.'

'OK. Look, I'm sorry. I'm just up against it and exhausted.' Simon sat down heavily. 'By the way, I'm sorry you two got hauled off to the police station earlier.' This comment was directed at his sister and Sylvie. 'It was just procedure. That's all.'

'Thought you'd have come to the rescue,' quipped Liz.

'Wouldn't have been allowed anywhere near you,' he said, shaking his head. His sister's teasing bypassed him. 'They'd have had my badge if I'd tried. Interfering in an active investigation. Anyway, enough of that. What makes you think that today's death is linked to the corpse found on Barney's estate?'

'A few years ago, a journalist named Donna Ashbourne wrote an article about DJ Juicer,' said Harriet. 'Though his actual name is Dominic John Liveland. He's a high-profile DJ who chose to call himself DJ Juicer as he and his wife, Madeline, have a company which creates juices. As he's a public figure, they use his public persona as one of their marketing tools.

'Much of the information Donna gathered was published in the magazine she works for. I spoke to her about an hour ago. Without any prompting, she told me that DJ Juicer owed his success to his former publicist. His name was Robin Thornton.'

'Where's this going?' asked Simon. He looked at his watch. 'I really need to get back.'

'Donna said that he stopped being DJ Juicer's publicist a while back, when he had a huge lottery win. The thing is, Robin Thornton had eleven toes. These were all things that DJ Juicer told Donna about at the time, but she agreed not to print them.'

'It's an interesting a coincidence,' said Simon. 'But as things stand, that's all it is. There's no actual proof that the remains found on the Cavendish-Mortimer estate were those of Robin Thornton. There's no actual proof he's even dead. Just out of interest, do you know how much money this Thornton guy won?'

'No. Donna said that DJ Juicer didn't go into specifics. All he said was that it was a substantial, lifechanging amount. He suggested millions.'

'Face it, for anyone who won that amount of money, the world's your oyster,' said Simon. 'It's likely he's sunning himself on some Caribbean Island, pina colada in hand as we speak.'

'But you will look into it, won't you, Simon?' asked Sylvie. 'To rule it out, if nothing else.'

'Best I can do is pass the information on to the investigating team. Now, if that's all?' He looked at each of them in turn. Satisfied there was no response, he stood up. 'In that case, I'll get back to my job, and I suggest that you don't meddle in this investigation. Don't get up, I'll see myself out.'

Simon slammed the door behind him, leaving the three women in a stunned silence.

'Your brother was uncharacteristically rude. I guess he must be feeling the pressure,' said Harriet at last. She huffed loudly, making no attempt to hide her annoyance. 'I'm sure these murders are connected, if only we could prove it.'

'And how dare he tell us not to meddle in this investigation,' said Sylvie. 'He wasn't exactly detective material when it came to finding Bertie's killer.'

'Well, in fairness, he's not a detective,' said Liz.

The others both gave her a withering look.

'I'm not trying to excuse him because he's my brother.' Liz held up her hands defensively. 'There's no denying he was out of order just then. All I'm saying is that he's a uniformed officer, not a detective . . . Then again, recent experience suggests the actual detectives aren't up to the job either.'

'We mustn't let this drop,' said Sylvie. She looked round at her friends, sounding resolute. 'I think we need to find out everything we can about Robin Thornton and DJ Juicer. If we accept that it's unlikely to be a coincidence, then it's likely that the killer knew both of them.'

'We should start by establishing who DJ Juicer had been in contact with in the last twenty-four hours, because unless it was a slow-acting poison it's likely to have been administered within that timeframe,' said Liz.

'Don't they say that poisoners are mainly women?' asked Harriet

'I researched this a while back,' said Liz.

They both stared at her open-mouthed. 'Well, you both know that crime is my genre of choice. Anyway, as I was saying, a study found that around sixty percent of poisoners are men, although women prefer poisoning to other types of murder. Essentially, if someone was poisoned, there's a forty per cent chance that the murder was committed by a woman — but if a woman does commit murder, it's more likely that she used poison as her weapon.'

'Ooh, get you!' said Sylvie, as she nodded approvingly. 'If you ever went on *Mastermind*, perhaps methods of murder should be your specialist subject.'

They all laughed.

'It would have taken a lot of physical effort to bury that body on Barney's estate,' said Harriet. 'Which means that if it's the same killer, and she is a woman, then she was a very strong woman ten years ago.'

'We need to approach this methodically. I'd like to find out about DJ Juicer's recent movements,' said Liz. 'I'll ask around to see who he interacted with this morning, and I'll find out what Simon knows. He won't stay grumpy with me for long, and he's more likely to open up to me than to either of you. But first, I think I'll head over to the Monksworthy Arms. I bet it'll still be packed out. Everyone will still be talking about what happened this morning. No doubt most of it will be wild speculation, but I might pick up a useful nugget or two of information.'

'That's a good idea,' said Harriet. 'I think I'll crack on here, if it's all right with both of you. I'll see what I can find out about Robin Thornton. It's possible he might have no connection to the Wye Valley. Just because he was DJ Juicer's agent doesn't mean that he lived locally. After all, we don't even know if he's dead. It could turn out that these two ghastly murders are entirely coincidental.'

'In that case, I'll see what I can find out about DJ Juicer and who he really was when he wasn't living it up in clubland,' said Sylvie. 'I'd like a copy of that magazine article you mentioned. It'll be as good a starting point as any.' As her phone pinged, she glanced down to see that she'd received a text from her daughter. 'Sorry, I'd better get home, Anna's on her way over. She's obviously heard about us getting hauled off to the police station.'

'You go and put her mind at rest. I'll send you the link,' said Harriet. 'We've a lot to get through, and I'm going to get started straightaway. As we've our usual table booked for Sunday evening, we can update each other on progress then.'

With a plan agreed, Liz and Sylvie headed off for the evening. It was getting late, but the three friends were determined not to waste any time in putting their investigative skills to the test. There was work to do before any of them went to bed.

CHAPTER 19

Despite knowing a murder had been committed earlier that day, Liz had felt completely safe as she headed to the pub alone. Although the heavy police presence of earlier had thinned out, no doubt because officers had gone off shift and the crime scene investigators had finished up, some crime-scene tape was still flapping in a slight breeze as she passed the hall. There was a police car stationed opposite, its windows slightly open, with a couple of uniformed officers sitting inside. Liz sensed their eyes on her as she made her way across the road.

As soon as Liz set foot inside the Monksworthy Arms, she knew that her instincts had been correct. The place was heaving. Most of the customers appeared to be either fellow villagers or other people she was familiar with from nearby villages, but as she looked around, she noted there were a number of faces she didn't recognise. The room pulsed with energy and the constant hum of chatter. If she was going to learn anything of interest, this was where it would happen.

Liz weaved her way through the crowd and eventually reached the bar. Duncan and Brendon were both working flat out, fulfilling drinks orders at record speed. The difference in their personalities was evident to even the casual observer.

Brendon was all smiles, managing to have a chat with each punter, even as he sped through their order. He thrived on being surrounded by so many people. Whereas Duncan's expression was businesslike, as he aimed to complete each task efficiently. Then again, he had been on his feet for much of the day, working single-handedly. So, it wasn't difficult to imagine that he was running on empty.

'Usual, Liz?' asked Duncan. He was already pouring the drink before she had time to answer. 'Try not to dwell on what could quite easily have turned out to be a miscarriage of justice. We all know you had nothing to do with what happened.'

Liz thanked him, paid for her drink and left the couple to get on with it. The last thing she wanted was to be reminded of the earlier horrible ordeal, though she knew Duncan was only being kind and supportive. Even before she had a chance to take her first sip, a local came up to speak to her.

'Hey, Liz. You've had a hell of a day,' said Julie Porter. 'That poor man dying like that has put me in a right pickle.' Julie ran the village hall. 'I had to cancel a birthday party at short notice. It was due to start at four o'clock. It was for a little six-year-old. As you can imagine, his parents weren't best pleased. But what could I do?'

'It was out of your hands, Julie.' Liz sympathised with her.

Having joined in various conversations with groups of neighbours, Liz was beginning to think that perhaps no one had any useful information to impart. Suddenly, the thought of heading home to soak in a warm bath, surrounded with fragrant candles, seemed so appealing. It might just prove to be the perfect antidote to the stresses and strains of the day and hopefully aid a good night's sleep. She'd been surrounded by people all day, and much of that time had been under extremely stressful circumstances. She started to extract herself from the group and make her goodbyes. But as she headed back to the bar to return her empty glass, she spotted Ian

Wyde chatting to Hannah Walters. Hannah waved and gestured for her to join them.

Liz smiled and headed in their direction. She'd join them for a short while, then make her excuses.

'We were just saying that there appears to be far too many nefarious deeds occurring in this neck of the woods,' said Ian. 'What with the body found by Sir Barnaby, and that poor man's life being cut short earlier today.'

'Not to mention Albert's untimely death,' added Hannah. The Albert she was referring to was Sylvie and Harriet's late husband.

'Yes, there does seem to have been a significant number of dreadful things happening in this area lately,' agreed Liz.

'I was just telling Ian that I was in Abbotsmead this morning, when the judges arrived. I believe it was their first stop of the day.'

'Yes, I think it was.' Sensing that there was a chance she might learn something useful, Liz's expression brightened. 'What were you doing over there?'

'I was walking a couple of golden labradors for one of my elderly clients.'

'Did you happen to see DJ Juicer?' asked Liz.

'Well, I was there when all the cars pulled up. Though I must admit my attention was focused on the dogs. But yes, I saw him standing there with the others. They'd just got out of their cars. Can you believe they gave each judge a chauffeur-driven car? Separate cars, mind. They weren't sharing.'

'What a waste of money,' said Ian. 'It would be far more cost-effective, not to mention better for the environment, to have had a minibus.'

Both women nodded their agreement.

'Easy come, easy go, if you ask me,' said Hannah. 'I'm no expert but they looked like expensive cars. Yet the chauffeurs didn't even bother locking them. When they dropped off their passengers, the drivers all headed down to the riverbank to have a smoke. They were still there when I returned with the dogs.'

'What makes you think they didn't lock the cars?' asked Liz. She raised an eyebrow questioningly.

'Because I was imagining what it would be like to be rich enough to have my own chauffeur. Perhaps one day, you never know—'

'That doesn't explain how you know that the cars were unlocked,' Liz interjected.

'Oh, it's probably nothing, but I glanced up at the cars as the drivers were making their way towards the river and saw the judges head off together,' said Hannah. 'Well, about five minutes later, I was still hanging about by some bushes because the dogs had picked up some sort of scent and were having a good old sniff. Anyway, while I was standing there, I spotted that head judge, you know who I mean, quite tall, looks as though she's chewing a wasp.'

Liz and Ian both laughed at the apt description.

'She was coming back to the cars without any of the others. Then she opened one of the doors and reached inside.'

'I suppose she must have forgotten to take something out of there,' said Ian.

'Sounds reasonable,' said Liz.

'Well, that's the thing.' Hannah frowned at the memory. 'From where I was standing, it didn't look like the car she arrived in.'

'Whose car was it?' Liz shivered as she felt the hairs rise on the back of her neck.

'I'm fairly certain it was one of the male judges,' said Hannah. 'Though I couldn't tell you which one. I wasn't really paying much attention to them. I was mostly just trying to keep the dogs in check. We've been working on their training, so I was focused on them. But when the vehicles arrived, I spotted Ms Holloway straight off. She's got a very distinctive voice, all false and hoity-toity. All fur coat and no knickers, as my mum would say. From the moment she got out of the vehicle, she was barking orders at everyone.' She sipped her drink, then continued.

'Then I saw Mrs Leverton getting out of one of the cars, a dark grey one. I remember that because she was one of my favourite teachers in primary school. I loved being in her class, and I'd know her anywhere. Anyway, when Christine Holloway returned moments later, I'm positive she opened the door of one of the other cars.'

'She must have been getting something for one of the other judges,' suggested Liz.

'Unlikely,' scoffed Ian. 'That woman has a reputation. My cousin Jim used to work at the council, and he said she was a right piece of work. Gave her staff hell.'

'Well, it does seem odd,' said Liz. 'Did you happen to see anyone else acting suspiciously?'

Hannah wrinkled her nose as she tried to recall the scene. 'I don't think so. Then again, I wasn't focused on what was going on with the judges. I was concentrating on getting the dogs back. I was conscious of the time, as I knew I would have to head off pretty soon to get over to another client to collect their pooch.'

'That's understandable,' said Ian. 'After all, no one had any idea of what was about to happen to that poor man.'

'I'd say that at least one person did,' said Liz. 'It's highly unlikely he poisoned himself.'

Hannah nodded her agreement. 'We heard he'd been poisoned. I hope they find the person responsible soon. Do you think I should mention what I saw to the police?'

'Absolutely,' said Liz. 'I'm sure there's a perfectly reasonable explanation for what Ms Holloway was doing in that car. Then again, someone poisoned that poor man, and I got the impression that Christine Holloway didn't think much of him.'

'I won't get into trouble, will I, if it turns out to be something and nothing?'

'Under the circumstances I think it's best they know everything you saw,' said Liz firmly. 'If Christine Holloway has nothing to hide, then they can rule her out as a suspect.

But the police need to investigate it. What you witnessed could be a vital piece of evidence. If you like, I can give my brother a call. I'm sure he'd be happy to listen to what you have to say.'

'OK. I suppose so.' Hannah sounded reluctant but appreciated that it was her civic duty to tell the police what she had seen.

CHAPTER 20

Having got the all-clear from the police, it was business as usual at the tearoom, and the venue was full to bursting, which was only to be expected as the weather was glorious. With no spare seats to be found anywhere in the establishment, some customers had resorted to either standing or squeezing up two to a seat. It was the busiest Liz and Sylvie had ever seen the place. Not that they were complaining. Following yesterday's shocking event, they had faced the very real possibility of going out of business. After all, once the word had got around, there was a chance that customers would shun the tearoom. But if today was anything to go by, it was apparent that they had been worrying over nothing. With hardly a minute to spare, they were both forced to eat and drink on the hoof. By the time they were ready to shut up shop at the end of the day, both women were exhausted.

It was their Sunday evening ritual to head home for a quick shower and change of clothes, before meeting up at the Monksworthy Arms with Harriet. The busy tearoom meant that, unlike many people, they were unable to indulge in a leisurely Sunday lunch. So instead, every Saturday, they each placed their order with Duncan, who ensured that the chef would have it ready for them for Sunday evening.

'I know you two wouldn't have had a chance to investigate anything today,' said Harriet. 'The village has been crazy busy again, and the couple of times I walked past the tearoom it looked as though it was chocka.'

'It was easily the busiest day of the year so far,' said Sylvie. 'Probably because the gossipmongers were out in force. Everyone without exception wanted to know what had happened, and why we'd all been taken in for questioning.'

As they ate, Liz updated them on the previous night's conversation she had with Hannah Walters. 'Simon's following up on it. I believe he was going to speak to Christine Holloway this afternoon. Let's face it, she's got a free day since the competition was cancelled.'

The others nodded their agreement.

'I know there's a general consensus that she's dodgy,' said Harriet. 'And Hannah's description does make it seem as though she was acting suspiciously, but that in itself doesn't mean that she's the one who poisoned DJ Juicer. There could be any number of reasons to explain away what she did.'

'Like what?' asked Sylvie.

'I've no idea,' admitted Harriet, 'but hopefully Simon will find out what she was up to. Did you manage to make any progress on finding out about DJ Juicer's life?'

'I spoke to Annabel last night,' said Sylvie. 'She was obviously shocked to learn what happened. But it turns out she knows who he is. He's been on the club scene for twenty years. She knew a bit about his personal life from a friend of a friend. Apparently, he was a decent man. Worked closely with a charity that aims to turn the lives of troubled kids around. Apparently, he's been committed to it for goodness knows how many years.'

'I know very little about the club scene,' said Liz. 'It was never my sort of thing. Even when I was younger, they'd have been kicking things off around the time I was getting ready for bed.'

'Hardly surprising,' said Harriet, 'given your early morning starts. It just wouldn't have been compatible.'

'Precisely,' agreed Sylvie. 'Anyway, as I was saying, Annabel told me DJ Juicer was a health freak. His wife is too. Their company produces healthy energy drinks using completely natural ingredients with no additives. Apparently, she wrote a book about healthy living a couple of years ago. It even made it onto the bestseller list. She and her husband co-author a blog where they promote the lifestyle. It seems they're very much against recreational drug use. They're anti-alcohol, anti-smoking and promoters of a healthy diet. They're big on yoga and meditation.'

Harriet's eyes widened. 'It just seems so at odds with his career as a DJ. I've built a career on trying not to stereotype anyone. Even so, it's difficult for me to reconcile the two parts of his life. Then again, we're only learning about him on a superficial level. I guess we need to dig deeper to get a real sense of the man.'

'I agree,' said Liz. 'Let's face it, until yesterday I'd never heard of him. So we're coming at this with no knowledge whatsoever.'

'How did you get on, Harriet? Did you manage to find out anything about Robin Thornton?'

'I worked on it until the early hours, pulling together all the information I could find online. His LinkedIn profile was quite useful, though it hadn't been updated for years. Still showed DJ Juicer as his client along with a couple of other high-profile artists. Which sent me off on a tangent. I think I'm going to have to get in touch with these other clients, which isn't as easy as it sounds.'

'I guess contact details for people in the public eye aren't generally available at the drop of a hat,' said Sylvie.

'You got that right,' agreed Harriet. She took another sip of her drink. 'It's a convoluted process, but one way or another I'll get there. At least I'm in the right industry to make inquiries. I've already put out feelers to various people. I'll chase them up tomorrow when they're back in the office and I'm hopeful I should get replies soon. It could turn out that Robin Thornton is still alive, and if I keep following this line of enquiry I could end up finding him.'

'The tearoom's closed on Mondays, so Sylvie and I should be able to spend more time on things tomorrow too,' said Liz. 'I think I'll head over to Abbotsmead and have a chat with some of the locals. I'll call into the SP. Ezra Tiverton would be a good start. He'll hear all sorts of things when he's serving customers. I think it's safe to say that however that poor man was poisoned, it happened before he got to our village. Which leaves three possibilities.' She counted them off on her fingers. 'He was poisoned the night before. He was poisoned at home. Or someone administered it after he left home on the morning of the competition. It seems unlikely that his wife poisoned him — Simon said she was devastated when the family liaison officer told her the news.'

'I don't know what security measures were in place wherever he was working,' said Harriet, 'but my guess is the DJ booth, or whatever it's called, would be away from the dance floor and he would have noticed anyone tampering with his water bottle. Although, I suppose it's possible someone could have administered the poison backstage.'

Sylvie and Liz exchanged a surprise glance. 'How come you're so knowledgeable about the club scene?'

'Every so often we have social events with the magazines. They're usually at some club or other and they often book VIP booths.'

'Perhaps we should do something like that for the tearoom Christmas party,' said Sylvie.

'But we don't have a tearoom Christmas party,' said Liz.

'Precisely. Perhaps it's time for a change. Oh, I forgot to say that Annabel knew where DJ Juicer lived,' said Sylvie. 'So I thought that first thing tomorrow I'd head over that way and see what I can find out about him. Given the circumstances, I'd have thought it's guaranteed that people will be gossiping, and I might be able to pick up some useful snippets. Find out if he had any skeletons in his closet. Or if he had any enemies.'

CHAPTER 21

Monday morning arrived and Sylvie was determined to avoid the rush-hour traffic. She was heading for the village of Appleby-in-the-Forest, which was about thirty miles from Monksworthy. Before Annabel had informed her that it was where DJ Juicer and his wife lived, she had never known the place existed, let alone where it was on a map. And having subsequently looked it up online to get a feel for the place, she quickly ascertained that under normal circumstances she would have no reason to go there.

Having arrived shortly after nine o'clock, Sylvie easily found a parking space just off the main street. The village itself was not on any tourist trail, though it was pretty enough. But as she got out of the car and glanced around, her first impressions were that it wasn't quite up to Monksworthy standards.

It lacked a focal point; there was nothing to make the heart leap when your eye caught it for the first time. In her opinion, the village could have been enhanced by a manicured village green or a duck pond. Though she had to admit that a second glance suggested that a lot of residents took pride in their homes. Many front gardens appeared well tended, with neatly cut grass, the occasional hanging basket and pots brimming with colourful flowers. These reassuringly familiar signs lead Sylvie to believe that the people who lived in this village might be the sort of people she could identify with. Hopefully, she would be able to strike up conversations which might enable her to glean useful snippets of information about DJ Juicer and his wife.

As Sylvie made her way towards the main street, a church bell began to chime. Up ahead she spotted a few groups of people and some lone individuals all walking in the same direction. Picking up her pace, she did her best to catch up with a woman who had recently come out of a nearby cottage.

'Looks as though we're set for a warm one,' said Sylvie. It was the most innocuous conversation opener she could think of.

'It does,' agreed the woman. 'Though it will be chilly inside the church.'

'Always the way.'

'Are you here for the service?'

'Absolutely,' said Sylvie.

The woman turned her head and looked Sylvie up and down. 'Not seen you in the village before. You're not from the press, are you? I don't want to talk to any journalists. This service is about coming to terms with the loss of a valued member of our community.'

It appeared that Sylvie had arrived in time to attend a service for the people who had known Dominic John Liveland. If she played this right, it would be the ideal opportunity to learn more about the man. Her honest, upfront nature immediately caused Sylvie to feel guilty about not being open about her motives for being there, but she knew it was essential she kept her cards close to her chest.

'No, I'm not a journalist, and you're right I'm not from the village. I'm from Monksworthy, and I'm one of the last people Dominic John spoke to before he died.' Sylvie sensed that the villagers would not refer to the man as DJ Juicer and would consider it be disrespectful for her to do so. 'I'd never met him before that morning, but in the short time I spent in his company I sensed he was a good person. I just wanted to come along today to pay my respects. I recently lost my husband. There was no warning, it just happened. So, I know what it's like to be blindsided by loss.' Sylvie decided it was best not to mention that Albert had been murdered too.

'Monksworthy?' The woman's eyes narrowed as she stared more intently at Sylvie. 'Was your husband the one who was murdered by that serial killer?'

Sylvie's composure crumbled. Swallowing hard, she hastily wiped away unanticipated tears. All of a sudden, she felt like a rabbit trapped in the headlights, and desperately wanted to move the conversation away from Albert's untimely death. Though her voice wobbled, she replied, 'Y-yes he was, so I'm sure you can understand why I want to come and pay my respects today.'

'Oh, I'm sorry, m'dear.' The woman reached out and squeezed Sylvie's shoulder in a supportive manner. 'Forgive me. That was really insensitive. I honestly didn't mean to upset you. I have a tendency of opening my mouth and putting my foot in it. And of course, I understand why you wanted to come here today. You don't owe me or anyone else an explanation.'

They made their way towards the church together. After a few minutes of companionable silence, the woman, whom Sylvie now knew was called Pam, began to make small talk, eventually suggesting that Sylvie might like to sit next to her in the church. Sylvie readily took her up on the kind offer.

The church was surprisingly modern, both inside and out, and Sylvie had to admit that it had a more homely feel than the one in Monksworthy. The female vicar was considerably younger than Sylvie and welcomed everyone as they arrived.

'I don't recall having seen you here before,' she said, as Sylvie approached. 'Are you new to the village?'

'No, I don't live here,' said Sylvie. 'I'm from Monksworthy, and I was part of the welcoming committee who met Dominic John shortly before he died. His death was profoundly shocking and incredibly sad. I just wanted to come and pay my respects.'

'That's an admirable sentiment. But how did you hear about this service?' asked the vicar. 'We didn't advertise it.'

Sylvie could have kicked herself for not thinking about coming up with an excuse before. She thought quickly. 'A close friend of mine is one of the police officers who attended the scene. He knows how upset we all are over this senseless loss of life, and we're a very close-knit community.'

'Ah, that explains it,' said the vicar. She nodded her understanding.

Sylvie couldn't imagine that it explained anything, but it appeared to put the vicar's suspicions to bed.

'We're a close-knit community too,' the vicar continued. 'Having connected with Dominic John for even a short while gives you every right to be here. We are all shocked to the core and united in grief. Please feel free to join us in the village hall after the service. We'll be serving refreshments, and I'm sure that as you were one of the last people to have seen him, there will be many of us who will be keen to learn of his last moments.'

The service was short and touching, and afterwards, the vicar insisted that Sylvie join them as everyone traipsed the short distance to the village hall. It seemed they were a welcoming lot, and having been introduced to various parishioners, Sylvie had no trouble joining in the conversation. Although Dominic John's widow, Madeline, had been unable to attend.

'Grief-stricken, poor thing,' confided Pam.

The villagers of Appleby-in-the-Forest were keen to have a first-hand account of what had happened to Dominic John on the morning of his death. However, Sylvie found out little of interest.

Having drunk two insipid cups of tea and nibbled a custard cream which must have been long past its 'best before' date, Sylvie was beginning to think that it was time to leave. It didn't appear that there was anything useful to learn about the poor man and his wife.

As she was about to say her goodbyes, an elderly woman whom Sylvie had not been introduced to beckoned her over to a small group of pensioners who were deep in discussion.

'The morning he died, did you happen to notice a young woman with shoulder-length dyed blond hair?'

'Can't say I did,' said Sylvie, after she tried hard to think about who she had seen in the village that morning.

'Are you sure? If your village is anything like ours, she would have stood out. I live next door to the Livelands and I got a good look at her on a couple of occasions. Seemed a bit brassy, wearing a skirt no bigger than a belt. And a face caked in far too much makeup.'

'You're being a bit harsh there, Maria,' said another villager.

'No, I'm not. She was brassy right enough. Always called round to their house when poor Madeline was there alone. First time I saw her was at the start of the year. Turned up regularly after that. Making a show of herself, saying all sorts. Claimed Dominic had got her pregnant and he was going to leave Madeline to set up home with her. If I remember rightly, that was in March. She was even there last Wednesday.'

'Are you saying Dominic was having an affair?' asked Sylvie.

'According to that lass he was.'

'I don't suppose you know her name?'

'Let me think . . . It was some sort of flower. Now, what was it?' She closed her eyes as she tried to recall it.

Another woman who was getting impatient started to list flowers. 'Petunia?'

Maria shook her head.

'Violet?'

There was another shake of the head.

'Lily?'

'That's it!' exclaimed Maria, with a look of satisfaction on her face.

'She was called Lily?' asked Sylvie.

'No. Her name was Rosie. And after she told Madeline about the pregnancy there was a right to-do at the house when Dominic got home. They were going at it hammer and tongs. Very inconsiderate, given the time of night. I've no idea whether that brassy piece was pregnant or not, but she had no intention of giving up. She was back and forth to that house at all hours for weeks on end.'

'But the Livelands stayed together?' asked Sylvie.

'They did,' said Maria. Gesturing to the group to huddle closer, she lowered her voice until it was no more than a conspiratorial whisper. 'Now, you all know that I have a lot of time for Madeline. I think of her as one of my own. But in recent weeks there's been a strange man visiting her when Dominic's not there.'

There were collective gasps, though no one asked the obvious question. As Maria looked at her captive audience, her eyes sparkled with mischief. 'Now, I'm not saying Madeline's having an affair as well, but something's going on between her and that man. And that's all I'm going to say on the matter.'

'Did you catch his name, Maria?' asked one of her friends.

'No. All I know for certain is that he looks older than her, and whatever's between them, they're very secretive about it. I've a feeling that our Madeline will have the sense to have a respectable period of mourning, and then we'll see her stepping out with his mystery man of hers.'

As Sylvie headed back to Monksworthy, she felt rather pleased with herself. As if Maria was to be believed, it appeared that DJ Juicer and his widow might not have had such a perfect marriage.

CHAPTER 22

After her regular morning run, followed by a shower and quick breakfast, Harriet set about providing detailed advice for the life questions submitted by seven different readers. Having fulfilled this role for more than two decades, she had long ago learned that whatever their background, most people's problems had similar solutions. Though each answer needed to be honed to fit the unique set of circumstances and individual personality traits, which caused people to act differently.

Harriet had allowed herself until ten o'clock that morning to undertake these tasks. After which she would switch her attention to progressing her investigation into Robin Thornton.

She had sent out emails on Sunday to various colleagues in the publishing industry, asking for information on Robin Thornton. Although she was keen to learn more, Harriet was loathe to chase anyone up too soon. She knew all too well that everyone had their own deadlines to meet, and a random request from an old acquaintance would inevitably be low on their to-do lists. The last thing she wanted was to annoy people and lose any goodwill she had built up over the years. So while she waited, she would trawl the internet, make a few calls and see what she could come up with, safe in the knowledge that as soon as one of her contacts came back to her, they would point her in the right direction.

She decided to start by taking another look at the Robin Thornton's LinkedIn profile. It hadn't been updated for many years. Nevertheless, it did contain some personal information about the man. She pondered what she knew about him. He'd been DJ Juicer's publicist, which surely meant he had lots of other clients. To do that, it was logical to assume that he was good at publicising himself. The world of publicity, much like the world of magazine publishing, was all about connections. There were gigs to be booked. Deals to be done. It was a career of confidence, cheek and charm. He would have had the gift of the gab, and the ability to sell sand in the proverbial desert. Someone somewhere would know him. It was just a case of tracking that person down.

After making a few phone calls, Harriet established that Robin Thornton had also been a publicist for Serena Bright. Not much had been heard of her in recent years, but there was a time when she was trumpeted as being an up-and-coming star. Having entered a national talent competition, she progressed through to the final stage, where the public vote awarded her third place.

Harriet was not one for watching reality TV of any kind, but she had a vague notion that when her children lived at home, she had seen Serena perform on that talent show. Over the years, Zara and Leo had compulsively watched the programme. Even though Harriet had no interest in it, she had occasionally joined them on the sofa and seemed to recall that Serena was a folk singer, with a pleasant though not exceptional voice.

Much of the next hour was spent trying to find a way of contacting Serena. Having found a clip of her singing in the talent show final, Harriet discovered that the finalists had been contracted to participate in a nationwide tour. It was a good earner for the producers of the show. There had been a number of pieces written about Serena in the national press, including by a couple of music journos who thought she should have won.

However, Harriet learned, Serena was destined to be a one-hit wonder. Her debut single made it into the top twenty, where it stalled. Following that, she was unable to capitalise on the success of the talent show and instead became a jobbing actor. She had a few minor roles here and there, including one on *Midsomer Murders*, but that all seemed to stop ten years ago. Try as she might, Harriet could find no further record of Serena Bright as either an actor or a singer after that date.

Harriet was deep in thought as she wracked her brain over a way to find and contact Serena, when her phone rang.

'Hi, Harriet. It's Janice Ingleby.' Janice was one of the people Harriet had emailed on the previous evening. She was her first point of contact on the most recent lifestyle magazine she was under contract to.

'Oh hi, Janice, it's good to hear from you. Thanks for getting back to me so soon.'

After a quick catch-up, Janice told Harriet about what she had found. 'Basically, there's nothing recent out there on Robin Thornton, though it was common knowledge that he won more than six million pounds in the lottery. So, I guess it was hardly surprising he packed in his career. Hey, I would too. I'd be off like a shot. You wouldn't see me for dust.'

'You and me both,' laughed Harriet. 'I don't suppose you happen to know where Robin went after he won the money?'

'Sorry, I've no idea.'

'In that case, do you have any information on Serena Bright? I think she was one of Robin's clients, and I'd like to speak to her.'

'Now, that's a name I haven't heard for a while. Got into the public eye when she appeared on that talent show, but the sparkle rubbed off pretty quickly. Never did much else as far as I know. Probably find she's so disillusioned that she left the business completely.'

'Many of them do,' said Harriet. 'It's not just about having talent; you need a lot of luck too.'

'Leave it with me, Harriet. I think I know a way to get my hands on her contact details. It might take an hour or so, but I'll get back to you.'

When Harriet's phone pinged almost twenty minutes later, she picked it up and saw that it was a text from Janice. As she opened it, she smiled broadly. Her contact had come up trumps, far quicker than anticipated, and she now had an address and phone number for Serena Bright.

Harriet's call went unanswered as the ringtone continued for more than a minute. But, as her thumb hovered above the red disconnect icon, someone finally answered.

'Hello? Sorry, I was in the shower.'

'Is that Serena Bright?'

'Y-yes.' There was a note of uncertainty in her voice. 'Who is this?'

'My name is Harriet Joyce. I'm trying to locate Robin Thornton. I believe he was your publicist?'

'Robin? Yes, that's right, he was, but I haven't seen or heard from him in years. Why are you trying to locate him?'

'I'm afraid I can't tell you that. All I'm at liberty to say is that I'm acting on behalf of a client, who needs to contact him about a personal matter.' Having spent her working life avoiding answering questions about what she did for a living, Harriet was used to lying convincingly.

'Ooh, that sounds so mysterious,' giggled Serena. 'Robin's such a lovely man. So kind and genuine. I'd love to get back in touch with him. I bet he's living a wonderful life with not a care in the world. Did you know that he was originally from the same town as me? We even went to the same school. Not that we ever spoke to each other back then. He was five years above me. I doubt he'd have been seen dead talking to a spotty kid like me.'

'Five years is a big difference when you're that age,' said Harriet. 'Do you happen to know where he went when he walked out on his career?'

'Well, that's the funny thing. You'd think winning all that money, you'd go and live it up in some tropical destination. Somewhere with a beach where it's hot and sunny all year round. But that wasn't Robin. He decided to move to a small village. When he moved out of his mother's house, he rented an apartment. He told me it was his dream to have cottage with a thatched roof. Each to their own, I suppose. If it were me, there'd be no contest. I'd opt for sunshine and cosmopolitans on tap.'

'Do you happen to know if any of his family are still alive and living locally?' asked Harriet.

'I don't think so. From what I recall, there was only him and his mum, but she died a couple of years after he finished school. They used to live three doors down from my auntie. My cousin Gina was in the same class as him. We used to joke about it being a small world.'

'Was your cousin friendly with him?'

'No, they wouldn't have hung out with each other.' Serena sounded thoughtful as she reflected. 'But as they were in the same class they might have connected on socials. Or she might know something about him from a friend of a friend. I think that year group was supposed to have a reunion a few years ago. It's the sort of thing people do as they get older.

'To be honest, Gina and I don't really socialise with each other either. We never did. When you're a kid, a five-year age gap is a lifetime of difference. Back then, I always wanted to hang out with her, but she avoided me like the plague. She was one of the cool kids in school. Good at sport. Pretty. Confident. Became Head Girl. Whereas I was a right ugly duckling. Didn't have anything going for me, what with having acne and braces.

'Though I guess the tables were well and truly turned when I made it to the televised rounds of the talent show. I was luckier than most. At least I got my fifteen minutes of fame in the end. Though that's way behind me now. These days I work for minimum wage at the local supermarket. But at least it's regular money.'

'You certainly did get your fifteen minutes, Serena. You're exceptionally talented.' Harriet sensed that the young woman was angling for a compliment and was happy to indulge her, if it kept her talking.

'Thanks, that's so sweet of you.'

'It's the truth, and you're welcome. Do you think there's any chance I could have Gina's contact details? My client won't be happy unless I chase down every possible lead to find Robin.'

'I don't have Gina's number, but I've got my auntie's address and telephone number if that's any help? I think she might have been friendly with Robin's mother. I've a feeling they used to go to bingo together.'

CHAPTER 23

While her two friends set about their own tasks that morning, Liz had already baked for a couple of hours and attended the group exercise session on the village green before heading off to Abbotsmead in the hope of learning more about DJ Juicer's movements on the morning of his death. Liz appreciated that she most likely had the easiest task, as she already knew quite a few people who lived in Abbotsmead and would have no problem getting them to talk about what they knew or even suspected.

Unlike the vibrancy of Monksworthy, Abbotsmead had never been a hub of activity. It was a smaller village, and apart from the Spotted Pig pub there were no other popular social amenities. At least in Monksworthy, they had a tearoom, a shop and a garden centre for people to congregate. Though Abbotsmead did have a village hall, it was run-down and only occasionally used. As such, the pub had become the hub of village life.

Ezra Tiverton was the owner and landlord of the Spotted Pig. His business model was a far cry from Duncan's, cheap beer and happy hours being the order of the day. And unlike the extensive menu at the Monksworthy Arms, here the only edible offerings were packets of crisps or pork scratchings. The premises was also more basic than the Monksworthy Arms, with no log fire to warm patrons on cold evenings, and a jukebox which blasted out tunes at a level far too loud to encourage conversation.

Having unlocked the door, Ezra was still ambling towards the bar when Liz entered the building. She was the first customer of the day, and from the state of the place it was obvious that he hadn't cleaned up from the night before. The bar and some of the tables were littered with dirty glasses, and the air smelled of stale alcohol.

Liz wrinkled her nose in distaste. 'You might want to open a window or two. Get some fresh air in the place.'

Ezra turned to face her. His eyes were bloodshot, his complexion sallow. 'Didn't hear you come in.' His voice sounded jaded.

'Are you all right, Ezra?' Liz was suddenly concerned.

'Had better days,' Ezra sighed miserably. 'The missus walked out on me, yesterday teatime. Said she'd had a bellyful. Gone to stay at her sister's. Things've been going downhill between us for a while. Think it might be time to call it a day.'

'I'm sorry to hear that. It's hard to keep all the balls in the air when you've a business to run too.' Liz was sympathetic.

'Tell me about it.' He sighed again. 'I've gotta get this place shipshape before the regulars arrive. Don't want to put them off. The place is only just ticking over as it is.' He picked up a couple of glasses.

'Why don't I give you a hand?' Before Ezra could answer, Liz headed to the nearest table and began to collect glasses.

'Oh, I couldn't ask you to—'

'You didn't. I offered. We all feel a little overwhelmed at times, and that's precisely the time to accept help if it's offered.'

Ezra's breath caught in his throat, and his voice croaked as he answered. 'Th-thanks, Liz. I won't forget this.'

'You're welcome. Now, let's crack on.' They worked together in silence. Liz collected the glasses and cleaned the tables, while Ezra opened some windows and loaded the dish-washer. Thirty minutes later, the pub was ready to serve the first of the customers. No one apart from Liz was any the wiser about Ezra's low point. His usual smile had already returned, and with his game face on, for all intents and purposes he was the very model of a genial host.

'What'd you like to drink, Liz? It's on the house.'

'Oh, thanks, Ezra,' said Liz, 'just an orange juice and soda for me. As far as I'm concerned, it's too early for the hard stuff.'

As no other customers had arrived, she sat at the bar and chatted with Ezra. 'Don't suppose you happened to see the judging panel when they were here on Saturday?' she asked eventually.

'Nah, didn't see them at all. Me and the missus were having a right ding-dong at the time. Plus, I'm a bit persona non grata at the moment, given the fact that I was serving the stag party that went and destroyed the flower arrangements.' Ezra sniffed dismissively. 'Some people round here are very good at holding grudges. But if you ask me, they should be directing their anger at the Joneses. They're the ones that let them lads book the Airbnb cottage. Ever since they went down that route, the village has gone to the dogs. It's not the sort of thing we need around here. And the word is they're after buying another place to do exactly the same thing again. Just because they've got money to burn, they seem to think they can treat the rest of us like dirt.'

Liz was about to respond when the door opened and two women walked in. Liz smiled as she recognised them both. Diane Potter and Gloria Norton were occasional customers at the tearoom.

'Didn't expect to see you here,' said Gloria, hanging her bag on the back of a chair by the window.

'I was at a loose end, so I thought I'd have a change of scenery,' said Liz.

'Come and join us,' said Diane. She went to order from Ezra.

Diane and Gloria were part of the Abbotsmead welcoming committee — something they had joked about the last time the pair had come into the tearoom. It was the perfect opportunity for Liz to find out if anything unusual had occurred on that Saturday morning. And it was immediately apparent that they were keen to speak to Liz for precisely the same reason.

'Awful business, that poor man dying like that,' said Diane, getting straight to the point.

'What exactly happened?' pressed Gloria. 'Does anyone know?'

Liz answered their questions in the vaguest of terms, and then managed to ask a few of her own. 'Did you notice anything out of the ordinary when the judges were here?'

'Not really,' said Diane. 'We knew we weren't in with a chance after those louts destroyed our floral arrangements. But we still had to see it through as the judges' timetable had already been agreed. They were nice enough. Sympathetic even.'

'I still can't believe that the Joneses had the brass neck to show their faces that morning,' said Gloria. 'Normally we don't see hide nor hair of them. Not that Rob Jones has any hair, at least not on his head. Bald as a coot, he is. Though I suppose he makes up for it with that big bushy beard.' She frowned. 'They're an arrogant pair. Can't take to them at all. They haven't even had the decency to apologise, even though it was their fault that our efforts were thwarted.'

'And that Rob had the damned cheek to have a go at me for calling the police about what those lads had done!' Diane added, outraged. 'Obviously didn't want them going to that cottage of theirs. He blamed me for sending the police to his door. I mean, who do they think they are? The very least they could have done is gone out and bought some replacement flowers. After all, everyone says they're loaded. Well, they've got to be, haven't they? Else they wouldn't have two properties.'

'Don't forget they're considering getting another one,' Gloria interjected.

'You're right, they are,' she harrumphed. 'People like that don't care about the likes of us.'

'What were the Joneses doing when the judges were here?' asked Liz.

'I don't recall seeing her. Though I did notice him,' said Gloria. 'He had one of those baseball caps on, which I thought was very strange. I've never seen him wear a cap before.'

Diane nodded. 'Gloria's right, he was wearing a cap and sunglasses, though you'd know him anywhere with that beard. He was watching the cars arrive. I wouldn't be surprised if it gave him ideas about getting his own chauffeur-driven car. I don't know what he did after that, because we were both helping to show the judges around.'

'As you spent some time with DJ Juicer, did you get a sense that he was feeling ill?' asked Liz.

'No, as I told the police, he seemed no different to any of the other judges,' said Diane. 'He was quite chatty, asking about the village. Said it was such a shame that those young louts destroyed our efforts.'

'Did anyone approach him or pass anything to him?'

'Not that I saw. He looked a bit tired. Then again, he explained that he'd been working for much of the night, so he'd naturally be tired. I remember him apologising a few times because he kept yawning. But he seemed happy enough. I didn't get the sense that he was worried about anybody or anything.'

Liz was starting to think that these two women hadn't spotted anything out of the ordinary while the judges were at Abbotsmead. But she still had one more question to ask. 'Did DJ Juicer wander away from the group at any time?'

'There wasn't time for that,' replied Gloria. 'That Christine Holloway made it plain that they were on a tight schedule. She was acting like a sergeant major on a parade ground, bossing everyone around. She kept the other judges on a tight leash. Us too, come to think of it. No, that poor man was with us the entire time.'

'Mind you, that woman had a bit of a cheek chivvying everyone along like she did,' Diane added. 'She kept banging on about their tight schedule, yet right at the start she was the one that kept everyone waiting.'

'Oh yes, I'd nearly forgotten about that,' said Gloria, rolling her eyes. 'She disappeared for a bit.'

'Why was that?' asked Liz.

'Well, we were about to start the tour of the village, when Christine Holloway pipes up and says she wanted to use the loo. I pointed her in the right direction and off she toddled. I've never known anyone take so long. We kept looking at our watches. She was gone for about ten minutes while we were standing around like spare parts until she returned.'

CHAPTER 24

Sylvie headed back to the car, keeping her head down as she walked far faster than felt comfortable. She couldn't wait to get home and tell her friends what she had found out. This was the first time she had played amateur sleuth by herself, and although she hadn't felt threatened, it had still made her feel jittery. She'd never been good at lying, and she'd dreaded the thought of going undercover to find out information about DJ Juicer. Yet here she was, a few hours later, feeling delighted at her success.

She dumped her bag on the front passenger seat and was about to start the engine when her phone rang.

'Sylvie? Beatrice Cornish here.' The crisp, efficient voice of Barney's PA came down the line. 'Sir Barnaby was wondering if you could meet him at the Hall at two o'clock? He's in back-to-back meetings today, but a small window has opened up at that time. He said it's important.'

'Do you want me to let the others know?' asked Sylvie.

'Thank you, but no. I've just spoken to Harriet, and Liz is next on my list. Oh, and he said to mention that there'll be refreshments.'

'In that case, tell Barney I'll be there.' When the call ended, Sylvie glanced at the clock on her phone and realised that if she was going to reach Barney's by two o'clock there would be no time for her to call in at home. She needed to set off.

As it turned out, she was stuck in a queue of traffic following a tractor along a narrow winding lane, which slowed her down considerably. And she eventually reached the Cavendish-Mortimer estate to find that she was the last to arrive.

'Nice of you to join us,' said Barney. There was a hint of annoyance in his tone.

'Sorry, I got stuck behind a tractor.' Sylvie's cheeks burned. She hated keeping people waiting.

'Never mind. But I am on a tight schedule today, so we better get started. Help yourself to some sushi and I'll tell you why I asked you all to come here.'

The others were already munching away, which made Sylvie feel even more guilty.

As Sylvie filled a plate with food, Barney began to tell them why he had asked them there. 'I've been mulling over recent events.'

'Precisely which events are you referring to Barney?' asked Liz. It seemed to her that so much had happened in recent days that he could be alluding do any number of things.

'Specifically, things to do with that dreadful woman Christine Holloway. She's a public servant. Our taxes fund her post at the council. Yet I'm certain she's corrupt.'

'Oh, I thought you were about to tell us that you'd found something out about one or both of the murders,' said Harriet through a mouthful of sashimi.

Barney looked surprised. 'No, I'm not equipped to investigate murders. I know I became embroiled in events with regards to Bertie's demise, but that was different. Lives were at stake, including my own.' Barney's complexioned paled at the recollection. Clearing his throat, he said, 'No, best leave murder investigations to the professionals. I asked you here today to talk about corruption.'

The three women glanced at each other in surprise.

Barney sounded as though he was making a political speech. 'In recent years there doesn't seem to be a week that goes by without instances of profligate waste and corruption in public service being reported in the media. In my opinion, we owe it to society to stamp out such abhorrent betrayals of public trust. And I believe that Christine Holloway stinks like a year-old fish supper.' Spotting that this statement had caused a confused expression to appear on Liz's face, he quickly added, 'I'm speaking morally, not aromatically.'

'Ah, yes, I'm with you,' agreed Liz. 'Though, just to set the record straight on the aromatic front, I think she was wearing Chanel No. 5.'

Barney continued, 'I'm considering hiring a private detective. That woman slipped up when she said that we were never going to win this year's award. That would indicate she'd already decided upon the winner.'

'And Christine Holloway's not the sort of woman to do something for nothing,' Sylvie interjected.

'Precisely. We need to find out which village was going to be awarded the accolade and then follow the money.'

'I'm in!' Liz practically jumped out of her seat. With all eyes suddenly on her, she stated her case. 'I'd be more than happy to investigate Christine Holloway's dodgy dealings. She was quite prepared to throw me to the wolves over DJ Juicer's poisoning. And that was after we'd given her free coffee and a Danish. She threatened to tell everyone it was our pastries that killed him and destroy our business. It was a horrible thing to do.'

'I'm in too,' said Sylvie. 'There's a witness who said she was acting in a shifty manner around the judges' cars. We'll show her that actions have consequences.'

'I'm glad you mentioned the judges' cars,' said Barney. 'I've had Beatrice make a few enquires this morning.' He extracted a piece of paper from his jacket pocket. 'This is the name and contact details for each of the drivers.'

He handed the document to Harriet.

'Barney, you sly old dog. I don't believe you had any intention of hiring a professional private detective,' said Harriet as she smiled knowingly. 'You asked us here because you wanted us to investigate Christine Holloway's potential dodgy dealings.'

He grinned back. 'I class myself as a good judge of character, and in my limited experience, I've found you to be very astute. And I think I've just proved myself to be correct. I know that once you ladies get the bit between your teeth, there's nothing stopping you.'

CHAPTER 25

After their sushi lunch, the three friends left Barney to get back to his hectic work schedule and returned to the village. They decided to meet back at the tearoom. There was a lot to discuss and baking to be done if Liz and Sylvie were to be sure of having enough stock when they opened the following morning. There was a delivery of cakes due from one of the contractors first thing. But for certain regulars, only Liz's cakes were good enough, and somehow they were able to tell the difference.

Sylvie ran home to freshen up and Harriet went past her cottage so that she could pick up some stationery. The ladies had previously found it enormously helpful to write down their findings and ideas on Post-it notes and arrange them accordingly to help make sense of information gathered throughout an investigation. That way they could add something whenever they thought of it, and common threads could emerge. It was a tried and tested method which they all approved of — when they were dealing with a lot of information, a visual aid helped to make sense of it.

After an hour or so of baking, they each selected a large sheet of paper, a pen and a pad of Post-it notes, which they took to separate tables to list out everything they had learned throughout their morning endeavours.

Liz was the first to finish, and as she sat back, a thought occurred to her. She called across to Harriet. 'Do you still have that list on you?'

'The chauffeur details Barney gave me?'

'Yes.'

Harriet rummaged through her bag.

'Here it is.' She handed it over.

Liz scanned the list, then glanced at her watch. 'Do you two fancy accompanying me to the funeral home?' Until his death, Liz's husband, Vince, had co-owned the funeral home, located a mile or so out of Monksworthy, with his business partner, David Pritchard. When Vince passed, his shares in the business were transferred to Liz, who remained a silent partner, but David still managed the day-to-day running of the place.

'That's a bit random, isn't it?' said Sylvie, as she put down her pen and stretched.

'You've found something, haven't you?' asked Harriet.

'Possibly. I just can't shake the idea that Christine Holloway might have something to do with the poisoning. What Hannah told me suggests that she was up to something around those cars. She saw her open one of the doors then bend down and reach inside, and Hannah didn't think it was the car that Christine had travelled in.'

'We agreed it sounds suspicious, when you first told us,' said Sylvie.

'Well, when I was speaking to Diane and Gloria today, I was told that Christine left the others before they started the judge's tour, claiming that she needed to use the loo. Apparently, she was gone for ten minutes.'

'Rather a long time for a comfort break,' added Harriet. 'Sounds to me as though she used the excuse of needing the loo as a cover story for whatever she was up to.'

'Precisely, and I don't know why it didn't occur to me when Barney gave you the contact details for the drivers that were ferrying the judges around. The council don't routinely do that sort of thing for council officials. They might have one official car and driver, but not five. Which lead me to think that most of those chauffeurs would have been individually contracted for the weekend. The rest of the time, their contracts would be unrelated to the council.'

'Of course. They'd be used on an ad hoc basis for funerals,' said Harriet.

Liz nodded. 'That's right. If there's a large funeral, it's not unusual to hire extra limousines and drivers. And I know at least two of those names on Barney's list. Brian Dinken and John Quigley. They're good men who regularly helped my Vince out. And I just happen to know that John is driving a limo for one of our funerals this afternoon and should be dropping Dai back at the funeral home within the hour. If we hurry, we should catch him.'

'It's worth a shot,' said Sylvie. 'Since he knows you, there's a good chance he'll tell you what happened that morning. Let's face it, it's unlikely we'll find out anything from the council's official driver. He wouldn't talk to the likes of us, in case it came back on him, and he'd end up losing his job.'

'My guess is that when you get a group of men like that together, standing around like spare parts while they're having a smoke, they let their guard down and dish the dirt on the people they're ferrying around,' said Liz. 'People never think the driver is going to listen, but there were occasions when my Vince told me things he'd overheard when he was travelling in the front of a limo. Things that would make your toes curl.'

'Then what are we waiting for? Let's go.' Harriet was already slinging her bag over her shoulder as she headed for the door.

As they entered the Valley View Funeral Home, they were hit by an overwhelming aroma of scented candles and lilies. It was a cloying but necessary measure for such an establishment.

The office manager looked up from the paperwork she was dealing with and smiled. 'Everything all right, Liz? We don't often have the pleasure of your company.'

'Everything's fine. I was just wondering if John Quigley was here. I know he was driving for us today.'

'He hasn't returned yet. Shouldn't be long though. Can I make you all a cuppa while you wait?'

'No, thanks. We'll head through to the car park and leave you in peace.' Liz led the way and the others followed.

Once they were outside, Harriet breathed deeply. 'I can't see how anyone can work in there. It gets you at the back of your throat. I could feel my airways closing.'

'You get used to it after a while. Can't say I notice it anymore. Ah, here they are.' The automatic gates clunked and screeched as they opened. Within seconds, a black limousine drove slowly into the car park.

'Ooh, don't usually get a welcoming committee,' said David Pritchard as he got out of the front passenger seat. 'Good to see you, Liz, but is there anything I should be worried about?' He raised a bushy eyebrow questioningly.

'Actually Dai, we're here to see John.'

'Well, that's put me in my place.' He chuckled and shook his head. 'I'll leave you all to it. There's plenty to do before we shut up shop for the day.'

'I promise we'll catch up soon, Dai. Why not call over to the tearoom on the weekend? I'll treat you to a free cuppa and slice of cake.'

'I might just take you up on that.' He said his goodbyes and headed into the building.

While this conversation was going on, John Quigley had got out of the car. He was a tall man, middle-aged, with a full head of hair and had a look of Rock Hudson about him. 'This looks ominous. I don't usually have three ladies queuing up to see to me. I don't know what my wife would make of this. How are you doing, Liz? It's been a while.'

'It certainly has, John. Look, I'll get straight to the point. There's nothing for you to worry about but we're after some information.'

'Sounds serious. Go on then, what do you want to know?'

'We understand that you were one of the drivers for the judges?'

John nodded and leaned against the car door. 'Yeah, I drove the poor guy that died. It was a shock, I can tell you. Seemed right as rain, apart from being a bit tired. Told me he'd only managed a few hours kip the night before. He seemed like a decent guy. Happy to make small talk. Not stuck up like a lot of punters.'

'Did you get a sense that he was worried about anything or anyone?' asked Sylvie.

'No, there was nothing out of the ordinary as far as I could tell.'

'Who decided which judge you'd drive?' asked Harriet.

'Oh, those decisions were above our pay grade. We were just the hired help. Though, if I had to make an educated guess, I'd say it was that Christine Holloway woman or someone working for her. She was the one calling the shots. But if you ask me, it was ridiculous them all having individual cars. It would've been more cost-effective ferrying them around in a minibus. Still, I can't complain. It was a nice little earner, and it means I'll be able to take the missus out for a slap-up dinner for her birthday.'

'I'm sure she'll appreciate it,' said Liz. Out of the blue, she thought of Vince and how he would sometimes surprise her with a little gift, or book a table for them to share an intimate dinner. Even after all these years, it was still painful to come to this place where he had spent much of his working life. It was why she had chosen to be a silent partner in the business. She didn't want to be involved in the day-to-day running of the place. Yet she didn't want to sell his shares either. Apart from her memories, this was the last link she had to Vince, and she still missed him so much.

'You all right, Liz?' When she didn't reply, Sylvie reached out and squeezed her friend's hand. 'You all right?' she repeated.

'Y-yeah, course I am. Momentary wobble, that's all. It's this place. It gets to me, you know? He's been gone for such a long time, but I half expect to turn around and see Vince standing there . . .' She sighed. 'Silly, I know.'

'Not at all. It's perfectly understandable,' said Harriet. She squeezed Liz's shoulder supportively.

With a sheepish expression, John lowered his gaze. 'Sorry, Liz. I didn't mean to upset you.'

'You didn't. It's just memories resurfacing. Caught me by surprise, that's all.' She forced her lips into a weak smile, though it failed to reach her eyes.

John gave her a sympathetic look. 'Actually, now I come to think about it, there was something strange on the competition day. Seemed like something and nothing at the time, but I suppose it could have been important.'

'What?' chorused the three friends.

'When we parked up in Abbotsmead, me and the other drivers all decided to head down to the river and have a smoke. Well, we'd be hanging around for a fair while, and it's good to get out of the car, stretch your legs and have a chat. Gets quite lonely sitting in the car by yourself,' John explained. 'Anyway, I didn't lock my car, as that Juicer chap asked if he could leave his drinks bottle in there. He didn't want to take it with him when he went on the tour of the village. I remember him having a quick swig of it before he set off with the others. He asked if I minded leaving the car unlocked as he might pop back for it later.'

'Annabel mentioned that Dominic's wife has quite a lucrative business selling juices,' interjected Sylvie. 'She's got a whole range of recipes and promoted them on her blog. I think the operation is now so big that she employs people to produce and distribute them. Apparently, it's a well-known fact that she tried every new recipe out on Dominic. He was her go-to guinea pig. They never left the house without taking a few juices with them.'

'I don't know about that,' said John. 'But I do know that I got back to the car before he did, and when he returned, he claimed that the bottle wasn't where he left it. Of course, there's not many places it could have been in the back the limo. But he was adamant it had been moved.'

'That's very interesting,' said Harriet.

'Which one of you drove Christine?' asked Liz.

'Neville . . . Neville Pointer. He's been a driver for the council for years. Decent bloke. We all felt sorry for him having to drive her about. She's got a bit of a rep for being a ballbreaker. Nev was telling us that some of the bigwigs in the council want rid of her, but they can't do it because over the years she's kept a lot of records. Things that could bring people down. Not just end careers but put them in the dock.'

CHAPTER 26

The three friends had spent much of the day in full-on investigative mode, and by that evening had gathered a lot of information. Just how much of it was useful had yet to be ascertained. As an obsessive fan of crime fiction, Liz knew that information was key to solving a case. Even the most random snippet of information could, when considered in the context of other evidence, crack a case wide open.

However, trying to solve just one case was challenging. Juggling all three was daunting. Firstly, they needed to establish the identity of someone murdered years earlier, an unfortunate eleven-toed individual who had seemingly not been missed. Next there was the murder of DJ Juicer, which might be connected to the murder of the eleven-toed man. And then, in the last few hours, there was the distinct possibility that a senior council employee might be corrupt. Yes, any one of these investigations would be time-consuming. But three . . . and that was on top of doing their day jobs.

On the way back from the Valley View Funeral Home, they collected their Post-it notes from the tearoom and headed to Sylvie's house. Knowing they would be back at work tomorrow, it was all the more important to press on with their investigations that evening.

They all agreed that it would be counterproductive to continue with a scattershot approach. They needed to study the information they already had and decide which of it was useful and which they could ignore. Hopefully, by talking things through and bouncing ideas off each other, they'd come up with a plan of action.

'I think right now we need to work out what needs to be passed on to the police,' said Harriet. 'There's no need for us to run a full-blown murder investigation.'

'There's plenty of ways we could help the police without putting ourselves in danger,' agreed Sylvie.

'Let's make a list of priorities,' said Liz, 'and then I'll try to get hold of Simon. He's on lates this week, so he should be at work now. Number one for me is making sure the police speak to John again. He obviously didn't tell them that DJ Juicer was convinced that his drinks bottle had been moved. While I'm at it, I'll try to find out if they tested the contents.'

'I'm sure they must have,' said Harriet. 'After all, they tested your pastries. But I agree, the police should speak to John.'

'And Simon needs to know that DJ Juicer might have been having an affair,' added Sylvie. 'Either that or he was being stalked. If someone was obsessed with him and he made it plain to them that he wasn't interested that could be the reason he was poisoned.'

Liz nodded. 'Stalkers don't play by the rules. Unrequited love could easily have been the reason he was poisoned. That young woman could have decided that if she couldn't have him, no one would.'

'I've seen on your notes that the Livelands' next-door neighbour thought that his wife may have been having an affair as well,' said Harriet to Sylvie. 'Do you think we should tell Simon about that?'

'To be honest, I'd prefer to check that one out ourselves before we say anything to the police,' said Sylvie. 'The next-door neighbour was adamant that an older man had been visiting the house when Dominic was out. But as things stand its only gossip. There's no real evidence to suggest that she's having an affair. The woman I spoke to seemed nice enough, but she could just have an overactive imagination.'

'You're right. You know what it's like in the tearoom. We hear all sorts. Some of our customers gossip and speculate about anything and everything. If it turns out that Madeline Liveland didn't poison her husband, and she's mourning the death of the man she loved, then allegations of an affair could push her over the edge,' said Liz. 'There could easily be a perfectly innocent explanation for that older man visiting her. It's just that we haven't figured it out yet.'

'Perhaps in a few days' time we could pop around and offer our condolences and subtly try to find out who that man is?' suggested Sylvie. 'We should let the dust settle first.'

'In that case, I suggest the first thing we should follow up is the conversation I had with Serena Bright,' said Harriet. 'She used to be one of Robin Thornton's clients when he was working as a publicist, and her aunt lived in the same street as Robin and his mother. I've no idea if we'll learn anything useful, but if she's happy to talk to us, we could get an insight as to what Robin was like as a child, which should help us build up a picture of him. We might even learn about what he's up to these days, because to all intents and purposes he seems to have dropped off the face of the earth, and no one seems bothered about it.'

'Sounds like a good idea,' said Sylvie. 'Let's face it, we don't even know whether he's alive or dead. We've just jumped on the coincidence that he apparently had eleven toes, and it just so happens that an eleven-toed man was found days before DJ Juicer's death. It's just as possible that someone else was buried on Barney's land.'

CHAPTER 27

The next morning it was full steam ahead with the day jobs, leaving no time to consider the three investigations. With the lunchtime rush over, Sylvie and Liz were about to take a well-earned break when the door opened once more and Harriet appeared, grinning broadly.

'You look like the cat that's got the cream,' said Liz. 'Fancy a cuppa? We were just about to have one.'

'Go on then, I could do with one. I haven't stopped all day.'

'What are you doing here?' asked Sylvie, as she came in from the kitchen. 'Thought you'd still be working.'

'Thought I'd pop by to give you both a quick update and see how you're fixed for later.'

'Ooh, sounds interesting,' said Liz. 'Give me two minutes. I'll get us some lemon drizzle cake to go with the tea.'

In no time at all, the three friends were sitting around a table sipping tea and nibbling cake.

'Umm, delicious,' said Harriet, as she wiped a few crumbs from the corner of her mouth.

'Never mind that,' said Sylvie. 'What were you going to tell us?'

'Well, I finally managed to speak to Serena's aunt. When I explained that we were trying to find Robin Thornton as there were concerns about his safety, she was very amenable. She said she's got something I might like to see, though she didn't go into specifics. I'm popping over there later and asked if I could bring both of you. She said it's fine.'

'In that case, what time will we need to leave?' asked Liz.

'Five o'clock.'

Sylvie and Liz glanced at each other and nodded their agreement.

Shortly after six o'clock, the ladies arrived at Serena's auntie's house. It was an unremarkable property located in the middle of a terraced row of houses set back from the pavement. A privet hedge cut at head height prevented passersby from looking directly into the downstairs window, while a low metal gate with flaking paintwork displayed more rust than its original black.

'What's the lady's name?' asked Sylvie.

'Monica Gaddick. Her daughter's called Gina.'

Harriet led the way to the front door, and as she pushed the gate open it squealed in protest.

'A few drops of oil wouldn't go amiss,' Liz winced, but she fell silent as Harriet pressed the doorbell.

As the door opened, Monica Gaddick smiled warmly and invited them inside. She was of average height, with a svelte figure and a pleasant face. Her dark, lustrous shoulder-length locks showed no sign of grey. Her sparkling blue eyes suggested she was someone who enjoyed life.

With introductions out of the way, they followed Monica along a surprisingly light and airy hallway towards the lounge, which appeared to be two rooms knocked into one. The lounge had been tastefully renovated, with clean lines, tiled floors and a minimalistic approach to decor and furniture. The result was both welcoming and open. A scented candle provided a fresh, comforting aroma. It was immediately apparent that a great deal of love and attention had gone into making this a stunning interior, which was at odds with poor condition of the gate.

'Sit, please,' said Monica. 'Anywhere's fine. We don't stand on ceremony.'

As they were making themselves comfortable, the sound of approaching footsteps could be heard. Moments later, a handsome man of a similar age to Monica strode into the room. Monica introduced him as her husband, Eddie, who worked at the local electronics factory.

'Would anyone like a cup of tea?' he asked.

'Thanks, love,' Monica said. 'Gina should be here soon. She texted to say she was on her way.'

As her husband headed back to the kitchen, Monica sat down too. 'Eddie didn't really know Robin, and he didn't have much time for Fiona — Robin's mum, that is. She smoked like a chimney. It's one of Eddie's pet hates. He can't abide it. So, you said on the phone you're trying to find Robin.'

'That's right,' said Harriet. 'Though I'm afraid I wasn't entirely honest with you.'

Monica stiffened. 'What do you mean?' There was a change of tone, and she sounded wary.

'Did you happen to hear about a body that was recently found the Cavendish-Mortimer estate on the outskirts of a village called Monksworthy?'

'Yes. I recall it being mentioned on the local radio. There were no real details about it. Just that the police were trying to establish the victim's identity.'

'Well, that's why we're here,' said Harriet. 'We don't have any actual proof, but we think there's a possibility that it could be Robin Thornton.'

'Oh my word! Robin? Are you serious? He was such a lovely lad. Fiona couldn't have asked for a better son. I hope you've got it wrong.'

At that moment Eddie returned with a tea tray laden with steaming cups. As he placed the tray down on the nearest surface, some of the hot liquid slopped into the saucers. 'What's happened?' he asked his wife.

'It's Robin. They think he might have been murdered. Oh, Eddie, it's a blessing that Fiona's no longer with us. This would have broken her. She doted on him.'

Eddie sat next to his wife and placed an arm around her. 'Are the three of you working with the police?' It was a reasonable question, as they hadn't yet explained their role in any investigation.

'We're private detectives,' said Liz. Eddie looked sceptical, and she quickly added, 'I know we don't look like your stereotypical detectives, but I can assure you that because of our efforts a serial killer was recently apprehended. And we work closely with the police, as my brother's on the force.'

Surprisingly, the explanation proved to be sufficient. Taking strength from her husband, Monica's composure quickly returned. 'I'm sorry, I was just taken by surprise. You obviously want to know more about him, although I'm not sure there's much I can tell you.'

'I don't want to distress you further,' said Harriet, 'but the body had been buried for a long time. And so far, the police haven't been able to identify it. But what we know is that the left foot had six toes.'

There was a noticeable tremor to Monica's voice as she replied. 'It must be him. Fiona told me that Robin had six toes on his left foot. There was an extra one in the middle.'

'Didn't they ever think of having it surgically removed?' asked Sylvie.

'I asked that, but Fiona said he liked the fact that it made him different, and it never seemed to bother him. He ran and played the same as anyone else. The only thing she wanted was for him to be happy, and he must've been. Otherwise, he'd have had it removed.'

'I don't suppose you happen to know which dentist they went to?' asked Liz. Being a crime fiction aficionado, it seemed a logical question to ask. If the dentist still had a copy of Robin's dental records, it could be used to verify whether it was his skeleton that had been found.

'The same as the rest of us, I guess. There's only one in this town. And as dentists are like gold dust in this country, you tend to stick with the one you've got.'

Everyone nodded their agreement.

'Though, I suppose Robin might have got himself a different one when he moved away,' added Monica, as an afterthought.

'It's a lot to ask,' said Harriet, 'but we'd appreciate it if you kept this conversation between us for now. We'll obviously let you know if it does turn out to be Robin. But if it ends up not being him, it could impede the police's efforts, and I don't think they'd take too kindly to the rumour mill making life difficult for them.'

'We won't say anything, will we, Eddie?'

'Absolutely not. Mum's the word.' He nodded solemnly.

'Oh, what about our Gina?' said Monica. 'She's on her way. I asked her to bring her school yearbook, so that you could see the photographs. You see, she'd obviously know who he was friendly with. Though I suppose that's not to say they'd have kept in touch over the years.'

'I think we should just keep the reason for our enquiries vague,' said Harriet. 'When I spoke to your niece, I said that I'd been asked to locate him for a client of mine.'

'We'll stick to that then,' said Eddie. 'Won't we, Mon?'

'Yes. No point in getting our Gina upset, when we don't know for a fact that it's Robin the police are trying to identify.'

As Liz was noting down the dentist's contact details, they heard the front door open.

'Hiya! Only me!' a voice called. A young woman walked into the room, a bag slung over one shoulder with a book poking out of the top of it.

'This is Gina,' said Monica, standing to greet her. Gina looked like a younger version of her mother.

With the introductions out of the way, Monica explained that the ladies were trying to locate Robin, and as it was proving difficult, they were hoping to speak to some of his school

138

friends, to establish whether any of them had kept in touch with him.

'Ah, just as well Mum asked me to bring my school year-book around. I wasn't really friends with Robin at school, apart from superficially. You know what I mean. We were sometimes put in the same group to work on a class project. But we didn't really hang out much outside of school. Anyway, that was years ago.'

'That's understandable,' said Sylvie. 'I imagine my daughter would be exactly the same with some of her classmates.'

Gina smiled. 'I'll do my best to try and recall the kids who might have been friends of his. But I doubt I'll be much help to you. I haven't looked at this tatty old thing for goodness knows how many years.'

'You can only do your best,' said Liz.

Having placed the book on a table, they crowded around Gina as she flicked through the pages. The photographs were of a time when what you saw was what you got. There was none of the airbrushed perfection of recent years, which might very well make the subject look great but often bore no resemblance to the person it claimed to be.

'I'm sure this boy, Sonny Jones, used to hang about with Robin.' Gina pointed at the photograph of a lad with mousey shoulder-length hair that looked in need of a wash.

'Was there anyone else?' Harriet asked.

'Him.' Gina pointed at a lad with short ginger hair and glasses. 'Joe, Joe Pettle. He was nice.'

'Are you implying that Sonny Jones wasn't?' asked Liz.

'No, Sonny was all right. I don't recall him being a troublemaker. But I spent more time with Joe.'

While they were talking, Harriet used her phone to photograph the images of Sonny and Joe. She liked having a record of everything they found out. You never knew when it might prove handy.

'I know Joe Pettle's father, if that's any help to you. I work with him,' piped up Eddie. 'His name's Peter, and when he first started at the factory, he used to get teased something awful.'

'Why's that?' asked Monica.

'Well, it's the name. Peter Pettle.'

'I've no idea what you mean.' Monica's brow was furrowed as she tried to make sense of what her husband was alluding to.

'Well, Peter Pettle, sounds a bit like Peter Piper.' Seeing his wife's still puzzled expression, he elaborated. 'The tongue twister. Peter Piper picked a peck of pickled peppers. Some of the lads changed it to Peter Pettle picked a peck of—'

'OK, Dad, no need to go on. I think we've all got the picture.' Gina smiled and shook her head in mock despair.

'Do you happen to have Peter's address or telephone number handy?' asked Sylvie.

'I can go one better than that. I'm meeting up with him this evening, in about . . .' He glanced at his watch. 'In fact, I'd better get going, else I'll be late. You can tag along if you like. We're off to the pub. I'm part of a darts team and we've a match scheduled.'

CHAPTER 28

The Dog and Duck pub was a five-minute walk from the Gaddicks' house. Eddie jogged along, eager to get there in time for the start of the match.

Sylvie huffed and puffed as she struggled to keep up, falling further behind with every step. As they took a shortcut down an alleyway, she was already ten yards behind the others. The sense of isolation from the group put her on edge. Normally she wouldn't have been so jittery, but the very fact that her thoughts were consumed with death and murder was unsettling. So it was no surprise that she screamed when a rat ran out in front of her, only inches from her feet.

Harriet and Liz both stopped abruptly and turned around.

'You all right back there?' called Harriet.

'I'm fine.' Sylvie's voice was higher than usual. 'It was a rat. Scared me half to death. Dirty creatures, I've never liked them.' The others doubled back.

'Not much further to go,' said Eddie. 'Sorry I should have warned you about the rat problem around here. It's a bone of contention. There's a derelict property a bit further down. I think it's infested.'

'No harm done,' said Sylvie. 'Just gave me a bit of a shock, that's all.'

'I'll slow down a bit so that we can all stay together,' said Eddie. 'Thing is, I run every day, and I'm used to moving at a reasonable pace. It just didn't occur to me that you wouldn't keep up. You're OK though? It didn't attack you?' His voice showed genuine concern.

'No, it didn't. I'm fine, honestly. Just not as physically fit as the rest of you.'

Even though the ladies were unfamiliar with the Dog and Duck, they knew without a shadow of doubt that it was going to be lively long before they arrived.

'Don't think I'd like to live on this street,' said Liz.

When they arrived at the entrance, Eddie grabbed the handle and held the door open for the three friends to enter. They were immediately hit by a wall of sound as a nineties ballad boomed. They squeezed a path through the crowd towards the bar.

With the music blasting, it was unsurprising that everyone in the place was forced to shout to be heard, but the mood was upbeat and relaxed, and they were all clearly enjoying themselves.

'Is it always like this?' yelled Harriet.

'Pretty much,' Eddie replied. 'The place is a bit of an outlier in these parts. Some of the locals complain, especially those who live across the road, but most of us love it. It's a great place if you like things lively. I've been coming here for years and never known any trouble. Everyone's welcome and rub along nicely, whatever your age.

'You'll find Peter Pettle over by the dartboard.' He gestured towards the back of the pub. 'We're a competitive lot, so if you want to have a word with him, I suggest you do it now, because the game's due to start in the next ten minutes.'

'Perhaps you could ask him to meet us outside?' shouted Sylvie. 'I don't think we could have a proper conversation in here. At least if we can all hear each other, we can find out what we need to know in a matter of minutes and then leave you to your match.'

'Fair enough,' agreed Eddie. 'You go outside, and I'll fetch him. Pete's a nice man. I'm sure he'll speak to you.'

'Imagine if the Monksworthy Arms was like that every night,' said Liz as they emerged into the relative quiet of the small beer garden. 'It'd be a nightmare.'

'Good for their profits,' said Sylvie. 'Though it wouldn't do much for the rest of us.'

'I can't imagine—' Harriet stopped speaking mid-sentence as the door opened and Eddie emerged, followed by a kind-looking man.

'Ladies, this is Peter Pettle,' said Eddie. 'I'll leave you all to it, if you don't mind. I want to get myself a drink before the match starts.'

Having quickly explained why they wanted to speak to him, Harriet took the lead in asking Peter a few questions.

'Robin Thornton, eh? I haven't heard that name for years. Yeah, my Joe was friendly with him. Robin was a nice lad too. As I recall, never got himself into any trouble. And he was smart as a whip. Helped Joe with his maths on numerous occasions. Joe really struggled with it. I don't think the teacher was much good, but Robin had the knack of explaining things. He was always thoughtful and patient.'

'Did Joe keep in touch with him after they left school?'

'I believe he did for a while. But I think they must've drifted apart, because I haven't heard him mention Robin for a long time. Then again Joe moved out of the village a few years back, so we don't see as much of him as we'd like. When he left school, he got a job as an estate agent. Learned the ropes and worked his way up for a few years until he decided to set up on his own. Doing quite well for himself now. We're very proud of him.'

'You must be,' said Sylvie. 'Does he live locally? We'd be interested in speaking to him.'

'He's based in Cheltenham. Been there for coming up to eight years. Married with two kids now.'

'Would you mind giving us his contact details?' asked Harriet.

'I'm sure he wouldn't object to you having his personal number. If you like, I'll give him a ring when I get home this evening and tell him you want to speak to him about Robin. Once he knows what it's about, I'm sure he'll be more than happy to talk to you. But if for one reason or another I don't manage to get back to you, you can always get hold of Joe through his business line. He owns Pettle Properties.'

The ladies thanked Peter and headed back to the car. It was time to call it a night and head back to the welcome tranquillity of Monksworthy.

CHAPTER 29

The following morning, Harriet's phone rang when she was in the middle of writing a response to one of the many requests for advice she had set aside to answer that day. As she was in full flow, she momentarily considered not picking up. A glance at the display told her that the caller had withheld their number. Thinking it might be a cold call, Harriet's finger hovered over the red icon. But with three investigations on the go, she thought better of it.

'Hello! Hello, can you hear me?' An announcement was being made in the background. Whoever was calling her was doing it from somewhere busy.

'Yes, I can hear you. Who is this?'

'I'm Joe Pettle. I had a message from my father, who said you wanted to speak to me about Robin Thornton. Is that Harriet?'

Harriet relaxed. 'Thanks for getting in touch, Joe. Yes, that's right. Do you mind if I ask where you're calling from? Only, there's a lot of background noise at your end.'

'Yeah, sorry about that. I'm in an airport. Our flight's been delayed, so I thought I'd use the time to call and find out what you wanted.'

'If your father hasn't already mentioned it, I'm trying to find Robin. He seems to have dropped off the face of the earth and I'm concerned for his well-being.' Harriet decided it was best at this stage not to tell Joe that she thought his old friend might be dead.

'What would you like to know? I'll help any way I can. Back in the day Robin was one of my closest friends . . .' Joe sighed. 'Scrub that. Robin was my best friend. I loved him like a brother.'

Harriet knew precisely what Joe meant. She felt that way about Sylvie and Liz. Being an only child, Harriet had learned to be resilient. Growing up, she had envied the closeness some of her friends had with their siblings and wished with all her heart that she'd had a brother or sister too. She knew sometimes siblings fell out, or perhaps had never really bonded in the first place. But when she looked at Liz and Simon, it was plain for everyone to see that despite living very different lives there was an unbreakable bond between them. It was special. Something to be nurtured, treasured and never taken for granted.

'Believe me, Joe, I understand. Friendships like that are rare.'

'Precisely. Robin and I were close for years after we finished school and went our separate ways. It wasn't always possible to meet up, but we'd text, email or chat on the phone. We still made the effort to see each other in person whenever we could.'

'As far as you know, did Robin have any enemies?' asked Harriet.

Joe laughed. 'Robin wasn't the sort of person to have enemies. Everyone liked him. He was a good-hearted guy, the sort who'd do anything for anyone. If he thought he could help someone, he would. Heck, he spent months on end helping me with maths. I really struggled with that subject, whereas he was a natural. Then again, he was good at so many things. I guess he was just very intelligent. He was one of those people who seemed to sail through exams without having to put much effort in.'

'I know the sort of person you're talking about,' said Harriet. 'Rare and talented.'

'Precisely. But you know, Robin wasn't a show-off. Things just seemed to come naturally with him. It was like his brain was a sponge. But he was also really down to earth, easy to talk to. He was the best friend you could ever hope to have.'

'So why did you lose touch?' Harriet was genuinely puzzled. If everything Joe was telling her was true, and she had no reason to doubt it, it seemed inexplicable that these two men would suddenly drift apart.

'To be honest, I've spent years wondering the same thing myself,' he sighed. 'I last spoke to him about six months before my wedding. He'd had a big lottery win about two months earlier, but it hadn't changed him. He had a career he loved. Clients whose careers he cared about. He was well respected in the business.' There was the sound of more announcements in the background. 'He told me that winning such a large amount of money wasn't going to change the way he lived his life. We had that conversation shortly after he told me about his big win, and I asked him what he was planning on doing now that he was so wealthy. And do you know what he said?'

'I've no idea,' said Harriet.

'He said that he wouldn't allow his lottery win to turn into a curse.'

'What did he mean by that?'

'He said that he'd heard so many horror stories of people who unexpectedly came into large sums of money and quickly went on to lose their purpose in life. And he wasn't about to let that to happen to him.'

Harriet was quickly building up a picture of Robin as a man who was grounded and sensible.

Joe continued to speak. 'Robin told me that he wasn't going to be miserly about it. He planned to buy himself the odd treat now and then. Stay in classy hotels. Fly first class whenever he went somewhere. Oh, and he was going to buy himself a new car. Ever since we were kids, he'd been a sucker for fancy cars, and said that one day he'd buy one. Come to think of it, I don't recall him ever having bought anything other than a second-hand one until then.'

'Sorry to interrupt,' said Harriet. 'Are you sure he had no intention of stepping away from his career?'

'Absolutely positive. He was one of those lucky people who loved what he did. It's what got him up in the morning. No matter how much money he had, he'd never step away from that.'

'And yet that's precisely what he seems to have done,' said Harriet. She shivered, despite the pleasant ambient temperature. Things didn't look good for Robin Thornton. 'He stopped representing his clients a few months after he had his win.'

'Really? I didn't know that,' said Joe. 'It was so weird, and gutting to be honest, but it was like he just dropped off the face of the earth. Robin was going to be my best man. He'd been planning my stag do for months. We were going to fly first class to Amsterdam. Spend four nights there. He was so enthusiastic and came up with some great ideas. Then there was nothing. No contact. No warning. He just ghosted me.'

'Did you try to reach out to him?'

'Of course I did. I called and left messages. Went across to his place but didn't get an answer. Weeks later I got an email from him. He said he was cutting ties, and I should find myself another best man as our friendship had run its course.' The change in his voice highlighted his emotional pain. 'I don't know what happened to cause such a change, but he was cold. Ice cold. And I never heard from him again.'

'That's dreadful. You must've felt so betrayed.'

'I did. Like I said, he was my best friend. It didn't matter to me whether he had money or not, and it's not like I expected anything from him. It was his good luck. I thought he knew that. I honestly believed we'd be friends forever.'

'Did Robin have any other close friends?'

'There was Sonny. Sonny Jones. He went to school with us. He was a laugh but there was a bit of an edge to him. I hung around with him sometimes after we graduated, but I'd never really trusted him.'

'Why is that?' Harriet asked.

'I couldn't put my finger on it, but I sensed that he only did things if they were to his advantage.'

'So he was calculating?'

'Yeah, that's the word I was looking for. But Robin didn't seem to see that side of him. In fact, he gave him a job. Nothing too taxing. Answering the phones, taking messages, arranging appointments, that sort of thing. I suppose you could say he was his PA. Truth is, Robin was a soft touch, and he felt sorry for him. Sonny used to come out with us occasionally, but I had a bust-up with him not long before I lost touch with Robin. So, he's another one I haven't seen for years.'

'Did Robin remain friendly with him after you and Sonny fell out?'

'Robin being Robin, he tried to get us to patch things up, but it was never going to happen. I'd seen Sonny for what he was and didn't want anything to do with him.'

'What did he do that was so awful?' asked Harriet.

'I saw him try to take money from Robin's wallet. I stopped him and called him out. He laughed it off and said that I'd got it wrong. But of course, I hadn't. I'd just seen him for the snake he is. Robin had a word with him, told him he was on a warning, but continued to employ him. Said he believed in giving people second chances. He always saw the best in people.'

'I don't suppose you have contact details for Sonny? I'd like to speak to him, as he might have some information about Robin that could help me find him.'

'Not on me. I deleted him from my phone contacts. There might be something in my box of papers from school days. I'm not sure. But my family and I are off to the Algarve for a week, so I won't be able to check things out until I get back. And it might take me a couple more days as I'll have a ton of things to catch up on. But I'll make of note of it, so I won't forget.'

'I'd appreciate it. One more thing, do you happen to have any photographs of you, Robin and Sonny as adults? I've seen the snaps of you in the school yearbook, but you've obviously changed over the years. It would just help me with the investigation. Especially if I need to show anyone photographs of Robin or Sonny.'

'Sure, no problem. Are you on WhatsApp?'

'Yes.'

'In that case I'll forward them to you at the same time.'

'That's great. Thanks, Joe.'

'No problem. Any chance you could do me a favour in return?'

'What's that?' asked Harriet.

'If you find Robin, could you let him know that I'd like to get back in touch with him? Tell him I hope he's all right and that as far as I'm concerned, whatever's gone wrong between us can be worked out. We can talk it through and move on from this.'

'Will do,' said Harriet, doing her best to sound upbeat. But she was more certain than ever that Robin Thornton would never get in touch with anyone again.

CHAPTER 30

That evening, the Monksworthy Arms was surprisingly quiet. As usual, Harriet was the first to arrive, and Brendon joined her at the table when he brought the drinks over.

'It's been like *Marie Celeste* in here all day,' he said. 'Didn't even get much trade at lunchtime. Hopefully it'll pick up later.' No sooner had Brendon said this than the door opened, and two men walked in. As they headed towards the bar, one of them glanced over. His brow furrowed momentarily and then he smiled and said hello.

It took Harriet a few seconds to put a name to the face, but she soon recognised him. She returned his smile and said hello too. Having only seen him once before, John Quigley looked remarkably different away from his car and wearing casual clothes.

'Who's that? I've not seen him before,' whispered Brendon.

Harriet was just explaining when Liz and Sylvie arrived, followed by a large group of customers. Brendon glanced up and saw Duncan raise an arm and point to the bar. It was obvious his other half needed his help.

'Better go and do some work,' he said. 'Catch you all later.' His chair almost toppled as he jumped up. Harriet reached out to steady it, and Brendon moved swiftly towards the bar.

'Any updates?' asked Harriet.

'Well, I spoke to Simon last night,' said Liz. 'I told him we'd gone to see the Gaddicks, and that Monica confirmed Robin had an extra middle toe on his left foot. I also passed on the contact details for Robin's dentist.'

'Did he tell you whether they'd made any progress on identifying the body?' asked Harriet.

'He didn't say, and there was no point pushing him for information. He already thinks we're too involved, and it would only wind him up. I'm sure he'll tell us when he's ready.'

Sylvie nodded in agreement. 'Best we keep investigating things on the down-low.'

'I spoke to Joe Pettle today.' Harriet went on to tell them everything she'd learned. 'There's no more we can do on that front until he sends me the photographs. It's a shame he couldn't do it straightaway, but he promised to do it when he returns from holiday.'

'From what he told you, it sounds completely out of character that Robin would have ended their friendship like that, or walked away from his career. Yet for all intents and purposes he did just that . . . Something's not right.' Sylvie stopped speaking as she spotted John Quigley and another man approach.

'We go months if not years without seeing each other and suddenly twice in as many days,' said Liz to John. 'Never seen you in this pub before.'

'Well, after our chat, I thought I might pay a visit.' He paused. 'But before I say any more, let me introduce you. Ladies, this is Neville Pointer. Nev, this is Liz Morgan — she's one of the owners of the funeral home ever since Vince passed — and, sorry, I mean no offence, but I can't remember your names.' He smiled sheepishly.

'There's no need to feel awkward, John. In your business, you get to meet so many people it's no wonder you can't remember everyone's name,' said Liz cheerfully. 'This is my business partner, Sylvie, and this is our friend Harriet.'

'I thought you might be interested in speaking to Nev,' said John, as the two men drew up seats and sat down.

'Yeah, in a past life I must have been really wicked, because in this one I've ended up working for the council as a driver,' said Nev. 'Last weekend I drew the short straw and got stuck with her ladyship. Christine La-di-da Holloway, that is.'

'You poor thing,' said Sylvie. 'And you're right, you must have done something really bad in a former life to have such a dreadful woman inflicted upon you.'

Everyone laughed.

'John said I could trust you.' He looked at each of them in turn.

'Absolutely,' said Liz. The others nodded their agreement.

'The thing is, Christine's got a bit of a reputation as a bully. It's common knowledge that she's clawed her way to the top. She's one of those people that doesn't care who she treads on, as long as she gets what she wants.'

'Ooh, I detest people like that.' Liz grimaced and shook her head. 'Though I'm not surprised. We all saw how she behaved when she was meant to be judging the Village of the Year competition. She just seemed to look down her nose at everyone. I don't think she gave a toss about anyone else. Not the sort of person you'd want to spend time with.' She shuddered at the thought.

'Is it just that she's a dreadful woman or is there more to it?' asked Harriet.

'I've heard rumours that she's been taking backhanders for years,' said Nev. 'Not that that's unusual in public service. The higher-ups are all cut from the same cloth as most politicians. They're a bunch of troughers.'

'I don't understand.' Sylvie looked puzzled. 'What are troughers?'

'He means pigs in a trough, Sylve,' explained Liz. 'You know the sort, public officials who are just there to improve their own lives. Take whatever they can get and to hell with the rest of us. It's about time people woke up and did something about it.'

'Which is precisely what we're hoping to do,' said Harriet.

'You're looking to expose her corruption?' asked Nev. His eyes sparkled as he waited for confirmation of their intentions. 'Because if you are, then I might be able to help. You see, I know something. Well, I know of something, but I don't know what it's about, if you get my drift.'

'It wouldn't happen to be about something that happened while you were waiting for the judges at Abbotsmead?' asked Harriet.

'Yes, but how do you know that?'

'We heard that Christine left the judges for a while and was seen by the limousines.'

'Hallelujah!' Nev slapped the table and smiled. 'See, John, I wasn't imagining it. She was acting shifty.'

'So you were right after all,' said John. 'You said that you thought you'd seen her open the driver's door to his car and lean inside. But I didn't see anything, and neither did Brian or David. And Charlie joked about you needing to get your eyes tested.'

'Well, you four were having a smoke, and I doubt you would have been able to see her, because I'd gone off to stretch my legs. Ever since I've given up smoking, I don't like being around people when they're puffing away. The temptation's too great. I don't have a problem with anyone having a fag break,' he added. 'It's just better for me to distance myself as I don't want to risk a relapse, and Charlie wasn't making it easy for me.'

'You're right,' said John. 'Charlie kept calling you back, didn't he? It's not as if you and him are that close. Come to think of it, he was the one who suggested we should head down to the path by the riverbank.'

'Was that unusual?' asked Liz.

'Well, we normally just stay with the cars. It's easier to keep an eye on them that way. But it was such a nice day and there's not exactly a lot of unsavouries hanging about tiny villages like Abbotsmead . . .' He furrowed his brow as he concentrated on recalling the scene. 'Didn't think much of it at the time. It was nice weather and an opportunity to stretch our legs before we had to drive off again. The Village of the Year competition covers a lot of ground. We're usually in the car for what feels like hours driving between places.'

'But they'd only recently had that trouble with the stag party,' said Liz. 'Couldn't get much more unsavoury types than that.'

The others nodded.

'Don't think I'd have left my car unlocked and then wandered away from it at that time of day,' said Sylvie. 'It's asking for trouble.'

'Who suggested you should leave the cars unlocked?' asked Harriet.

'Come to think of it, it was Charlie,' said Nev.

'Well, in fairness, I'd agreed to leave mine unlocked as that poor DJ asked me to,' said John. 'He said he might want to retrieve his bottle.'

'When you told Charlie that you'd seen Christine open the door of his car, was he worried that she might have taken something?' asked Sylvie.

'Nah, he just shrugged it off. Reckoned I was mistaken,' said Nev. 'Which is odd in itself. If I'd been told that someone had opened one of the doors and leaned into my vehicle, I sure as hell would want to know what they'd been doing, because I wouldn't want whatever they were up to coming back on me.'

'I'd have thought most people would feel that way,' said Harriet. 'Which begs the question, did Charlie know what Christine was up to?'

'If he did, there's a chance it was something dodgy, since he wasn't curious in the first place,' said Liz.

'I don't suppose either of you know whether there's a link between Christine and Charlie?' asked Sylvie.

John wrinkled his nose as he thought about it. 'No, they wouldn't move in the same circles. She's far too hoity-toity.'

'And Charlie's much too rough around the edges,' said Nev. 'Comes from one of those families who are always in trouble. He's a bit smarter than some of them. Got the nous to act nice to get what he wants, but I wouldn't trust him further than I could throw him.'

'Do you know where Charlie lives?' asked Liz.

'No, sorry, I don't,' said John. 'But a word to the wise, Liz, Charlie Baines is bad news. I'd advise you to stay away from him. You ladies are far too nice to get mixed up with the likes of him.'

'Don't worry, we won't confront him. We just want to figure out what was going on between him and Christine.'

They chatted a bit more, then John and Neville finished up their drinks and headed off.

'What are your thoughts, ladies?' asked Sylvie.

'Charlie Baines set something up,' said Liz. 'But I've no idea what it was.'

'Well, we know that it involved Christine. So something was going on between the two of them.' Sylvie's brow furrowed as she tried to make sense of what they'd just learned.

'But we know that Christine opened Charlie's car and leaned inside,' said Harriet. 'Though there's nothing to suggest that she went to John's car and tampered with DJ Juicer's bottle.'

'But DJ Juicer told John that he thought the bottle had been moved,' said Liz. 'Oh, this is all so confusing.'

'What if someone else moved the bottle?' suggested Sylvie. 'Someone that no one noticed.'

'As far as I'm concerned, we made two promises,' said Harriet. 'We promised Simon that we'd stay away from DJ Juicer's murder investigation, and we also promised Barney that we'd do our best to establish whether Christine Holloway is corrupt.'

'And from what we've just learned,' Liz interjected, 'it looks as though something dodgy might be going on between Christine and Charlie.'

'Don't forget that Charlie comes from a dodgy family,' added Sylvie.

Try as they might, the ladies could come up with no rational explanation to satisfactorily explain Christine's actions and Charlie's apparent disinterest when told that she had opened up his vehicle and leaned inside.

The things they'd just learned left the ladies determined to put their detective skills to good use by trying to find out more about the personal lives of both Christine Holloway and Charlie Baines.

The three friends were about to agree a plan for the following day's investigations when someone opened the door so forcefully that it thudded against the frame. All heads turned to discover it was Simon.

'Take it easy, Si!' called Duncan. 'Hope you didn't damage the woodwork.'

'Sorry, Duncan. Don't know my own strength at times.' He held up a hand in a conciliatory gesture. Then, spotting his sister and the others, he pointed and moved his index finger in a circular motion to save asking them if they wanted another round of drinks. All three ladies smiled and gave him the thumbs-up.

When Simon returned with a tray of drinks, he placed it on the table and allowed them to reach for their favoured tipple. 'Sorry I'm late,' he said, as he pulled out a chair and sat down.

'What time do you call this?' teased Liz. 'We've been waiting for you for ages.'

'I know. But there's a reason I'm late, and believe me, you're going to want to hear it.'

The three friends all leaned towards him.

'Go on, spill,' urged Liz.

'Don't go telling anyone yet, but you were right all along. The body Barney found really was Robin Thornton's.'

'Oh, no! Poor man.' Sylvie's complexion paled. 'Even though I didn't know him, I felt as though I did.'

'I know what you mean,' said Liz.

'Everyone said he was a genuinely lovely person,' said Harriet.

Simon shot them a warning look. 'You mustn't say anything. At least not until it's made public. It's an active investigation.'

'OK, Si,' whispered Sylvie. She clamped her lips together and mimed pulling a zipper closed.

'How did they finally identify him?' asked Liz.

'I passed on your information about his dentist. They followed up on it straightaway and sent an old X-ray of his teeth. Once that came through, there was no doubt in the pathologist's mind that it was a match. So, well done, everyone. Here's to your investigative endeavours.' He held out his glass in a toast.

'Does this mean you're looking at a link between the murders, then?' asked Harriet.

Simon sighed. 'You know I can't divulge details of active investigations. My hands are tied. You've done us a service in helping to identify Robin Thornton as the victim, but I hope you have the sense to take a step back and allow us to get on with the investigation. The last thing I want is for any of you to put yourselves in danger. You can pat yourselves on the back for a job well done, then leave the rest of it to the professionals.' His stern tone left them in no doubt that this was an end to the discussion.

CHAPTER 31

The next day, Liz and Sylvie found themselves with some unexpected free time. A coachload of tourists had cancelled due to unforeseen circumstances, which meant the tearoom would be quiet. So they left it in the capable hands of Marjorie, who had been brought in to help with the extra load.

'You're paying me for the day, and I can manage myself,' she pointed out.

'Are you sure you don't mind?' asked Sylvie.

But Marjorie was insistent. 'Wouldn't have suggested it if I did. Go on — get off, the pair of you. Make the most of the rest of the day. Do something fun for a change. You both work far too hard.'

So off they went.

* * *

Marjorie promised she'd call them should a sudden influx of customers appear, and so the two friends set off for Harriet's house. They rang the doorbell, but to their surprise got no answer. They were just deciding whether to go to Sylvie's or Liz's instead when the door suddenly opened.

'Sorry, I was in the middle of something, but come in,' Harriet said.

'Anything interesting?' asked Liz.

'Yes, actually. I got through my work quicker than expected, so I decided to do some background research on Christine Holloway.' Harriet's eyes glittered mischievously. 'Turns out she's got quite the social media presence. I get the impression she loves being centre of attention. Which makes it easier to follow her digital trail. I've been trawling through years of photographs and posts.'

'Ooh, did you find anything?' asked Sylvie.

'For one thing, she's got a daughter we didn't know about. I'm not sure how that will help us, but it's something, and who knows where it might lead. Anyway, I've made a start at mapping out her contacts. You can tell some are just acquaintances, whereas others appear frequently. From there, we need to see who each of those people interact with.'

'That will take forever,' Sylvie grumbled. 'And most of it will probably turn out to be irrelevant.'

'But it's what needs to be done, Sylve,' said Liz. 'Any half-decent detective would tell you the same. If Christine Holloway's corrupt, she'll have done her best to cover her tracks. Otherwise, her dodgy dealings would have been discovered years ago. Harriet's approaching this in a logical way. If we're going to get anywhere with this investigation, we need to establish who the real Christine is: the one that does grubby deals, takes backhanders, or whatever it is that she's into. We've got to delve into her private life, because we won't find anything in the public image she portrays to the world. She'll have made sure of that.'

Resigned to the fact that her friends made sense, Sylvie sighed. 'I suppose you're right. Detective work is the same as any other job. Most of it's a hard slog.'

'Precisely,' agreed Harriet. 'Look, I'm making headway with this now. So how about you two leave me alone to get on with it, and perhaps you could make a start on finding out about Charlie Baines? We could meet back here at four o'clock to update each other on our findings. And with a bit of luck, we should have a clearer idea of who we're dealing with.'

'Sounds like a plan,' said Liz, as she linked arms with her friend and led her towards the front door. 'C'mon, Sylve. Let's leave Harriet to it. We need to get organised as we've plenty to get on with.'

As they left Harriet's, Sylvie was in a huff. 'When we left the tearoom, I had visions of us spending a few hours staking out the council offices,' she complained. 'You know, carrying out real surveillance work, or taking photographs of Christine to build a case against her.'

'But we don't know where Christine is today,' replied Liz reasonably. 'If she is at work, how would we get inside the council offices without causing suspicion? In any case, she spent enough time with us on Saturday to be able to recognise us. She'd be suspicious the moment she saw us, and if she realised we were following her, she'd hardly be likely to do anything dodgy.

'No, if Christine Holloway and Charlie Baines are up to something, then the best use of our time will be to find out everything we can about Baines. There must be some area of their lives where they intersect. They must have someone or something in common, and if we can find that, we can start to figure out what they're up to.'

'I guess you're right. But where do we even start?' Sylvie looked and sounded defeated. 'I'm no good at this sort of thing, Liz. I'll just hold you back.'

'Nonsense, Sylve. We'll work together and map out what we find as we go along, just like Harriet's doing. We already know that Charlie Baines comes from a rough-and-ready family.'

'So chances are there'll be things about him or at least some of his associates in the local press,' said Sylvie. 'Shall I look at press reports?'

'Great idea, Sylve,' encouraged Liz. 'Meanwhile, I'll concentrate on social media. That way we can cover more ground. Come on, we need to make the most of the next few hours, so let's get started.'

Sylvie collected her laptop and headed to Liz's house. They set themselves up at either end of the dining table and worked diligently for the next few hours. A couple of hours in, Liz looked up at her friend and smiled. Sylvie had a tendency to overthink things and always worried about letting people down. But Liz knew from long experience that Sylvie was more than capable. She had known that once Sylvie got started, she would become immersed in her search through the local news websites, and she'd been right — it was the same when they'd opened the tearoom. Sylvie had the occasional wobble, but nothing could stop her once she got going.

Time passed quickly and the only sounds were from the clacking of computer keys, the clicking of mice and the scribbling of notes.

Liz had had the foresight to set an alarm on her phone, and when it went off at 15:45, the sound was so loud that it made them both jump. 'Oh, that's gone quickly. Is it that time already?'

Sylvie put down her pen and sat back in the chair. 'My hand is aching. I'd forgotten what it was like to write so much. It was a bit like taking our exams at school.' She laughed at the distant memory.

'I never liked exams. Weeks of trying to memorise facts you knew you were never going to use. But even though the last few hours have been quite intense, I feel as though I've made some headway. This was a useful study period.' Liz glanced over to Sylvie's side of the table. 'And you seem to have made a lot of notes too.'

'No point in discussing anything now,' said Sylvie. 'We may as well head over to Harriet's and share our findings there. Let's hope that between the three of us we've come up with some useful facts and can formulate a plan of action.'

And so, a couple of hours later, the three women found themselves back together in Harriet's dining room, staring intently at a fresh patchwork of coloured Post-it notes linked by numerous inked lines which looked like the industrious workings of a manic spider. Concentration etched across each of their foreheads as though they were studying a scene for imminent recall in the once iconic quiz show *The Krypton Factor*. The show had been compulsive viewing in their younger days, with contestants pitted against each other to prove their physical and mental prowess.

Unsurprisingly, Harriet was the first to spot the link hidden in the mass of information. Liz and Sylvie interacted with customers daily and were skilled in many ways, and Harriet was the first to admit that her culinary credentials and business acumen were no match for theirs. But when it came to logical thinking and looking for patterns of behaviour, the others were no match for her. Throughout her working life, she'd had to sift through vast amounts of data, which required a keen analytical eye.

When Harriet pointed out the link to the others, Liz clapped her hands in delight.

'Winning in Wye!' she exclaimed.

'Definitely,' agreed Harriet. 'And I bet Barney will be up for it. He's already asked us to find proof that Christine's corrupt, so if we manage to pull it off at that event, it'll be the icing on the cake.'

'This is so exciting,' said Sylvie. 'We can finally get to do some undercover work and go in disguise.'

CHAPTER 32

Barney's synapses were firing at lightning speed as he listened to what the ladies had discovered. His eyes sparkled as he nodded his approval. 'I'm impressed, ladies. Very impressed. You've made remarkable inroads, and so quickly too.'

After further discussion, he decided to go all-in on their broadbrush plan for obtaining proof that Christine Holloway was corrupt. 'But first things first. There's work to be done. We've only one chance to do this, and it has to be done right. I appreciate this is a big ask, given you all have jobs to attend to, but I need your commitment for the next few days.'

'You've got it,' said Liz, without any hesitation.

'Whatever you need,' agreed Harriet. 'I can just juggle my workload.'

'Yes, Marjorie can look after the tearoom.' Sylvie nodded her agreement too.

'Excellent! Game on!' Barney rubbed his hands together in delight. 'There's a lot to organise in such a short space of time. But it's doable if we put our minds to it.'

Winning in Wye was the brainchild of Sir Barnaby Cavendish-Mortimer. Its inaugural event was a whole-day affair, and attendance was by invite only. The venue was his conference centre located in one of the far-flung reaches of the Cavendish-Mortimer estate. And the aim was to attract high-quality businesses to the Wye Valley. The event would give entrepreneurs and existing business owners the opportunity to have face-to-face discussions with public officials, who in turn would advise them of government grants and other inducements to encourage them to invest in the local area.

Barney had first come up with the idea after becoming hooked on watching *Dragons Den*. Being a highly successful businessman with many interests, he liked the idea of diversifying his portfolio even further, and this seemed like the ideal way of identifying one or more companies which might be a good fit. As far as he was concerned, this was a win–win situation and could eventually see a healthy return on his investment.

As Sir Barnaby's PA of many years, Beatrice Cornish was used to her employer asking her to do the unexpected at short notice. He had complete trust in her abilities and knew that she was loyal and tight-lipped about his dealings. In return, she was paid and treated exceptionally well, as the pair respected each other.

Beatrice knew Sir Barnaby to be an honest and honourable man. Though when he asked her to purchase a large quantity of state-of-the-art surveillance equipment which cost more than her annual salary, even she raised an eyebrow. And when she spotted it being delivered to the conference centre the following evening, just as she was leaving for the day, it piqued her curiosity even more. The sign on the van in which it was delivered stated that it came from a soft-furnishing company. Yet Barney and his three friends from the village were there to oversee the work.

Try as she might, Beatrice couldn't begin to fathom what was going on. All Sir Barnaby had said when she went to ask him about it was, 'Mum's the word for now, Bea. I'll fill you in when the time's right, and I guarantee there'll be a generous bonus coming your way.'

It was gone midnight when Barney and the others locked up the conference centre. The security company had long since left the premises, having installed and instructed them on how the various devices worked. The three friends were to stay at Barney's that night, which was just as well as Liz was so tired that she could barely put one foot in front of the other.

As they traipsed up the stairs to retire for the night, they all longed for sleep. They were well aware that it would be a short night. Alarms were set for five o'clock. There was a lot riding on the day ahead, and there were still plenty of last-minute preparations to be taken care of.

Despite each of them feeling as though their heads had only just hit the pillow when their alarms went off at that early hour, everyone woke feeling refreshed and raring to go. The smell of bacon and coffee drifted upstairs, and as each of them walked into the kitchen, Liz, Sylvie and Harriet were surprised to find Barney preparing breakfast.

'Didn't know you knew your way around the kitchen,' said Liz.

'Needs must, old girl. Given the enormity of the task we're about to undertake, it's best all round to approach it on a full stomach. Minimise the potential distraction of thinking about food. If we're to triumph over the enemy, and by that I specifically mean Christine Holloway, today needs to go off with military precision. We need our wits about us. I'm a firm believer in Maslow's Hierarchy of Needs. So, first things first, if you know what I mean.'

Liz didn't, but nodded anyway. 'Absolutely, Barney. Absolutely.'

By quarter to six, the four co-conspirators were sitting around the kitchen table, tucking in to a full English breakfast and helping themselves to a pile of hot buttered toast.

As soon as Barney swallowed his final mouthful, he got down to business. 'OK, everyone, follow me into my office.' They traipsed after him, still clutching steaming mugs of fresh coffee. Barney sat behind his oversized desk, and the three friends took seats facing him. 'Right, a final recap of what is expected of each of us today. Each delegate will be expected to wear a name badge. This should make it easy to know who's who.' Barney looked at each of them to make sure they were paying attention.

'Harriet, as you are relatively new to the village, and you weren't part of the welcoming committee for the Village of the Year competition, there's very little chance that Christine or any of the other delegates will recognise you. That makes you our secret weapon. As far as everyone else is concerned, you are someone hoping to set up a business in the area. You'll be free to mingle with the other delegates without raising suspicion, while keeping an eye on Christine.'

'I can do that.'

'Have you decided what your business will be?'

'I thought I'd go for something innocuous. Like professional organising services. You know the sort of thing, helping clients organise their workspace to an optimum level. It's the sort of thing which only requires good old-fashioned common sense. And as it doesn't require any specialist knowledge, I'd feel confident in winging it without giving myself away.'

Barney nodded his approval. 'Excellent choice. Just remember in any conversations you have, to keep your contribution to a minimum and be as vague as possible about any personal details you divulge. Over the years I've had plenty of experience at similar events, and believe me, most delegates are usually self-obsessed egomaniacs. They're there to make an impression. All they want is to do a deal and come away with connections and funding. Which means they're more than happy to talk ad nauseum about themselves and their business.' He rolled his eyes, and the three ladies grinned.

'Some might say, "Pot, kettle," Barney. We wouldn't, of course,' said Liz, as the three friends laughed uncontrollably.

'Ha-ha, Liz. Very funny. But this isn't the time for flippancy. There's too much riding on this.' Barney's tone was serious. 'Now, Harriet, I've acquired an item which you need to keep with you at all times.' He reached down and retrieved a black leather shoulder bag from the side of his chair. 'This isn't any ordinary bag. As you can see, if you look closely at the stud on this side panel, it's a camera. There's also a microphone built into it. Which means it's essential that you keep this side panel unobstructed and facing forward.'

'So the zipper closes in the direction of the recording equipment?' Harriet examined the bag with interest.

'Yes, which will make it easy for you to remember which way the bag should face. I'll set it to record before you go in.'

'Is Christine my only target?'

'She'll be your main one, but there's another council official on the list. His name's—' Barney scanned the list of delegates — 'Niall O'Leary. I know nothing about the man, apart from the fact that he's another bigwig. But his name crops up from time to time, so I guess we need to check him out. Which will be one of Beatrice's tasks for today.'

'Oh, I wish I had one of those bags,' said Sylvie. 'It's amazing. You'd never guess there was a camera and microphone in there.'

'Not today, Sylvie,' said Barney. 'Perhaps I'll get you one for your birthday.'

'Yes, please. I'd love one.' She nodded enthusiastically.

'I don't think it would be very ethical,' said Liz. 'I'm sure you could get into all sorts of trouble recording people without their knowledge.'

Barney sensed that the ladies were losing focus. 'Right, moving on! Liz, Sylvie, as Christine already knows what you both look like, you'll have to go in disguise. You'll be meeting and greeting as people come in and serve as part of the general organisational team. Taking coats, offering drinks and nibbles, helping people find their way around, that sort of thing. Those roles will afford you the opportunity to mingle with the delegates.'

'I've seen the wig, glasses and uniform,' said Liz.

'Me too,' said Sylvie. 'It's so exciting getting to pretend to be someone else.'

'Yes, I left them in your rooms.' Barney's tone became firm as he continued. 'For this operation to succeed, everyone needs to put their excitement, nerves or whatever else you might be feeling to one side. This is a job, and you need to approach it as professionals. Think of yourselves as thespians. You'll become your character. If you convince yourself of that, then you'll have no problem hoodwinking others.'

The two women nodded their understanding.

Barney opened a drawer in the pedestal beneath his desk and took out two substantial plastic name badges. One name was Claudine. The other Fran. 'Take your pick, ladies. These badges each have an embedded camera and microphone, so always ensure they're unobstructed.'

Liz and Sylvie each took a badge and marvelled at the tiny devices.

'As for me, I have this rather nifty tie pin, which I'm assured will record events more than adequately. And as luck would have it, the man you've identified through your thorough detective work as linking Christine Holloway with that odious toerag Charlie Baines was already on the list of delegates. And as it's already widely known that I'm actively looking to expand my portfolio of business interests, I shall put my own needs aside and feign an interest in his company.'

'You're ever so impressive, Barney.' Liz looked and sounded a little starstruck.

'I like to think so,' he replied. 'Right, chop-chop, ladies.' He clapped his hands. 'With showtime almost upon us, it's time to pull out all the stops and make sure that Christine Holloway walks into the trap we've set for her.'

'Whatever it takes, Barney,' said Harriet.

'Absolutely,' agreed Liz and Sylvie.

CHAPTER 33

Beatrice Cornish was already at her desk, beavering away on her fact-finding mission about discovering everything there was to know about Niall O'Leary, as Barney and the three ladies set about getting ready for the Wye Valley business event of the year.

Harriet, as always, was dressed to impress. She put the finishing touches to her hair and makeup, then studied herself in the mirror and was buoyed by the fact that she scrubbed up well. Since their get-together in Barney's study, she'd noticed a fluttering of anxiety in the pit of her stomach. Since carving out a career as an agony aunt, she'd always felt completely in control of things. There was never any reason to feel nervous giving people advice. After all, apart from attending the odd meeting at the headquarters of the various magazines and newspapers she worked for, she undertook most of her work at arm's length.

Today, however, was a foray into the unknown. For a few hours it would be essential that she played her role convincingly to a roomful of strangers. She knew that Barney had spent a great deal of money on hosting this event. But it was for an excellent cause: to help regenerate the area by encouraging businesses to invest in the Wye Valley and in turn provide good-quality, well-paid jobs for local people, and she didn't want to let him down. She was aware that if, collectively, they failed to pull this off in a covert manner, it could have untold implications for him further down the line, as others in the business world might not trust him again.

Harriet gave her reflection one last look, then made her way over to the venue. She wondered if she would be able to spot Liz and Sylvie. They were already in place at the conference centre before the delegates arrived. Sylvie had texted her earlier to say they were so well disguised that even close family and friends would be hard pushed to recognise them.

Harriet looked around curiously. She was one of the first delegates to arrive, but she couldn't see either of her friends. So she headed over to a long table covered in tote bags, where a petite woman in glasses was checking names off a long list.

'May I have your name, madam?'

'Yes, it's—' Harriet began.

'I know who you are, silly.' Liz's familiar eyes twinkled over the thick-framed glasses.

'Oh my God, Liz!' Harriet hissed, trying to quash her surprise, lest anyone was watching. She took in Liz's carefully applied cosmetics, spectacles and stylish wig. She looked ten years younger.

'You're mistaken, madam. My name's Fran.' Liz pointed to her name badge and forced herself to keep a straight face. 'I'm a member of Sir Barnaby's team tasked with ensuring that delegates make the most of the day.'

'The transformation's remarkable,' whispered Harriet. 'Where's—'

'My colleague Claudine's over there. Please feel free to approach either of us if there's anything we can help you with.' Liz gestured towards Sylvie, who nodded hello. 'Can I have your name, then?'

'Samantha Follet.' Harriet recovered herself and gave the name she was going by for the event.

'Ah yes, now I see your name on the list, Ms Follet. This is your badge. Please ensure it's visible at all times, as it will save you having to introduce yourself to everyone, and I hope you get everything you need from this event. Now, if you head over to my colleague, Claudine, she'll explain where the amenities are, and give you a timetable to enable you to make the most of the day.'

Over the next half hour or so, Liz and Sylvie worked flat out as the other delegates continued to arrive. Barney was busy working the room, and Harriet was somewhere in the crowd. Having just given a name badge and the now all too familiar spiel to the latest delegate in the queue, Liz glanced up and forced herself not to react when she realised who was next in line.

'Christine Holloway.' The woman all but barked her name.

Liz averted her gaze as she made a show of scanning the list for her name.

'C'mon, c'mon, I don't have all day,' Christine snapped.

Liz clamped her lips tightly together in an effort not to react. This woman was every bit as rude and objectionable as she had been on the day of the Village of the Year competition.

'Ah yes, I have you on the list.' Her voice was sugary sweet. 'Just let me locate your name badge.'

'I don't need that.' Christine attempted to walk off.

'Then I'm afraid you won't be allowed inside, Ms Holloway.'

'Don't be ri—' snapped Christine.

'It's the event policy,' Liz interjected. Her tone was resolute. 'Health and safety. There are to be no exceptions. Should you be involved in any unfortunate mishap without your badge, you will be deemed to be personally liable.' Liz beamed beatifically, covertly crossing her fingers behind her back. They needed Christine to wear her name badge as Harriet hadn't seen her up close, and she needed to be able to recognise her.

'Oh, just give it here.' Christine held out a hand and clicked her fingers.

In any other circumstances Liz would have happily given her a piece of her mind. But with so much at stake, she resigned herself to just pushing the badge across the table. Then she turned her attention to the next delegate.

Christine harrumphed loudly, but snatched up her badge and marched off, presumably in search of potential movers and shakers.

The line of delegates seemed to have multiplied during their short exchange, so Liz was forced to work faster. She glanced at the clock and realised that there was less than ten minutes to go until Barney was scheduled to give his welcome speech in one of the inner rooms. Working on autopilot, she efficiently checked people in, and it wasn't until her brain caught up with her actions that she looked up to see a tall, slender man with a shock of ginger hair walking away, having collected his name badge. She'd been so focused on her task that even his soft Irish accent had passed her by. It was Niall O'Leary.

Fortunately, Sylvie's role was less time-consuming than Liz's. Though, in fairness, it was virtually impossible not to notice the councillor. His height and hair colour made a striking combination. Sylvie quickly explained to him where everything was and pointed him in the right direction. As he walked away, she discretely nodded to Harriet, who was standing nearby.

Harriet stared intently at the timetable in her hand as she walked towards the room where Barney's welcome address was about to begin. From the corner of her eye, she sensed Niall approaching from her right, changed tack at the last moment and stepped straight into his path.

'I'm sorry, are you OK?' He reached out to grasp her elbow, to steady her. 'I didn't mean to bump into you.' His Irish burr was as smooth as chocolate.

'Umm, yes, no, I mean yes.' Instinct told Harriet that Niall would respond well to a vulnerable woman. 'No, no, I should apologise to you. It was entirely my fault. I changed direction, though I can't for the life of me think why.'

Niall smiled. 'We'd better get in there before Sir Barnaby gives his speech. It won't make a good impression if we're late.'

'You're right. We'd better go. I'm just finding it all a bit daunting.'

'First time?'

'Yes, and you?'

'No. Well, obviously first time here, but I've been attending these sorts of events for years. Though I'm not here for investment. I'm a local councillor. So I'm here in an advisory capacity. Anyway, I must go. Good luck, and you never know, our paths may cross later.'

As most of the delegates had already taken their seats, there were few vacant ones remaining. Harriet selected one near the end of the back row, while Niall sat at the end of the next row down, slightly to the left of Harriet's.

Above the stage, a timer counted down the seconds to Barney's appearance. It seemed very un-British and over the top. Yet Harriet appreciated why her friend had had it installed. It was all part of hyping up the event. Raising expectations. Getting people excited. A subliminal message that every person in the room was pitting themselves against the clock. It was motivational.

There was only a couple of minutes to go until Barney's address. Harriet glanced curiously at the man sitting next to O'Leary. She could only see the back of his head, but she could tell they weren't strangers. As soon as Niall sat down, the other man's posture stiffened.

Harriet positioned the bag on her lap, angling it so that the camera and microphone would record something of the exchange. She couldn't hear what Niall was saying, but the acrimony between the two men was palpable. Harriet wondered why the councillor had approached him in a roomful of people. It seemed unfathomably indiscreet for a politician.

'It's nothing to do with me, so leave me alone. We're done.' Even from her position several seats away, Harriet could hear the venom in the man's words.

Niall O'Leary leaped out of his seat and walked briskly for the door as the room erupted into applause and Barney bounded onto the stage like a gameshow host. But Niall just kept moving without a backward glance. Harriet watched him go, hoping the camera had captured the scene. Even the most casual observer would have been able to tell that this man was barely keeping a lid on his emotions. His expression was murderous.

CHAPTER 34

Harriet watched Barney give his welcome speech. He was a magnificent public speaker. Like everyone else in the room, her gaze was fixed upon him. However, while the crowd were hanging off his every word, Harriet found herself unable to concentrate on what he was saying. Instead, her thoughts were drawn to the tense encounter which had occurred only a few feet away. What had gone on between Niall O'Leary and the other man to have caused so much animosity? And was it connected to any fraudulent activity?

It was only the sound of rousing applause that broke through these thoughts. Harriet blinked and realised Barney was leaving the stage to a standing ovation. She looked over at the man who'd had a run-in with Niall O'Leary, waiting patiently until he made a move. He stood to go and she pushed her chair back. She headed towards him, all the while pretending to be preoccupied with her phone. When the inevitable happened and she bumped into him, it gave the stranger no cause to doubt that their encounter was anything other than her not paying attention to where she was going.

She squeaked a feigned surprise, playing to the stereotype of a scatterbrained middle-aged woman.

'Oh, I'm so sorry, Mr, er . . . ?' She squinted, straining to see his name badge, which was partially obscured by a booklet he held close to his chest.

'Phillip. Phillip Stanwell,' he replied. 'No harm done. Though, given the number of people in such a confined area, it's probably best to be more aware of the immediate surroundings.'

'Noted. Lesson learned, and apologies once more.'

It was apparent that Stanwell was in no mood to prolong their encounter. Nodding his acceptance of her apology, he headed out the door in the direction of one of the smaller break-out rooms. Harriet wended her way discreetly through the crowd to a small room where it had been agreed that the four friends would meet after the welcome address.

'Niall O'Leary's gone,' said Liz, once the door had closed behind Barney. 'Missed the whole speech. He looked fit to kill.'

'He had a tense exchange with another delegate,' said Harriet. 'Someone named Phillip Stanwell. They were in the row in front of me. I'm hoping the recording equipment picked up the entire conversation, as I could only catch a couple of words.' She went on to relay what she had overheard.

'We'll have to wait until later to download that conversation,' said Barney. 'I'll be interested to know why Councillor O'Leary and this Stanwell chap are not on the best of terms.'

'Was our target there?' asked Harriet.

'Yes,' said Sylvie. 'Denzil Bartholomew was seated near the front.'

'I need to get going. Otherwise, people will notice my absence,' said Barney. 'Harriet, I want you to go and take a soft approach with Denzil. I'll give you a few minutes, then I'll come across to have a chat with him myself. I'll make out that I might be interested in investing in his business, but I need to speak to some other delegates first. I don't want Denzil to get suspicious over my motives.'

'Liz and I will keep mingling,' said Sylvie. 'And we'll do our best to keep eyes and ears on Christine.'

As the event was about making contacts and doing deals, it proved easy for Harriet to strike up a conversation with Denzil. Of course, it helped that the plumber had an eye for the ladies. And as luck would have it, he spotted her standing there alone and made a beeline in her direction.

'First time, is it, love?'

'Sorry, I don't understand,' said Harriet.

'First time at one of these events? I don't mean to sound condescending or nothing, but you're looking a bit overwhelmed.'

Well, he's right about one thing, Harriet thought. It was her first time at an event such as this, but the man was absolutely condescending. She hitched a timid smile onto her face. He had given her a way in, and she was quite prepared to play up to his stereotypical view of the vulnerable woman.

'Y-yes. It's all a bit much.' Harriet's voice was meek and breathy. 'Everyone seems so confident, and I'm quickly starting to feel out of my depth. I've only recently started up my business and I'm beginning to think I should have come here better prepared. I've got so much riding on this, and I just know things are going to go horribly wrong and I'm going to end up making an absolute idiot of myself.'

'Now, now, don't be so quick to do yourself down. You just need to learn a few tricks, that's all.' Placing a hand on her waist, he led her aside.

His touch was so unexpected, Harriet had to compel herself not to pull away. Her instinct to demand he get his grubby hand off her was at odds with the role she was playing. And for the time being, she needed him to believe that she was indeed the vulnerable, inadequate female he clearly considered her to be.

'What tricks are you referring to?' She sounded naive, even to her own ears.

'Well, take me for example. I've been in business for yonks, and for quite a while I was happy with the way things were going. But, what with the pandemic and the political climate, me profits have taken a hit. So, I did what I had to do.'

'Which is what, exactly?' Harriet entreated, gazing up at him with wide eyes.

'Oh no, lady. No specifics. That's privileged info.' He smirked and tapped the side of his nose. 'But what I will say is that you've gotta get in with the right sort of people. And when you make yourself known, you make them an offer they can't refuse. Everyone has their price, if you know what I mean.'

'I'm not sure that I do.' Harriet shook her head and looked thoroughly perplexed.

'Don't be so naive, love. It's a dog-eat-dog world.' As he spoke, he scanned the room. 'If you want to get ahead in business, you've gotta do a bit of bartering.'

'Bartering?'

'Yeah, you know. Offer up something to get something in return. These days, no one does something for nothing. It's the way of the world, love. The way of the world.'

'But where should I start?'

'Well, and this is my own opinion, but I'd say you could do worse than getting the council on your side. Could open a few doors for you if you play it right. Now, you've had the benefit of my wisdom free of charge, so it's time for me to go and do something for meself. Good luck.' And with that, he walked away.

Harriet's eyes narrowed as she watched the odious plumber wander through the assembled crowd. She knew the whiff of corruption when she smelled it. And from what Denzil had just alluded to, there'd be less of a stench emanating from a packet of prawns stuffed behind a warm radiator.

Scanning the room, she spotted Barney in the distance. He was looking directly at her and her heart skipped a beat. Putting it down to the stress of their covert operation, she shrugged it off and discreetly gave him a wink.

Barney nodded in acknowledgement and seamlessly homed in on his target. An Exocet missile had nothing on his focus. 'Mr Batholomew! You're just the man who's next on my list. Now, I believe you're in plumbing, am I correct?'

Denzil stopped in his tracks and turned to face him. He'd not anticipated the likes of Sir Barnaby knowing his name, let alone making a point of speaking to him. 'Yes, sir. Yes, that's correct.'

'Good. Good. Good. Though I'm afraid the name of your company eludes me.' Barney maintained eye contact.

'Eh, it's Abbey Well Plumbing.' Denzil's mind raced as he tried to imagine why Sir Barnaby would want to speak to him. 'Are you needing a plumber, sir?'

'No, no, no, my good chap. I'm afraid you have the wrong end of the stick. I have numerous interests, and I'm looking to diversify. I believe the term is *expanding one's portfolio*. I've already been speaking to one or two delegates about the possibility of me providing a cash injection in return for a commensurate share in their respective businesses. I must admit that your field would be new to me, but it is one I have an interest in.'

Afraid of saying something silly, Denzil made a conscious effort to clamp his lips together, as he needed a moment to compose himself. Of all the things he had hoped would happen today, the possibility of Sir Barnaby Cavendish-Mortimer wanting to buy into his company hadn't even crossed his mind. Swallowing hard, he discreetly pinched his thigh to make sure that he wasn't dreaming. 'Wh-why me? What I mean is that I'm delighted. But to say I'm surprised is an understatement.'

'As far as I'm concerned, it's a logical diversification. I don't have any financial interests in that sector. You're a local outfit on the way up, and I believe that as well as providing a cash injection I'm also in a unique position of being able to put a lot of business your way. As far as I'm concerned, it's a no-brainer.' Barney tossed him a winning smile.

Having listened to Sir Barnaby's reasoning, Denzil felt his heart begin to race. He could visualise the pound signs mounting up.

'We should talk. I'd be very interested in your vision.'

'My vision?' Denzil failed to understand what Sir Barnaby meant.

'You know: where you see the business heading. How much of an investment you would need to take it to the elusive next level. That sort of thing. If we reach the stage of agreeing in principle to a collaboration, I'd contact my solicitor and get the ball rolling — with all due diligence, of course.'

'Due diligence?' Denzil felt his heart sink. He'd inherited Abbey Well Plumbing from his father, who'd taught him everything he knew about how to work the books so as not to alert the taxman, with plenty of cash-in-hand and bartering for favours if it happened to be advantageous. But if Sir Barnaby wanted to check the books, he wasn't going to argue. He'd just need to sort them out beforehand.

'Standard procedure, old chap, but must be done. My accountant frowns on handshake agreements these days. A load of old box-ticking, if you ask me. Got to get him to scan your books and be double sure of the turnover, profits, commitments. All the standard but necessary sort of guff. Caveat emptor, as they say. Caveat emptor. All being well, I sense that Abbey Well Plumbing will go from strength to strength. You could soon be the premier plumbing company in the Wye Valley and beyond. And who knows, give it a year or two, you could be spending your days on the golf course, instead of sticking your hand up someone's T-bend.'

Denzil was mesmerised by Sir Barnaby's vision of what the future could hold. If a collaboration with Sir Barnaby could change his life for the better, then as far as he was concerned, the man could carry on calling a U-bend a T-bend. After all, he was only substituting one letter for another.

'When I get an idea in my head,' Barney continued breezily, 'I push ahead PDQ. So, if you could drop your books off with me the day after tomorrow, I'll get the ball rolling. That should give you time to get them up to date.'

'Of course.' Denzil felt rather dazed. On the one hand, Sir Barnaby was offering a quick path to wealth and success. On the other, he'd have to fix his accounts pretty quickly if he was going to convince Sir Barnaby to invest in his firm. So long as he didn't ask to see the contract with the council.

'I'll leave you to get on, old chap, as there are other potential investment opportunities I'm considering. By the way, what most impressed me is the deal you've recently closed with the council. Very impressive.' Barney pursed his lips and nodded his head to emphasise the point. 'Naturally, I'll need full disclosure of the contract.'

'Of course,' Denzil said again. But Barney had already walked away, leaving the plumber to steady himself against a nearby table.

CHAPTER 35

Christine Holloway was easy to spot as Harriet made her way across the room. The councillor was in full flow, talking to a middle-aged man who had a bulbous red nose and a patchwork of thread veins that would have given a map of the London Underground a run for its money.

'Anything I can help you with, Ms, umm, Foley?' Sylvie made a show of looking at Harriet's name badge.

'She said anything incriminating yet?' Harriet's voice was low enough to ensure that anyone near was unable to hear their conversation. She pulled out her timetable and mimed confusion.

'Nothing at all. You going to speak to her?'

'Yes. Denzil's already suggested that I should. Gave strong hints about getting on better in business if you know the right people, and he was definitely referring to her.'

'Any word or update on Councillor O'Leary?' asked Sylvie.

'Not as far as I know.'

'In that case, I'll leave you to it. I can't keep standing in the same spot as it might raise suspicion,' said Sylvie. Raising her voice, she added, 'The next workshop is through those doors to your left. You have plenty of time, though. It doesn't start for another ten minutes.'

Harriet thanked Sylvie and was pleased to see that Christine and the bulbous-nosed man had finished their conversation. She was quick to approach the councillor. The last thing she wanted was for some other delegate to get there first.

'Councillor, I was hoping for some advice and possibly some help too,' said Harriet. As she was introducing herself, she smiled warmly and offered her hand in greeting.

Christine responded in kind, giving no suggestion that she suspected that this was anything other than a normal conversation with a delegate. 'So how can I help?'

If Harriet hadn't known better, she would have had no inkling that the councillor was anything other than a helpful public servant. It appeared that when it suited her, Christine was more than capable of hiding her horrible nature and playing nice.

Harriet spoke about her fictious business with passion, enthusiasm and vision. Indeed, her performance was so convincing that even she began to believe it was quite a good idea.

She had just started to ask what help and incentives were available from the council, when from the corner of her eye she spotted Denzil heading rapidly in their direction.

There was a marked change in the plumber's body language since his chat with Sir Barnaby. His brow was furrowed; his shoulders tense and his eyes betrayed his anxiety.

He barged passed Harriet and grasped Christine's arm, his knuckles white.

'We need to have a talk,' he hissed, mouth merely inches from her ear.

Christine yelped in surprise, but quickly regained her composure. 'Get off me. You're causing a scene. Can't you see I'm in the middle of something?' Using her free hand to cover his, she dug her nails into his flesh until he released his grip. 'Please excuse my cousin, Ms Foley. He's always had the tendency to act like a Neanderthal whenever he wants to get attention.'

A momentary puzzled expression crossed Denzil's face, but he was not to be put off. 'We need to talk. Outside. Now.'

Without waiting for a response, he headed for the door.

Christine's eyes narrowed, but she smiled and then sighed in a theatrical manner. 'I'm sorry, Ms Foley. I'd better go see what he wants. Family, eh? Often more trouble than they're worth. Here, take my card.' She rummaged in her bag and pulled one from a small stack, held in place with an elastic band. 'If you head over to the table at the far end of the room, there's a booklet you may find useful. It has names and contact numbers. It's well worth a look.'

Taking her leave, Christine made a beeline for the doorway through which Denzil had just gone and into a corridor beyond. Harriet caught Liz's eye and discreetly nodded for her to follow the councillor. Liz gave her a thumbs-up and set off to tail their mark.

After taking one of the booklets Christine had referred to, Harriet spotted Barney among the crowd of delegates and wound her way through various groups until she drew level with him. As luck would have it, the conversation he was having with a younger man was reaching a natural conclusion. As they shook hands, there were others loitering nearby in the hope of speaking to Sir Barnaby too. But Barney made his excuses and promised to return soon, before following Harriet to a quiet corner. Once they were out of earshot of the others, she updated him on what had just happened.

'The fact that our favourite councillor claimed that Denzil Bartholomew is her cousin doesn't ring true to me. If they were related in any way, it would surely have raised a red flag when he was awarded that council contract. Denzil's got the wind up because I mentioned that in order for me to invest in his company, I'll need to see his books and have sight of any contracts he already has in place.'

'And if the council contract isn't totally above board, it would explain why he was so insistent on speaking to Christine and wouldn't take no for an answer,' said Harriet.

'Precisely. However, as things stand, I'm up to my eyes in it. There're so many people who want to have a word with me. Which means I can't just slip out,' he said. 'You've done everything you can, and you can't speak to either Christine or Denzil again without raising suspicion.'

'I agree.' She nodded. 'They're not stupid.'

'Do me a favour and go back to my office. Ask Beatrice to log you on to the system and then see if you can verify any familial or other such link between them. I'll meet you and the others back there, once this event has finished.'

CHAPTER 36

It was several hours later before Barney finally stood at the podium once again to give the assembled delegates his closing remarks. The room was packed with a sea of eager faces, and the sense of optimism and self-determination was palpable. They all hung on every word, and when he ended with some carefully chosen closing remarks, his motivational speech was received with a chorus of cheers and rapturous applause.

The event had been a success. Yet Barney knew that he had to put the excitement of the day aside and focus on other more pressing matters.

If he was right about Christine's dodgy dealings, she could be hand in glove with any number of unsavoury characters who would have a lot to lose should their nefarious deeds be exposed. And should he and his friends blunder blindly into a situation they didn't fully understand, the repercussions could be too awful to contemplate. People he cared about could get hurt. After all, there was the distinct possibility that Christine Holloway had somehow been involved in the murder of that poor man, DJ Juicer.

Barney's first port of call when he returned to the house was to check in with Beatrice. As usual, there were a ton of messages for him to deal with, which was only to be expected given the extent of his business interests. These could wait until the following morning. Instead, he sat with his PA as she briefed him on what she had discovered about Niall O'Leary. Eventually satisfied that he was abreast of the information, he thanked her and told her that she could leave for the day.

As he made his way to the sitting room, he could hear his friends' voices drifting up the hallway. They were clearly feeling upbeat about the day's events.

Liz was the first to spot him. 'Ooh, that was so much fun, Barney. Dressing up and going undercover like that.'

'It was quite the adrenaline rush,' agreed Sylvie. 'It almost seemed a shame to take off the wig and uniform. I quite liked being Claudine for a while.'

'Glad you enjoyed it!' Barney replied. 'You all played your parts to perfection, and I'm sure no one suspected what we were up to. I've taken the liberty of informing Eliza that there'll be four of us for dinner, I hope you're all able to stay.'

'Thank goodness for that. My stomach thinks my throat's been cut,' said Liz, as her stomach growled.

'She's planning to serve up in half an hour. Let's pool our information between now and then.' His phone pinged. 'To that end, Beatrice has just updated me on her findings, so I'll kick things off. Budge up, Harriet,' he ordered, as he plonked himself on his favourite sofa. He continued, 'According to Beatrice, there is nothing to suggest that Niall O'Leary was or indeed has ever been implicated in anything underhanded.'

'Which in itself might raise a red flag,' interjected Sylvie. 'Let's face it, no one's squeaky clean.'

'Umm, I suppose it's a possibility.' Barney sounded sceptical. 'Though for now, I'd suggest we stick to what we know.'

'Which is?' asked Harriet.

'Niall's been a council employee for twenty-six years. He's worked his way up the ranks and has apparently ruffled quite a few feathers along the way, as he's a stickler for the rules.'

'Could be a double bluff?' suggested Liz. 'Deflect attention away from any impropriety on his part.'

Barney cleared his throat. 'Once again, that's merely a presumption. Which means we're in danger of veering off track.'

'Sorry,' Liz said ruefully. 'I'm just getting carried away. Since we don't like Christine, it's easy to tar anyone associated with her with the same brush.'

'As I was about to say,' he pressed on, 'Beatrice uncovered some posts on social media which suggest that Niall's marriage is in trouble.'

Sylvie gasped. After what had happened to Albert, she and Harriet both had first-hand experience of what it was like to discover that all was not well in a marriage.

'Any idea what Niall's wife's name is?' asked Harriet.

Barney scanned the email Beatrice had sent him. 'I believe it's Jasmine.'

'Ahh, at least that's one mystery solved.' Harriet gave a satisfied nod.

'I don't follow.' Barney's eyes narrowed as he tried to make sense of what she'd said.

'Me neither,' chorused both Liz and Sylvie.

'After witnessing the tense encounter between Niall and Phillip Stanwell, I did some digging on Phillip. I came across some cryptic comments from some of his friends, which suggested that about four months ago, Phillip had started seeing a woman named Jasmine. It seemed that he was trying to keep their relationship quiet, but someone had spotted the couple together and even posted a photograph of the two of them together. Phillip got quite shirty about it, demanding that the photograph be taken down, but of course it wasn't.'

'Did Beatrice find any photographs of Niall and his wife?' asked Liz. 'If she did, we could check them against the one on Phillip's profile.'

'That's a good idea,' said Sylvie.

Moments later, the friends had proof that Phillip Stanwell was indeed having an affair with Niall O'Leary's wife.

'It appears that at least for now, we can discount O'Leary and Stanwell from our investigation,' said Barney. 'That argument you witnessed wasn't anything to do with our investigation, Harriet. Instead, it was about affairs of the heart and therefore, I suspect, none of our business.'

'I agree.' Harriet nodded. 'Though from what I witnessed today, there's definitely something fishy going on between Christine and Denzil. He was really worked up after speaking to you. I'd even go as far as to say that he was panicking when he interrupted my conversation with Christine. And as for her, well, it didn't ring true when she claimed he was her cousin. I got the impression that it was the first thing that popped into her head as she was caught off-guard and wanted to cover up whatever was going on between them. I don't suppose either of you overheard Christine and Denzil's conversation when they headed outside?'

Sylvie shook her head. 'I could see that they were having a heated discussion, but I wasn't able to get close enough to hear what they were saying.'

'I had a little more luck,' said Liz. 'I grabbed a stack of folders, to make it look as though I had a genuine reason to be out there. They were standing outside conference room three, so I marched past and was able to overhear a couple of snippets. Though it wasn't much. Denzil was panicking, and I'm certain Christine mentioned something about blackmail, but they moved away from the door, and I couldn't hear any more.'

'Did she, indeed? Now, that's very interesting,' said Barney. 'After we've eaten, we should call it a day. Go home and get some much-needed rest. At some stage soon we'll have to listen to those audio files. But not tonight. We're all tired and need to get some sleep.'

'I agree,' said Sylvie. 'We need to be fresh when we listen to those recordings. Otherwise, we might just miss something important.'

'First thing tomorrow, I'll inform Beatrice that I'm taking her off her usual duties and ask her to make a start on the recordings from my long-term security setup and turn them into transcripts,' said Barney. 'That'll leave us free to trawl though the others. You never know, if the councillor and the plumber were standing in range of the equipment, it could have recorded their entire conversation.'

'Fingers crossed,' said Liz. 'And since we know when they both went outside, we can narrow down the timeframe for her, which should help her enormously.'

CHAPTER 37

Without exception, each of them had difficulty getting to sleep that night, as the exhilaration of the day's events proved impossible not to think about. And so, it was inevitable that when morning arrived no one felt refreshed.

At the tearoom, there was a steady stream of day trippers, though it was nowhere near full capacity. It was the sort of day that Liz and Sylvie enjoyed, with a relaxed atmosphere filled with chatter and laughter, and all the while the till kept ringing.

As usual in recent days, customers were keen to chat about DJ Juicer. They made no attempt to hide their eagerness to get the inside information about what had happened. Sylvie was working front of house and was asked numerous questions about what had happened on that fateful Saturday morning. Mindful of the ongoing police investigation, Sylvie kept her answers vague yet seemingly informative.

When two women strolled into the tearoom that afternoon, Sylvie braced herself for more questions. She had a sense that she somehow knew them, though she couldn't place where from. And sure enough, as soon as she heard them speak, her thoughts were transported back to her school days.

She hadn't seen them or given them a second thought since her teenage years, and it was immediately apparent that the trauma of that time had lain dormant but not entirely forgotten. Her stomach flipped, and she suddenly noticed her hands begin to shake. The rational side of her brain told her that it was a ridiculous overreaction. That awful time had been decades ago, and there had been a lot of water under the bridge since then. But still . . .

As teenagers, these women had been a couple of mean girls. They came from well-to-do families, and had been pretty enough, but they had looked down on the likes of Sylvie, Liz and the other girls. Though, unlike Sylvie and Liz, Felicity Durbin and Bella Gormley had both flunked their O levels and left school at the age of sixteen.

The two women selected a table near the window, no doubt with the intention of keeping an eye on what was going on outside. Sylvie forced her lips into what she hoped was a welcoming smile and headed over to take their order.

'Good afternoon, ladies. What can I get you?'

'Oh hello, Sylvie love. I didn't realise you worked here,' said Felicity. There was no suggestion of condescension in her tone.

'Actually, I co-own the establishment.' Despite Sylvie's hackles already beginning to rise, she managed to mask her annoyance.

Seeing them up close, she noticed Felicity and Bella hadn't aged well. Their looks had faded, waistlines expanded, and their lustrous hair colour was almost guaranteed to be no longer natural.

'Have you decided what you'd like to order?' pressed Sylvie. She was keen to keep their interaction to a minimum.

'Could you give us a couple of minutes, Sylvie, love?' asked Bella.

'Sure, no problem. Take your time.' Sylvie smiled and walked back to the counter. She breathed deeply, forcing herself to act naturally, despite wanting to put as much distance as possible between herself and these women. She felt more or less composed when another customer arrived. This time it was a familiar friendly face, which took her mind off the two unwelcome customers.

After five minutes or so, Sylvie returned to the table nearest the window.

'Have you decided yet?' Her tone was no different to the one she used for all her customers.

The two women placed their order, and as Sylvie was about to leave, Bella spoke. 'I know we haven't seen each other since our school days, and you probably haven't given us a second thought over the years, but I just want to apologise for the way I acted back then.'

Sylvie stared at them in disbelief.

'Me too, Sylvie. We were a couple of bitches back then. It makes me shiver when I think how awful we were, and I'm truly sorry.'

'Don't worry about it,' said Sylvie. 'It was a long time ago. We're different people now.'

'That's the truth,' said Bella. 'But we were rotten to you, Liz, and so many other girls. I think it was because you were both cleverer than us. Everything seemed to come easy to you.'

'But you were the pretty girls, and your families were far better off than ours,' said Sylvie.

'It doesn't mean we were happy,' said Bella. 'Anyway, we just want to make amends. Say sorry and move on.'

'Apology accepted. I'll be back with your order,' said Sylvie, before she headed into the kitchen to tell Liz about this unexpected turn of events.

When Sylvie returned carrying a tray with the ordered refreshments, she carefully set it down on the table.

'We were just saying that what happened to that poor man was awful,' said Felicity.

Sylvie nodded but said nothing. It occurred to her that the reason these two women had turned up in the village out

194

of the blue was because they were after salacious details of DJ Juicer's death.

'My sister lives next door but one to them,' said Bella. 'They were a lovely couple. Kindness itself. I can't begin to imagine why anyone would do such a thing. It beggars belief.'

'I heard that dreadful councillor was playing up, trying to make it all about her as usual,' said Felicity. 'She lives near me in Friars Way.' This was a village a few miles from Monksworthy. 'Horrible woman. Only out for what she can get.'

'Not the nicest of people,' agreed Sylvie. Her resolve to say nothing evaporated as soon as Christine Holloway was mentioned.

'By all accounts her daughter's no better,' added Felicity. 'My Helena is friendly with her Shannon, but only on social media,' she added quickly. 'She's more sense than to have anything to do with the likes of Shannon Holloway in real life. Anyway, according to my Helena, Shannon's been boasting about a new bathroom she's had installed, completely free of charge.'

'How'd she manage to wangle that?' asked Sylvie. With her interest suddenly piqued, she pulled out a chair and sat down at the table.

'Most likely something to do with her mother. That Christine's always got some dodgy deal on the go. She's as bent as a butcher's hook. I'm telling you, the police should be looking into her. After all, it's our council tax that pays her wages.' Bella's lip curled in disgust.

'I agree that one's as bent as a nine-bob note,' said Felicity. All the while, her head nodded so vigorously that she almost resembled the Churchill dog.

'Any chance I could take a look at Shannon's socials?' asked Sylvie.

'Absolutely,' said Felicity. She picked up her phone and fiddled with it for a short while, then thrust it towards Sylvie. 'Here, take a look for yourself. She's being as brazen as anything about it.'

Sylvie looked at the image and felt her heart begin to pound. A pretty young woman who shared her mother's eyes and hard smile was posing next to none other than Denzil Bartholomew. Beneath the image was a caption, which read:

Me with the best plumber in the world. Love my new bathroom. #AbbeyWellPlumbing #thanksMum

This was the lead they'd been waiting for. True, Shannon hadn't explicitly stated that the bathroom was free of charge. But who on earth posed with their bathroom fitter? 'Any chance you could forward that to me? And give me Shannon's address?'

'Sure . . . but why?' asked Felicity.

'Because this looks like fraud,' said Sylvie with great satisfaction, 'and someone needs to do something about it.'

CHAPTER 38

Sylvie's unexpected discovery meant that there would be no opportunity for the three friends to take it easy that evening.

'I've always tried to be a live and let live sort of person,' said Harriet. 'After all, it doesn't pay in my line of work to be judgemental about people. Especially since everyone who asks for my help has somehow got themselves into a mess and finds it difficult to extricate themselves from it. But I can't just sit back and do nothing about this. This is not just making a few bad choices. This is corruption, and it makes my blood boil.'

Liz and Sylvie shared a glance. They had never seen Harriet this worked up before.

'I'm not being unreasonable, am I? I mean, you're both as angry as I am, right?' She looked at them in turn.

'Yes. That woman is vile. There's no way she should be allowed to continue in a high-paid council job. Or any job that's paid for out of people's taxes. It's down to us to expose her. After all, if we don't then who will?'

'You're right, Sylve. We've a public duty to do something about this,' agreed Liz. 'But what are we going to do?'

'First off, I think we should stake out the daughter. Do another bit of proper detective work and see if we can find any more incriminating evidence before going to the police,' said Sylvie.

'How do you propose we do that?' asked Harriet.

'I've got her address,' said Sylvie. 'We could drive around there and keep watch from the car.'

'I hate to say this, but I don't think that will achieve much. Let's face it, it's not as though Denzil's going to go back there any time soon. He's already spooked after yesterday. The only reason he'd go back there is if something went wrong with the plumbing.'

'I suppose we could knock on the door, say we're lost and ask if we could use the loo,' said Sylvie.

'Seriously? No one in their right mind would allow a stranger in to use their toilet,' said Harriet. 'And anyway, what would that achieve? We need her to admit on record that she had the bathroom installed for free.'

'We could say that we're doing market research for a national company,' said Liz. 'You know the sort. The ones that sell their goods online. We could make it more general and say that it covers kitchens and bathrooms, and that we're canvassing properties in the Wye Valley to establish if there'd be a potential customer base.'

'I suppose that might work,' said Harriet. Her brow furrowed as her thoughts raced ahead. 'Although, if we get caught out it could lead to all sorts of problems. We could even get arrested.'

Sylvie shuddered. 'Oh, I don't like the sound of that. It was bad enough spending hours in the police station after that poor man died.'

'If it came to that, I'm sure we could talk our way out of it,' reassured Liz. 'Simon wouldn't like it, but he'd be in our corner.'

'I guess the key would be to keep things vague,' said Harriet. 'It's far too risky to say that we're linked to a national company. That could easily be checked. It'd be better for us to say that we're representing a mystery startup company that's considering holding a launch competition with a prize of either a new kitchen or bathroom. We're undertaking market research in the area. Just sounding out potential interest at this stage. That way we're under no obligation to name a company, so we're unlikely to get caught out in a lie.'

'But how would that help us to get Shannon to admit that she's recently had a new bathroom installed free of charge?' asked Sylvie.

'Because as part of our spiel we'd say that we need to know if the householder has had any recent upgrades to their kitchen or bathroom, and if so when, by whom, and how much it cost. We'd also make sure to say that just because she'd had her bathroom upgraded it wouldn't preclude her from a free kitchen upgrade.'

'That could work,' said Liz.

'It could, but I think we should give ourselves a couple of days to rehearse what we're going to say,' said Harriet. 'We'll only have one shot at it, so we need to be believable. If we go there acting all gung-ho, we risk our lies unravelling. Preparation is the key.'

'I think we should tell Barney what we're planning to do,' said Sylvie. 'He's already persuaded Denzil that he's considering investing in his company. Perhaps this could be linked into his plans. That way, if anyone wants to dig deeper, we're not leaving ourselves wide open to being caught out in a massive lie.'

'That's such a good idea,' said Harriet. 'I'm sure he'll be able to coach us to sound authentic. If you can sort that out with him, I'll look up the electoral register to see if there's anyone living in that street who might pose a problem to us.'

'Like whom?' asked Liz.

'There's always a chance that someone might know us. I know it's a belt-and-braces approach, but I'd just feel easier about pulling it off if we gather as many facts as possible before we show up on their doorstep.'

CHAPTER 39

It took longer than anyone expected for the four friends to put their plan into action. Such was Barney's determination to get to the bottom of what had gone on between Christine and Denzil that he had tasked Beatrice with devising a fictitious company logo and a vague mission statement to accompany it.

Meanwhile, Harriet had discovered that, like many public services, there were reams of red tape to get through in order to be able to examine the electoral register. It had to be done in person at the council offices, and under supervision. This meant that she had to make an appointment, and that in turn meant she needed a plausible reason to view the information. She concocted a cover story based on her professional link with the press.

Finally, having eventually located the appropriate section of the register, Harriet set about her task. Despite taking this precaution, she didn't anticipate finding anything of importance. In fact, she'd half convinced herself that this exercise would be a waste of time. So when the name of one resident did jump out at her, she did a double take.

Suddenly, everything seemed to slot into place to help explain why Christine Holloway had acted so strangely while the judges were in Abbotsmead.

Harriet quickly checked through the rest of the street, just in case there were any other surprises in store, then she rushed back to Sylvie's house, where they'd all agreed to meet. Barney's car was already parked outside.

'Finally! Where've you been?' said Liz. 'We expected you ages ago.'

'I've brought along the props,' said Barney, pointing to a big box by the door. 'Clip boards and headed notepaper with a stonking fictitious company logo. And I decided to go the whole hog, so I've got lanyards with name badges and a selection of wigs and other accoutrements for everyone to choose from.' His tone became wistful as he continued. 'To be perfectly honest, I'm a little jealous. I love a bit of role play. Flex my thespian muscles. But it's not to be . . .'

Sylvie was the only one to sense that Harriet was about to burst their bubble. Her eyes narrowed as she focused her attention on her friend's face. 'You're about to tell us that our little deception isn't going to happen, aren't you?'

'Possibly,' admitted Harriet. 'At least, before we make any decisions, I think you all need to hear what I've just found out. It might make sense of a few things.' With everyone sat around the kitchen table, Harriet plonked herself on the nearest available seat.

'Did you find something on the register?' asked Liz.

'I did,' confirmed Harriet. 'In fact, there was one name that jumped out at me.'

'Go on,' urged Barney.

Harriet took a deep breath, placed the list of names on the table and explained her findings. 'I'm still new to this neck of the woods, so there could very well be other people on this list that some of you might know. But look at this.' She pointed to one of the entries.

'Charlie Baines!' Liz's voice rose to a squeak.

Sylvie gasped. Barney looked from one to the other and shook his head.

'That chap's name obviously means something to the rest of you, but quite frankly I'm at a loss to understand its significance.'

'He was one of the chauffeurs for the judges, and by all accounts he's a nasty piece of work,' said Sylvie.

'What's more, we've had it on good authority that when Christine was acting shiftily in Abbotsmead, it was his car door she opened and leaned inside,' said Liz.

'Wouldn't that just have been the car she was travelling in?' said Barney.

All three ladies spoke in unison. 'No.'

'I'm confused. Why is this so important? What am I missing?' Barney's brow furrowed.

'We've also been told that when the chauffeurs parked up in Abbotsmead, Charlie insisted that they all head down to the riverbank for a smoke,' said Liz. 'He led the way and chose where they stopped. It was a place where they couldn't quite see the cars.'

'But one of the drivers had recently given up smoking,' added Sylvie, 'and he walked away because he didn't want the temptation.'

'And by all accounts, Charlie wasn't happy with that, he was trying to keep all the drivers together,' continued Liz. 'And when the non-smoker walked away from the others, he saw Christine open the driver's door of Charlie's car and lean inside.'

Harriet picked up the story. 'Now, put that information together with Liz thinking she overheard Christine use the word "blackmail" when she was talking to Denzil, and we find Charlie lives in the same street as Christine's daughter, Shannon, who has already posted a photograph of her and Denzil together and is boasting that she had a new bathroom fitted, courtesy of her mother.'

'Let me get this right, you're suggesting that this unsavoury Baines character had found out about this and has been blackmailing Christine?' asked Barney.

'Yes!' said the three women together.

'In that case, we're in way over our heads,' said Barney. 'We still haven't watched the security feeds yet. Why don't we do that to establish whether the surveillance equipment picked up enough of the conversation between Christine and Denzil to tell us what they were discussing? And, Liz, I think you should tell Simon about this. Give him a chance to show some initiative. If he says we don't have enough to go on, I'll sound out Andy. But I'd prefer not to get the chief constable involved at this stage. At least not until we've assessed all the evidence and got our ducks in a row.'

'No time like the present,' said Harriet. 'I'm a firm believer of not putting things off.' She looked at each of them, silently willing her friends to agree with her.

'You're right,' said Sylvie, as she nodded agreement. 'And it shouldn't take too long. We made a note of the time that the conversation took place.'

'I'd suggest it's full steam ahead to the old AP,' said Barney. He stood up and gathered his things together, and they all headed out of the house.

With everything set up in Barney's office, the four of them watched with bated breath as they listened to the recorded conversation. Christine was clearly heard saying that Charlie Baines was blackmailing her, and it was obvious that Denzil knew why the blackmail was taking place. Though throughout the short conversation between the pair, there was no mention of why Christine was being blackmailed.

'We should let Simon have this recording,' insisted Barney. 'It's time they did some digging into what's going on. After all, you don't get blackmailed for no reason.'

'It'll have to wait until the morning,' Liz replied. 'I have the impression that something's up with Si. He's not himself. Been a bit cagey, and it's so unlike him. When I spoke to him earlier, he said he was tied up all evening. I tried to find out what he was doing but he shut me down. Said he would call at the tearoom before his shift tomorrow.'

CHAPTER 40

Simon popped into the tearoom the next morning on his way to the station. It was in the golden hour when they had finished their early morning preparations and had yet to open. Liz and Sylvie were about to sit down and enjoy a continental breakfast.

'Hello, hello,' he said as he came through the door.

'You're not wearing your uniform,' exclaimed Liz.

'You noticed,' he grinned. 'Got some spare for me?'

'We've always got enough spare for you,' said Sylvie. Her welcoming smile caused his cheeks to glow.

'Thought you were on shift this morning?' said Liz.

'Well, that's the thing. I've got some news.' Simon pulled out a chair and sat down.

'As you look like the cat that got the cream, I'd say it's something good.'

'Nothing gets past you, sis,' quipped Simon. He'd hardly stopped smiling since he'd arrived. 'Right, first off, I'm not in uniform anymore.'

'You've been promoted?'

'No. I'm still a sergeant, but I'm a bit long in the tooth to be out on the frontline day after day. To be honest, I'd started thinking about retirement. But as you already know, your tip-off about Robin Thornton and his dental records paid off. And as you allowed me to take credit for it, well, long story short, I've been given a different role. More of a back-room data analysis type of thing, which means I'm doing more real detective work, but from the comfort of a desk. And I think I'm going to like it. So thanks, both of you. And I'll also thank Harriet when I see her.'

Liz and Sylvie both jumped out of their seats to hug him.

'I'm so pleased for you, Si,' cooed Liz.

'Me too,' added Sylvie as she ruffled his hair.

'Thanks. I only found out late yesterday, and I'm starting today.'

'Have they given you a case yet?' asked Liz.

'Funny you should mention it, yes, they have. Now, you really must keep this to yourselves, as I don't want to get into trouble—'

'What is it?' interjected Liz.

'Well, after what happened at the village hall, the chief constable took a real dislike to Christine Holloway,' said Simon. 'There've been numerous rumours about dodgy dealings with the council for a while, and I've been tasked with looking into things.'

'That's an amazing coincidence,' said Sylvie.

'Coincidence? Don't tell me, you've found something out about her, haven't you?' He looked from one to the other and shook his head in disbelief as they both nodded. 'Go on then, tell me what you think you know.'

Simon sat there agog as he listened to everything they'd managed to find out. 'You're in the wrong job. You'd make brilliant detectives. But it'd be best if you to allow me to take it from here.'

'Don't worry, we'd no intention of taking this forward,' said Sylvie. 'Not when it became apparent that Charlie Baines was involved and has most likely been blackmailing Christine. We'd be way out of our depth.'

'I'm glad to hear it. Baines and his family are not the sort of people you want to mess with. Best that you steer clear. And let's get this clear, this is a recording of Christine Holloway speaking to some plumber about her being blackmailed by Charlie Bains?'

'Yes, it's from Barney's surveillance system,' said Liz. 'It was recorded during the Winning in Wye event. We only got around to looking at it last night, but we're none the wiser about why Baines is blackmailing her.'

* * *

For the three friends, the next few days passed without thoughts of corruption or murder. As far as they were concerned, they'd done everything they could and were more than happy to pass the investigative baton on to the police. Their days were filled with work, and their evenings with socialising. And when they met up for the pub quiz, Simon assured them that he was making headway with the investigation into Christine.

'By the way, thanks for sending across the security footage from your business event,' said Simon.

'You're welcome,' said Barney. I'm glad you're taking things forward and hope you'll find something useful in there. I'm afraid we bit off more than we could chew, as they say. We could only take things so far. Frankly, I don't have the skillset for this sort of thing. And I'm sure we're both agreed that despite their proven investigative prowess, neither of us want these three lovely ladies put in harm's way. Especially since there's a real possibility of links to hardened criminals.'

'Couldn't agree more, Barney,' said Simon. He looked pointedly at each of the women. 'Fortunately, the chief constable has specifically tasked me with investigating possible corruption within the council. And I intend to pull out all the stops.' Simon's chest puffed out as he spoke. 'Anyway, this round of drinks is on me.'

'That's the spirit, old bean. I'm sure you're more than up to the challenge. My advice is, be methodical, keep digging and follow the money, as they say. I'm convinced there's a trail to lead you in the right direction, once you know where to look. To use common parlance, Councillor Holloway is a wrong'un.'

Harriet's phone pinged to announce the arrival of a message. But before she could look at it, there was a squeal of feedback over the speakers and everyone winced at the sound.

'Listen up, everyone,' Duncan's voice boomed over the speakers, 'it's time to switch your phones off and put them out of sight! The quiz is about to start.'

'Better put it away,' said Sylvie.

The order had barely left Duncan's lips when there was a rummage as everyone in the room turned off their phones. Harriet pressed the button on the edge of her phone to put it on silent and slipped it into her bag.

'Are we all set?' asked Barney. Everyone on the team nodded. 'Good-oh. Let's show them what we're made of.'

At the end of the quiz, the Yabbadabbadoos had come in third place.

'We should be pleased with that result,' said Barney.

'How d'you make that out?' asked Simon. In contrast to Barney's ebullient mood, he seemed a bit deflated by it.

'We scored two more points that last week, when, as I recall, we ended up in fourth place. We're improving.'

'Yeah, you're right,' agreed Sylvie. 'We should be pleased.'

Liz gave Harriet a nudge. 'So who was the message from then, one of your contacts about the case?'

'Oh, yes, I forgot all about that. I suppose I should take a look.' She reached into her bag and switched off the silent setting, then opened the message. 'It's from Joe Pettle. He's forwarded the most recent photographs he has of Robin. Oh, and there's one of their friend Sonny. Though I got the impression that they tolerated him more than liked him.'

'Let's have a look,' said Sylvie.

Harriet placed the phone on the table and they all scootched in to take a look.

'They all look so young,' she said as her breath caught in her throat. 'Look at the long hair.'

'I'd say it's a given that Joe and Sonny would be nearly unrecognisable after this amount of time,' said Simon.

'It's so sad to think that Robin was buried on your estate, and no one realised he was there,' said Sylvie.

'He was a good-looking young man too,' said Liz.

'He was,' sighed Harriet. 'And from what Joe said, he was a one-in-a-million, all-round good guy. Kind. Considerate. And a good friend. With everything to live for. He had a career he loved and was good at. And then to win all of that money too . . .'

'Money's a good reason for murder,' said Simon.

'His lottery win could very well have been the reason he was killed,' added Liz. 'Didn't you say that Joe last saw him a few months after he won that money?'

'That's what he said.' Harriet nodded. 'Joe was getting married, and Robin was going to be his best man. Then without warning he just disappeared off the face of the earth. Though I'm sure Joe said that after a few weeks, he received an email from Robin telling him he was cutting ties and that Joe needed to find himself another best man as their friendship had run its course. Joe told me that it just didn't ring true, and I have to admit, it doesn't sit right.'

'Have they established a cause of death for Robin?' asked Liz.

'Blunt force trauma to the skull,' said Simon.

'Horrible way to go.' Sylvie shuddered.

The five of them sat in silence for a moment, each contemplating these new findings and the loss of a young man who had seemed so promising.

'Has anyone spoken to their other friend, Sonny?' asked Barney, breaking their reverie. 'Seems to me that someone should.'

'Not as far as I know,' said Simon. 'Though I'm not on that case, so there could've been developments I'm not aware of.'

'Perhaps you should ask Joe if he's still got Sonny's contact details or even his family's,' suggested Liz. 'We might be able to track him down.'

'I already have, but I guess he's forgotten.' Harriet glanced at the time. 'It's getting late now. I'll ring him in the morning.'

CHAPTER 41

A welcome breeze stung Harriet's cheeks as she ran, which helped focus her thoughts. As usual, at this early hour she was pounding the footpath on her morning run. When the alarm had gone off, she toyed with the idea of hitting the snooze button. That in itself was unusual, as she couldn't recall the last time she relied on an alarm to wake her.

She prided herself on an ability to fall asleep relatively quickly. But last night had been different. The image of Joe, Robin and Sonny, each looking so young, hopeful and happy, kept swimming in front of her and she had been overcome with sadness. Knowing that Robin had been killed less than a year after that photograph had been taken was heartbreaking. Try as she might to think of other things, Harriet hadn't been able to shut down thoughts of how cruelly Robin's life had ended. And it was those thoughts which had kept her awake for hours and filled her dreams when she finally managed to get some sleep.

Even though she had never known him in life, she had spent so long trying to find out who he was, and he now felt familiar. Little by little, she had learned things about him. Spoken to people who had known and valued what he brought to their lives.

Back home, with a pot of coffee brewing, she hit the shower and turned her face upwards to allow the jets of water to pummel her as she washed away the endeavours of her morning's exertion. As usual, Harriet had a tight schedule ahead of her, but for once she lacked the enthusiasm to get to grips with the day's tasks. She knew that she wouldn't be able to give her full attention to those individuals who sought her help until she had spoken to Joe, so she decided that she would ring him while she was having breakfast.

The call rang out and Joe answered almost immediately. He sounded upbeat.

'Joe Pettle here.'

'Hi, Joe. It's Harriet Joyce. Sorry to call so early.'

'Oh, hi. Did the photograph help?'

'Yes. Thanks, Joe. About that, look, there's no easy way of saying this, but I'm afraid it's bad news about Robin.'

'Bad news?'

It was now apparent that he hadn't yet learned of his friend's death. 'I'm sorry to have to tell you that Robin's dead.'

'H-he c-can't be.' Joe's voice faltered, as he struggled to control his emotions. Harriet gave him a moment to collect his thoughts. After a second or two of silence, he cleared his throat and asked, 'When? How?'

Harriet told him everything she knew, then asked if Joe could tell her anything about Sonny, as she was determined to contact him.

'Yeah, sorry. I forgot that you asked for his contact details when I spoke to you at the airport. All I know is where he lived back then, and I seem to recall that his father's name was John . . . John Jones. I never met him, but Sonny always said that his father was a drunk. Apparently, his mother died young. I don't know any more than that.'

'I'm so sorry to hear that,' said Harriet. 'It sounds like he had a tough childhood.'

'Yeah, I think his homelife was pretty awful.' Joe sounded thoughtful. 'But Sonny rarely spoke about his family, and he never invited us around to his house. Given what he'd told us about his dad, we weren't inclined to go there.'

Harriet waited until after the tearoom closed for the day to tell Sylvie and Liz what Joe had said. As soon as they'd been told, they didn't need convincing: they needed to find Sonny Jones's father. Robin's remains had lain undiscovered for a decade, with no one to mourn him. The least they could do was to find Sonny and tell him what had happened. According to Joe Pettle, Sonny had been Robin's friend. Even if the young men hadn't been close, a friend was still a friend, and Sonny deserved to know what had happened to Robin, so that he could mourn his loss.

* * *

'Are you sure this is the right address?' asked Sylvie.

'I spotted the street sign as we turned onto the road. It's definitely our destination,' said Liz, once again checking the scrap of paper where she had scrawled the address.

'Unless Joe got it wrong,' said Harriet. 'I must admit, I wasn't expecting this.'

They gazed about at the leafy street, where each house seemed to be larger and more expensive than the last. It seemed a far cry from the childhood home Sonny had described to his friends.

'Well, we're here now,' said Liz. 'We might as well knock at the door and find out if this is where Sonny's father lives.'

'I guess so. Let's face it, just because Sonny's father was an alcoholic doesn't mean that he couldn't have been wealthy,' said Sylvie.

They parked on the side of the road and walked up a driveway that would have been large enough to fit half a dozen cars. At the end was a triple garage. A Lexus convertible and a Range Rover were parked outside, and there was the faint hum of music.

'Whoever lives here isn't short of a bob or two,' whispered Liz as she eyed the vehicles. She squealed as a sudden movement surprised her, and a man's head appeared at the side of the Range Rover's bonnet.

'Can I help you?' His voice was friendly but firm, and he appeared to be of a similar age to them.

'Oh, I almost jumped out of my skin!' gasped Liz as she reached out to steady herself on Sylvie's arm.

'I hope so,' said Harriet. 'We were told that Sonny Jones's father lived here.'

The man shook his head and sighed. 'He's my son. What's he done?'

'Done?' Harriet sensed that Sonny and his father weren't close. 'No, you misunderstand. He hasn't done anything. We just want to—' Her explanation was cut short when the front door opened and a slender woman with vibrant blue eyes came outside.

'Hello?' she said.

'They're asking about Robson,' said the man, then turned his attention back to the three ladies. 'His name's Robson, not Sonny.'

'Have you seen our son?' asked the woman.

'Your son?' Sylvie's eyebrows arched.

'Let me guess, you thought I was dead?' The woman's laugh was hollow.

'And no doubt, I'm an alcoholic widower?' supplied the man. 'We've heard it many times before. Sadly, our son is an inveterate liar.'

'I'm Ella.' She closed the gap between them and extended her hand. 'Robson's mother. And this is Thomas, my husband and Robson's father.'

'I won't shake if you don't mind,' said Thomas. He held up his hands to reveal a sudsy sponge. 'Rather wet and messy. You caught me washing the cars.'

Sylvie, Liz and Harriet introduced themselves.

'Look, as you're here, would you like to come into the garden?' Ella asked. 'We've plenty of seating and we can talk in comfort.'

The rear garden turned out to be both impressive and expansive, with a large lawn and an array of shrubs which wouldn't have looked out of place in the Chelsea Flower Show. Ella showed them to the seating area, excused herself for a moment, and returned shortly with a tray containing a pitcher of homemade lemonade, an ice bucket and four tumblers. 'Would you like some? I made it myself.' They all readily agreed, and she began pouring the drink into the glasses. 'Help yourselves to ice if you wish,' she added.

'Thank you,' said Liz appreciatively.

'We were led to believe that Sonny's mother was dead. I'm sorry to ask, but can we just check that this is your son?' Harriet held out her phone, which displayed the photograph Joe had recently forwarded.

Ella sighed, then nodded. 'Yes, that's Robson. He doesn't seem to have aged. Is that a recent photograph of him?'

'I believe it's more than ten years old. Are you saying that you haven't seen him for a while?'

'He walked out of this house about ten years ago, when he told us he wanted nothing more to do with us. We haven't seen or heard from him since.' Ella's voice cracked as she struggled to suppress her emotions.

'I'm sorry. I didn't mean to upset you,' said Harriet. 'I know it's not always easy being a parent. You bring them into the world, and you've such hopes, dreams and love for them. But no parent knows how their child will turn out.'

'Robson was never easy. He was challenging from a young age.'

'Let's be honest, Ella. That's an understatement. He was worse than that,' Thomas said, striding across the patio to join them. 'We tried. We really did. Gave him every opportunity in life, poured ourselves into loving him. Eventually we took him to see a specialist, only to be told he had some sort of personality disorder. Well, antisocial personality disorder, actually. Which means that, apparently, he has no regard for right or wrong.'

'Why do you want to speak to Robson?' Ella asked. 'Has he defrauded you too?'

Ella's question was so out of left field that Harriet thought she must've misheard. 'Sorry, what did you say?'

'Did he defraud you? It's what he did to us. The same day we discovered what he was up to and challenged him about his behaviour, he walked out.'

'No, no,' said Sylvie. 'Your son's done nothing to us.'

Harriet's mind was racing as a thought entered her head, and she wondered whether it was plausible. 'Did you know Robin Thornton?'

'The name sounds familiar, but I can't say I know him,' said Ella. 'Do you know him, Tom?'

Thomas looked thoughtfully at his wife. 'Yes, I think he might have been in school with Robson. Didn't he go on to win the lottery?'

'He did,' said Liz.

'That's right, I recall Robson being up in arms about it. Saying how unfair it was,' said Thomas. 'That was a couple of weeks before we found out that he'd stolen some of our money. Lucky for us that we have numerous bank accounts and investments. Ones that Robson didn't know about. Otherwise, I'm sure he'd have cleaned us out.'

'It must've been awful to discover that he'd betrayed you like that,' said Sylvie.

'Heartbreaking,' said Ella. 'But at least we found out before it was too late.'

'We lost quite a lot of money before he left, though,' said Thomas. 'He'd forged my signature to take out loans. We'd known he was struggling. But still, you don't expect your own flesh and blood to steal from you like that. We would have given him the money if he'd asked.'

'Did you report him to the police?'

'No. Thomas wanted to — I think you were at your wits' end, by that point, weren't you? But I wouldn't have been able to live with myself if we'd gone down that route,' said Ella. 'No. We cancelled those cards, paid off the debts and closed the account. And that was that. We haven't heard from him since.'

'You still haven't explained why you need to speak to Robson,' said Thomas.

'Ahh, yes,' said Harriet. 'A body was found buried near our village. It was eventually ascertained that it was Robin Thornton.'

'What!' Thomas's complexion paled. 'And you think that Robson—' Thomas and Ella glanced at each other, and from the expression on their faces it was apparent that they both thought their son was capable of murder if it meant that he could get his hands on such a large amount of money.

'No, no. That's not it,' said Harriet quickly. The very thought had occurred to her the moment she learned of Robson defrauding his parents. But until there was proof, there was no justification for distressing his parents, both of whom seemed like genuinely decent people. 'No, we learned that your son was one of Robin's friends, and we just thought he should know what had happened to him. That's all there was to it.'

They spoke some more, the couple filling in some of the details of Sonny's life, and then Thomas offered to walk them out. As they neared the car, he touched Harriet's shoulder.

'I didn't want to say this in front of Ella. She doted on Robson and has missed him terribly since he walked out.' Thomas's expression was pained. 'But I know from personal experience that my son is capable of violence. You see, when I realised what he was up to with our bank account, I challenged him.' He shuddered at the memory. 'Thankfully Ella was out at the time, and I've never told her what happened, but Robson threatened me with a knife. Luckily my neighbour called by as we'd arranged to play tennis. I'd left the front

216

door unlocked for him, and he called out to ask if I was ready. Robson panicked and ran out of the back door. That was the last I saw of my son. But I know from the look in his eyes that he would have killed me, given half the chance.'

'But presumably you didn't report him to the police?' asked Liz.

'No. He's my son, and it would have broken Ella's heart. I couldn't do that to her. Instead, I cancelled my bank cards and closed the account. I also changed the locks and had heightened security measures installed at the house.'

'Wasn't your wife suspicious?' asked Sylvie.

'Not really, a few days earlier one of the neighbouring houses had been broken into. It was a wake-up call and a few of us were already considering upgrading our security systems. So Ella didn't question it when I went ahead and arranged it at short notice.

'I can't tell you ladies what to do. But what I will say is don't underestimate my son. I did, and I was fortunate to get away with it.'

On the journey back to Monksworthy, Liz was the first to speak. 'Are you thinking what I'm thinking?'

'Absolutely,' said Harriet.

'How do we set about finding him?' asked Sylvie.

CHAPTER 42

As usual, Liz was busily baking when her phone rang. A quick glance at the screen told her that it was Simon. Her brother was on shift, and she knew that he would only be contacting her if it was urgent. Liz hurriedly wiped her hands on her apron to remove the worst of the flour, then accepted the call.

'Everything all right, Si?' Her heart thudded. She'd told Simon about their conversation with Thomas Jones and he'd assured them that the team investigating Robin Thornton's death would examine his finances, to try to establish what, if anything, had happened to his money.

'Turn the radio on.' Instead of his usual calm tone, he sounded excited.

'Wha—'

'Don't ask questions,' he interjected. 'Just turn the radio on.'

Liz did as Simon requested and called Sylvie into the kitchen. Both women listened in silence to a news report on the local radio station. With various voices speaking over each other in the background, the reporter struggled to get her voice heard.

I'm Alice Batley with a sensational breaking news story. I'm reporting live from outside the Wye Valley police headquarters, where a crowd gathered when news broke that Councillor Christine Holloway has been arrested on suspicion of corruption and malfeasance in public office.

I can confirm that the Wye Valley police have not yet issued a statement on this matter.

Early this morning, we received information from an anonymous source at the council. We arrived at the police headquarters in time to see the councillor being escorted into the station by two uniformed officers. And I can confirm to our listeners that Councillor Holloway was handcuffed when she arrived.

As this is a developing situation, we will remain outside the station to give you up to date information as and when things happen. But for now, back to the main broadcast.

Sylvie switched off the radio, and the two friends stared at each other in stunned silence. It was only when they heard Simon's voice coming through the speakerphone that they remembered he was still on the line.

'We've got her, sis. It's a rock-solid case. She's not going to walk away from this.'

'Well done, Si. You've played a blinder,' said Liz. 'I'm proud of you.'

'Me too, Si,' echoed Sylvie. 'This calls for a celebration. Mine tonight, seven o'clock, and I'm not taking no for an answer.'

'Yeah, see you then. Gotta go. Cases to build. Criminals to catch.' He disconnected the call before either of them had a chance to reply.

Learning of Christine Holloway's arrest was the highlight of the day and knowing that they had played a small part in her downfall was its own reward.

'Hello? Anyone serving?' a voice called from the customer area.

'Oops, what with all the excitement, I forgot we were open,' said Sylvie. Her cheeks flushed with embarrassment as she headed out of the kitchen to find a middle-aged couple seated at a recently cleared table. As she approached to take their order, she realised that it was Roger and Kath White who lived in Abbotsmead.

'This is a nice surprise,' said Sylvie. 'Haven't seen either of you for a while. How are things?'

'All's well, thanks,' replied Kath.

'As it's such a nice day we thought we'd go for a walk, so we headed down this way,' said Roger. 'I take it that everything's returned to normal?'

'As normal as it ever is in these parts. Though as you've been out walking, I guess you haven't heard the news?'

When they both stared at her blankly, Sylvie pulled out a seat and sat down to tell them about Christine Holloway's arrest.

'That woman deserves everything she gets,' said Kath. 'I hope they throw the book at her.'

'I know we didn't stand a chance in that competition after those young hooligans ruined our efforts,' said Roger, 'but she was extremely rude when they arrived to tour the village. We did the best we could to put things right, but it takes time, effort and good-quality plants. And we had very little time, and all the best plants were gone.'

'There'll always be next year,' said Kath. She gently squeezed her husband's arm.

'I'm keeping my fingers crossed that the Joneses will be gone before the end of the year,' said Roger. 'But selling two properties is going to be a big ask.'

'The Joneses?' asked Sylvie.

'Yes, Rob Jones and his wife. Moved to Abbotsmead, must be about ten years ago. Thinks he's God's gift, flashing the cash.' Roger's mouth curled as he made a sucking sound to emphasise his dislike of the man.

'I don't trust that Rob,' said Kath. 'I don't think he's a nice man.'

'What do you mean by that?' asked Sylvie.

'I don't know.' Kath wrinkled her nose as she searched for a reason. 'There's just something about him. I can't put my finger on it, but he makes me feel on edge.'

'He ruined our village when he bought that other property, just so that he could make money out of it at everyone else's expense!' Roger's complexion had darkened.

'We were all up in arms about it,' said Kath. 'A newcomer like that, spoiling it for the rest of us. It's just not on — all and sundry turning up, with goodness knows how many cars. Music blaring. Barbeques. Parties. Drinking.'

'We're not unreasonable people, but that's not the sort of thing you expect to have to put up with. Not in these parts anyway,' said Roger.

'Well, at least if they're selling that property as well as their own, it's a win for the village,' said Sylvie. 'With a bit of luck, they'll soon be gone, and you won't have to put up with all the shenanigans.'

'We're keeping our fingers crossed that everything goes smoothly,' said Kath. 'It's tearing our village apart. There was no choice but to call the police after what those lads did. But Rob was up in arms about it. He seemed to think that we all had it in for him after the police had a word.'

'We know it wasn't directly his fault. Those lads were responsible for their own actions. But Rob Jones has responsibilities too. Just because he wants to earn money that way, it shouldn't mean that the rest of us have pay for it. It's not right.'

'Was there any suggestion he was thinking of selling up before all of that happened?' asked Sylvie.

'Not a hint of it. But things have been simmering beneath the surface for a while now, and those thugs were the final straw,' said Roger. 'I can only think that he's finally realised that no one wants him or his holiday let in the village. The sooner he's gone, the better.'

Sylvie experienced a flutter of excitement. Rob was a common name. And as for Jones . . . Well, there were more Joneses in the country than you could shake a stick at. But there was a nagging voice in her mind telling her that she was correct. Was the Rob Jones this couple were talking about, and Robson Jones who in the past had insisted upon being called Sonny, one and the same person?

'Any idea what made Rob Jones move to the village in the first place? Does he have any links to the area?'

'No idea whatsoever,' said Kath. 'Him and that wife of his have kept themselves to themselves from the moment they arrived. Not interested in socialising with the likes of us. A bit snooty if you ask me.'

'But they've obviously got plenty of money,' said Roger. 'When you think about how much properties, even doer-uppers, go for in these parts. You're talking a huge financial commitment.'

'Do you know if he has a job?' asked Sylvie, trying her best to appear casual. 'Surely he couldn't make enough from one holiday let to live comfortably.'

'Never noticed him go out at regular times. Then again, there're so many people working from home these days.'

'What about social media, is he on Facebook or Instagram?' Even as she asked the question, Sylvie knew that it must sound odd.

'Funnily enough, no,' said Roger. 'I've searched for him, but couldn't find any social media account, and considering his age, I think that's strange.'

'And are they still in the village, or have they moved on?'

'Still in the village,' said Kath. 'They haven't been able to sell their cottage yet, although it's on the market.'

'But that cottage of theirs is still booked for the foreseeable,' added Roger. 'At least that's what it shows on the website.

They'll milk it for all its worth during the summer months and make a fortune at everyone else's expense.'

Having eventually taken the Whites' order, Sylvie rushed back to the kitchen. She was so excited that she almost skipped with delight but resisted the urge.

'Liz, Liz, I think I know where he is,' she said.

'Where who is?' As she wiped her hands on a tea towel, Liz listened to what her friend had to say.

'Robson Jones.'

CHAPTER 43

That evening, as they all sat around Sylvie's kitchen table celebrating the arrest of Christine Holloway, Sylvie told everyone that she thought she knew where Robson Jones lived.

'It's best you stay out of it,' warned Simon. 'I'll pass on the information, but I want all of you to stay away from Abbotsmead.'

'I agree,' said Barney. 'If that man does turn out to be the killer, then you shouldn't put yourselves in harm's way.'

'We've got a photograph of Robson, though it was taken at least ten years ago,' said Harriet. She handed her phone to Simon.

'But he'll look way different now,' said Liz. 'Ten years is a long time, and the Rob Jones from Abbotsmead is completely bald.'

'That shouldn't matter. You told me that you spoke to his parents, so if he's arrested, and one or other of his parents are prepared to provide a DNA sample for comparison purposes, it should be easy enough to prove his identity. The trouble is that the investigating team are still trying to establish whether Robin's money was transferred into Robson's account. So until they've proof of that happening, they don't have anything to connect him to the murder.'

'But—' countered Sylvie.

'No if or buts, I'm telling you to back off and let the officers do their job,' ordered Simon. His tone was uncharacteristically firm. 'You're all way out of your depth on this one, and if you get caught up in something you can't handle, you won't just be putting your own lives at risk. You'll be putting police officers and possibly other members of the public at risk too.'

The three women felt this was entirely unfair. It was their hard work that had got them this far in the first place. But Simon was resolute. The team investigating Robson would take it from there.

Over the next few days, Sylvie, Liz and Harriet did their best to wheedle, cajole and plead information out of him, to no avail. Simon remained uncharacteristically firm. He also cut Liz's calls short and stayed away from the tearoom.

They were all eagerly looking forward to the quiz night, when they might finally get some news, but it wasn't to be.

For once, Simon made a quick getaway at the end of the quiz, and as Barney was deep in conversation with Brendon, the ladies decided to call it a night. It had been a frustrating evening, and to make matters worse, their team had come last, which had never happened before.

'Simon's really digging his heals in on this,' said Sylvie irritably. 'I've never known him to be so pig-headed.'

'I don't know what's wrong with him,' huffed Liz. 'I've always been able to get him to spill the beans about anything. Even when what he's told me is supposed to be confidential. But for some unfathomable reason he's sticking to his guns and shutting me out. He even put the phone down on me yesterday when I mentioned Rob Jones's name.'

'I know he's ordered us to back off,' said Harriet, 'but there's nothing stopping us going to Abbotsmead whenever we want . . .'

'You're right. It can't hurt to go to the village, can it? As long as we're not breaking any laws, we have the same right to be there as anyone else.' Sylvie looked at her watch. 'Shall we head over there now? It's not even nine o'clock.'

'We could pop into the Spotted Pig,' said Liz. 'See how Ezra Tiverton's doing. He was in a right state the last time I spoke to him. Having a hard time with his wife.'

The roads were reasonably quiet and so the three friends pulled into Abbotsmead shortly before nine fifteen. It was the golden hour, and the country lanes seemed to glow in the gentle light of the summer sun. The balmy evening was perfect for relaxing in a beer garden with friends.

'It's smaller than I imagined,' said Harriet. Despite its close proximity to Monksworthy, this was the first time she had visited the village.

'Not a patch on Monksworthy,' said Liz. 'Nothing here to attract tourists.'

'Given the size of the place, I can see why the villagers dislike the Airbnb so much,' said Harriet. 'It might bring the occasional group to the village, but it's taken an entire home out of the market for residents.'

They were walking across the deserted car park to the Spotted Pig, when from somewhere nearby there was the sound of breaking glass, followed immediately by a scream. Had it happened in a built-up area, where a melee of background sounds was a constant of life, it might very well have gone unnoticed. But in a village of this size, at this time of night, the sounds meant one thing. Someone was in trouble.

'What was that?' Harriet exclaimed, staring around.

'I think it came from down that lane.' As Liz pointed, there was another scream.

'Quick, you go. I'll raise the alarm and follow on behind,' said Sylvie as she reached for her phone. She was already dialling the emergency services as her two friends ran down the lane towards whatever was happening.

An operator answered and Sylvie shouted down the phone that all three services might very well be required. The operator promised help was on the way, but it would take at least ten minutes to arrive.

'But we don't have that long!' Sylvie ran towards in the pub to alert everyone that there was some sort of emergency in the village. She tugged on the door but was shocked to discover it was locked. She was so distracted that it took a few moments for her to notice a message pinned to the door:

Closed until further notice.

Sylvie began to bang on the front doors of the nearest houses. Yet she got no response. It didn't make sense. The village was like a ghost town. No one answered, despite her repeatedly hammering on doors and windows.

The operator had advised that the emergency services had been despatched, but given the distance they had to travel, they were unlikely to make it to the village any time soon. And with no sign of her friends, it was possible that they could be in danger too.

Sylvie set off in the direction of the lane, breathing heavily. She dialled Simon's number, only for it to go straight to answerphone, so she decided to leave a message. 'Si, it's Sylvie. Don't be cross, but we're in Abbotsmead. Something's happened. There were screams. Someone shouting. And we heard glass breaking too. I'm not with the others, they've gone on ahead, down the lane just past the Spotted Pig. Hurry!' Her speech was rushed, and as she disconnected the call, she hoped that Simon would be able to understand what she was saying.

She dialled Barney's number. But instead of her call being answered by his friendly, reassuring voice, it rang out unanswered. He must have forgotten to take his phone off silent after the pub quiz.

Sylvie stopped to catch her breath and tried to calm herself. She suddenly felt cold, despite the balminess of the night air. It occurred to her that she hadn't felt this scared since she had briefly been held hostage by her husband's killer.

* * *

While Sylvie stayed back to raise the alarm that something was terribly wrong, Harriet and Liz raced in the direction of the terrifying sounds, with no thought about what they were running towards, or indeed whether it was even safe to do so. They ran hell-for-leather along the lane. Despite the fact that the sun had not yet sunk over the hills, it was dark here. The houses and fences pressed close together on either side.

They streaked past several properties, the windows dark and empty. There could be no one at home, else they would surely have heard the confrontation and come to help. Further down the track, light blazed from some windows. In a stark contrast to the surroundings, the cottage seemed like a prop on a stage. But this was no theatre where people paid to be entertained. This was real-life drama, and it was clear, even without seeing what was happening, that someone was in distress.

Unsurprisingly, Harriet, who ran every morning, was way ahead of Liz. She stopped abruptly at the sound of a man's voice shouting. She listened intently. He was incandescent with rage.

'I'm not letting you take everything away from me! You tried it once before and I came back bigger and better than ever. You're pathetic. Ever since I was born you never did anything in my best interests. All you ever did was whine on about how I was an embarrassment. How I disappointed you. Well, news flash. You mean nothing to me.'

'P-please, Robson. I'm begging you, don't do this. I'm your mother. I've only ever wanted what's best for you.' Harriet recognised Ella Jones's voice. It was unnaturally high and quivering with emotion. 'Let me help your father. Look at him, he's not moving.'

'You stay where you are!' screamed the unseen man. 'You've asked for this, turning up at my home uninvited.'

Liz panted as she drew level with Harriet.

228

'Quiet,' Harriet whispered. 'Robson's got his parents in there. It doesn't sound good. I think he's done something to his father and his mother's terrified. We've got to help.'

'I hope Sylvie's managed to raise the alarm,' said Liz in an undertone. 'I thought some of the villagers would have headed over here once they knew that something was happening.'

'We can't afford to wait,' said Harriet. 'At least we've got the element of surprise on our side.'

'That's all we've got. I really don't fancy our chances. Robson's younger and fitter than we are, and you said he's already overpowered his father.'

The next words to carry from the cottage were chilling. 'Have you mixed the drink, Ange?'

Harriet was the first to appreciate the significance of Robson's question.

'They're going to poison his parents,' she hissed. 'Just like they did with DJ Juicer. We can't afford to wait.'

'I'll hold her mouth open. You pour it in.' Following this order, there was an immediate sound of a struggle.

Harriet could stand it no longer. She raced to the cottage's front door. As she neared, she could see a mound of shattered glass from one of the downstairs windows. Through the jagged pane, three people were now in clear sight.

Ella Jones was tied to a chair. Robson stood behind her and struggled to hold his mother's head still. Yet despite her precarious situation she struggled for all she was worth to free herself from her son's grip.

A younger woman calmly walked towards them with a pipette.

'Are you sure that's enough?' asked Robson.

'It's more than we used on Juicer,' she replied.

As this scene was playing out, Liz reached into her bag and pulled out an attack alarm which Simon had recently given her. She pressed the button, and the device emitted a relentless ear-splitting wail. Then she threw it into a nearby hawthorn hedge which bordered the lane. Then, spotting

Thomas Jones's car up ahead, she ran towards it and used her momentum to set off the car alarm too.

Liz had always been good at improvising, and that's what she did now. She upended her bag and the contents clattered to the ground. Then she scooped up a loose coping stone and dropped it inside, testing the strap to ensure it would take the weight. When she was satisfied that it would not break, she twisted the handle securely around her hand and powered towards the house.

In the ensuing chaos, Robson flung open the door at the precise moment that Harriet charged at it. The pair collided, and found themselves instantly entangled, grappling furiously as each tried to get away from their unexpected attacker.

'Who the hell are you?' growled Robson, his mouth so close that Harriet could smell the alcohol fumes on his breath. He was far stronger than Harriet, but they were both taken by surprise when someone barrelled into them.

'Get your hands off her!' cried Liz, battling to be heard over the noise of the alarms. But as she turned to face him again, weighted bag held high, ready to strike, she didn't spot Angela Jones. The younger woman pelted out of the house, bent low and running flat out as though dipping for the winning tape in the final few metres of a race.

Liz was knocked sideways and sent staggering into a bush. Liz's heart hammered at the force of the unexpected collision, but she pushed herself upright, determined to save her friend who had just been slammed into the wall. Having listened to Simon's tales of tackling criminals, Liz had often wondered how she'd react. Would she, a usually mild-mannered woman, fight? Or would she run away? She was already on the move, racing, determined to rescue Harriet, when she realised that she already had the answer to that particular question. Liz was a fighter.

No one had spotted Sylvie, who turned up just in time to see Liz being pushed aside. The fight between Harriet and the young man had moved just inside the threshold, but Angela

Jones was running fast towards her, in an apparent effort to make a quick escape.

Sylvie gripped the only impromptu weapon she had — a bottle of perfume given to her by her late husband that she always carried in her handbag. Planting her feet firmly apart, using the cover of darkness to her advantage, she raised the perfume bottle. She waited until the young woman was no more than a foot away from her and sprayed the perfume directly in her face, making sure to keep her finger depressed, to use as much of the perfume as possible.

Angela screamed and stumbled, falling to her knees. 'I'm blind.'

'No one pushes my friend and gets away with it,' snapped Sylvie. 'See how you like it, you bully!' She pushed the young woman face first to the floor, then deftly sat on her to ensure that she couldn't get up again. 'I'm making a citizen's arrest.'

Back in the house, subduing Harriet was not as easy as Robson had anticipated. For an older lady, she was strong and agile. And he was soon about to learn that she was prepared to fight dirty. He used his bulk to force her into the wall, sneering as her head thudded against the Farrow & Ball–painted surface. That should be enough to stun her, he thought with malice, and loosened his grip to change his stance now that he had the upper hand.

But the smirk was soon wiped off his face as Harriet forced her knee into his groin.

Harriet staggered out of the hallway and into the living room, her head spinning. Behind her, Liz hefted the bag and twirled it above her head. In her school days she'd loved doing field events such as javelin, discus, shotput and hammer. This substantial stone in her bag made the perfect hammer, and she knew just where she was aiming.

There were tears in Robson Jones's eyes as he clutched his groin and raised his head. The timing couldn't have been better as he took a direct hit from the flying handbag and fell back, stars dancing before his eyes.

CHAPTER 44

Liz dragged Robson into the living room, where Harriet had freed Ella and was seeing to Thomas. Liz tied the slightly concussed young man securely to the chair in which he had incapacitated his mother.

'He'll never work his way out of these,' she declared proudly. 'I got my knotter's badge in the Girl Guides, and I've practiced them ever since, so I know how to make them secure.'

With Robson no longer posing a threat, Liz headed outside to help Sylvie with Angela.

'Almost finished the bottle keeping this one in check,' said Sylvie, hauling the younger woman across the lawn. 'Good thing I decided not to bin it. It never was my favourite fragrance.'

Angela had stopped wailing but was still muttering mutinously.

'Well, it would have been such a waste to use one you really liked,' laughed Liz. 'Come on, let's get her inside. We can tie her up next to that husband of hers.'

Thomas had regained consciousness by now, though he was pale and clammy. They'd managed to get him onto the sofa, where he was propped up with cushions, and Ella dabbed his brow with a damp tea towel.

As they waited for the emergency services to arrive, the friends asked Ella how she and her husband had ended up at the Joneses cottage.

'A police officer came to speak to us about Robson,' Ella said, 'and in passing mentioned Abbotsmead. So, we decided to come and find out for ourselves whether Rob Jones was our boy.' As she mentioned his name, her breath caught in her throat. 'It was a mistake to have come.'

'It was a mistake not to have reported him to the police when he defrauded us all those years ago,' said Thomas. 'People have died because of that decision, and that's on us.'

'No, it's not,' said Harriet. 'You had no idea what he was capable of. Robson is an adult. He makes his own decisions.'

'I am here, you know!' he bellowed. 'None of this is my fault.'

'Oh, do be quiet, we've all had quite enough out of you,' snapped Sylvie. 'If you interrupt again, I'll use what's left of this perfume on you.' She waved the bottle menacingly in his direction.

At last, the police arrived, followed swiftly by the ambulance. Angela and Robson were arrested. The three ladies were checked over by paramedics. Thomas was taken to hospital, where he remained until the following day. It was a standard precautionary measure for someone who had suffered a head injury.

Liz, Sylvie and Harriet spent the following morning being questioned by the police, before giving statements about what had occurred at the Abbotsmead property. And it was then that they learned the reason why there had seemingly been no one at home in Abbotsmead when they tried to raise the alarm that something was wrong. With community spirit at a low ebb because of recent events, the villagers had clubbed together to hire a bus to take them all to the cinema.

Later that afternoon, Simon popped into the tearoom, where he joined the three ladies for a fortifying piece of cake.

Robson had been officially charged with the murders of Robin Thornton and DJ Juicer, and the attempted murder of his parents. Angela was charged with DJ Juicer's murder and the attempted murder of her in-laws. Although Robson had committed the act, it was Angela who had concocted the poison that had killed the DJ, using knowledge gained from her degree in pharmaceutical chemistry.

Between mouthfuls of cake, Simon enthusiastically updated them on what the police had learned. 'Robson admitted that he had panicked when he realised that DJ Juicer was the celebrity guest judge,' he said. 'As soon as Robin's remains were found, he'd been worried his identity would be discovered, and of course, DJ Juicer knew that Robson had worked for Robin. They'd bumped into each other on numerous occasions at Robin's office. Robson was certain that if Juicer recognised him, he'd be suspicious of how a former administrative assistant could afford two properties in such an expensive part of the country.'

'So he killed the man rather than risk his secret being exposed.' Liz sighed. 'How awful.'

'But what about Angela, how much did she know?' asked Sylvie.

'Robson never told her he had killed anyone or disposed of the corpse,' said Simon. 'Not even when she had insisted they live in Abbotsmead. But she's just as ruthless as he is. When she learned what he had done, she agreed that they couldn't risk DJ Juicer putting two and two together. They needed a plan, and they needed to come up with it quickly. And that was when they agreed that they had to kill DJ Juicer.'

'Over the years Dominic had made no secret that he always carried a bottle of his wife's juices,' said Harriet. 'They actively promoted them on social media and in the press. It was obviously the reason they came up with the moniker DJ Juicer.'

'That's right. Well, when Robson knew Dominic was going to be a judge, he made sure to be there when the judges arrived,' said Simon. 'Robson noticed that Dominic left his drinks bottle unattended in the car. He took note of which car he had travelled in and went to see if he could break in. As luck would have it, the cars were unlocked. The chauffeurs were out of sight, so he took the opportunity to poison the juice.'

'The audacity,' breathed Liz.

'That was a major risk he took. He could have been caught at any moment,' said Sylvie.

'But he knew he had to chance it,' said Harriet, 'and it paid off.'

'How did he get Robin's money, though, Simon?' asked Liz.

'Through his job as an administrator,' said Simon. 'Robson siphoned money from his friend's account, both before and after his death. That took a nifty bit of detective work to uncover. Me and the other detectives spent weeks tracing Robin's money. Robson wasn't as clever as he thought, though. True, he sent it all to an offshore account. But he'd set the account up in his own name.'

'Rookie mistake,' said Liz knowledgably.

'He made a lot of those.' Simon laughed grimly. 'We were also able to prove that he had sent emails from Robin's account, because he was still logged into that email address on his home laptop. He had drafts saved in a personal folder of all the letters he sent as Robin, advising clients that he was stepping away from his career and would no longer represent them. He used the same account to email Joe Pettle, as Robin, to say that he had decided not to be his best man.'

'But what about Christine Holloway? We know she's been charged with fraud, including awarding a council contract to Denzil Bartholomew of Abbey Well Plumbing without it going out to tender.'

'We had a tough time getting anything out of that one,' said Simon. 'Christine Holloway refused to say anything about her wrongdoing for ages. It was Denzil who told us, under questioning, that he had fitted a bathroom free of charge for

Christine's daughter, as Christine had promised to award Abbey Well the accolade of Village of the Year. The village had never won, and Denzil was Chair of their village committee. It was yet another reward for his generosity towards Christine's daughter.'

'I still don't understand what she was doing by the cars,' said Sylvie. 'She was seen acting suspiciously by the judges' cars in the Abbotsmead car park. If she wasn't poisoning DJ Juicer, what was she up to?'

Simon's eyes gleamed. 'Well, that's where it gets interesting.'

'More interesting than conspiring to cover up a murder by committing another murder?' Liz was aghast.

'Maybe not as interesting as that,' Simon acknowledged. 'But it took a lot of persistence to learn what Christine had been up to. After some pretty intensive questioning, she revealed that she was being blackmailed by Charlie Baines, who himself had discovered the dodgy dealings between Christine and Denzil. It transpired that when Christine had opened the door of Charlie's car and leaned inside, she was depositing the latest instalment of hush money.'

There was a long silence as the three women reflected on what they'd just heard.

'It's sad,' said Liz at last. 'So many lives ruined by so much greed.'

* * *

Life eventually returned to normal. That is, until Harriet, Liz and Sylvie were all summoned to attend the police headquarters. Simon assured them that he had no idea why they had been ordered to go there. Which made the three friends worry even more.

'Do you think we're going to be charged with assaulting Angela and Robson Jones?' asked Harriet.

'It's possible,' said Barney unhelpfully.

'I don't suppose you could ring the chief constable and put a word in for us?' asked Sylvie. She had an awful feeling that they would end up in trouble, when all they had done was catch the killers and save some lives.

'It wouldn't be appropriate to use my friendship in such a way. Sorry, ladies. But I'll take you there myself,' said Barney. 'And if necessary, I'll be a character witness for each of you. I'm afraid that under the circumstances it's the best I can do.'

No one uttered a word throughout the entire journey. When they arrived at the station, Barney told them all to take a seat while he had a word with the desk sergeant. After a brief conversation which was undertaken in hushed tones, he headed towards them. 'I've been informed it shouldn't be long. Someone will be out to escort you inside.'

'Oh no, we *are* going to be arrested,' said Liz. She was close to tears.

Moments later, a door opened, and a uniformed officer appeared. 'Follow me, please.'

'You'll stay with us, won't you Barney?' asked Harriet.

'Absolutely. After you, ladies.' He followed along, and none of them saw him wink at the desk sergeant.

They walked in single file behind the uniformed officer along a narrow corridor and into a lift which took them to the third floor. As the lift doors opened, he pointed at a door. 'Please go inside.'

Each of the ladies had the same thought. It was so unfair that they should be treated like they were the criminals, when they had been responsible for capturing the killers and had placed themselves in danger while doing it.

Liz opened the door indicated, but the room before them was in complete darkness.

'I'll get the light,' said Sylvie, as she patted the wall for the switch.

As the light came on, there was a collective shout of, 'Surprise!'

It was the last thing any of them had expected. A banner stretched across the wall bearing the words *Citizens Bravery Awards*. Reporters. Photographers. A crowd of friends and family, all there to congratulate them. Barney, Simon and the chief constable clapped and smiled along with everyone else.

And, for once in their lives, Harriet, Liz and Sylvie were lost for words.

THE END

THE JOFFE BOOKS STORY

We began in 2014 when Jasper agreed to publish his mum's much-rejected romance novel and it became a bestseller.

Since then we've grown into the largest independent publisher in the UK. We're extremely proud to publish some of the very best writers in the world, including Joy Ellis, Faith Martin, Caro Ramsay, Helen Forrester, Simon Brett and Robert Goddard. Everyone at Joffe Books loves reading and we never forget that it all begins with the magic of an author telling a story.

We are proud to publish talented first-time authors, as well as established writers whose books we love introducing to a new generation of readers.

We won Trade Publisher of the Year at the Independent Publishing Awards in 2023 and Best Publisher Award in 2024 at the People's Book Prize. We have been shortlisted for Independent Publisher of the Year at the British Book Awards for the last five years, and were shortlisted for the Diversity and Inclusivity Award at the 2022 Independent Publishing Awards. In 2023 we were shortlisted for Publisher of the Year at the RNA Industry Awards, and in 2024 we were shortlisted at the CWA Daggers for the Best Crime and Mystery Publisher.

We built this company with your help, and we love to hear from you, so please email us about absolutely anything bookish at feedback@joffebooks.com.

If you want to receive free books every Friday and hear about all our new releases, join our mailing list here: www.joffebooks.com/freebooks.

And when you tell your friends about us, just remember: it's pronounced Joffe as in coffee or toffee!